Praise

"Absolutely loved t̄ ... ̄ cover to cover – everythin̄ ... ̄ u̇ı ṫhe same please!"
Clark Osell

"Very enjoyable! Really brilliant engaging story that kept me hooked from page one. Creative and visceral language builds a very believable universe. I especially liked the fact that the author used the chronology in an original way, telling a story from multiple perspectives and keeping me guessing as to how it would all come together. Good stuff."
Pete E

"An original and out of the ordinary read with a different spin on the fantasy genre. All of the characters seem to come more alive as you read through the book as each is so well crafted yet individual."
J Bailey

"This is a book to move you."
Sheila Price

"I knew I would love this book – and it completely delivers! I was gripped from the start. Each chapter adds a layer to the story, delving back into the past to reveal what twists and turns of fate brought the four young men to this desolate place in the dark of night. This book is constantly shocking – every step is a surprise. At times it is funny, and the shocking descriptions of violence are beautifully contrasted to the real pain of the group's awful split."
Alison Brown

"Such a compelling story, it was hard to tear myself away and get on with everything else!"
Meriel J D Britton

"I found it curiously gripping from the start and then I just had to keep reading it!"
Random Kindle Reader

Spyrus

Philip T McNeill

Text ©2014 Philip T McNeill
Cover ©2014 Philip T McNeill

First Edition – July 14

Also by Philip T McNeill
Shadows

Bethan,

I can't believe
you got same on
it after only half
an hour! TCh!

And now you're
insulting my
writing!

To Ofsted – your constant 'attention' encourages me to pursue my writing with increased vigour

SPYRUS

Prologue – Running Out Of Air
October 10

The lights flickered on as Altair entered his apartment and closed the door behind him. It was the end of a particularly arduous day of meetings and appearances around the city, and he was eager to get started on the routine that he was resorting to more and more frequently.

First, he went to the bar counter at the back of the living room and poured himself a double vodka with a dash of crushed snowdrop. With a flick of his hand, the eighty-eight piano chimes hanging from the ceiling rippled into motion, a slow and soothing melody drifting through the room as he knocked the drink back in one, then poured another.

Next, he walked over to the mirror that hung proudly in the centre of the far wall. It had been a present from some government official or other, and Altair had become extremely fond of it of late. The frame was chrome and crafted into the shape of billowing clouds, a silver lining to surround the gloom he usually saw when he looked into the black lacquered glass. He still looked remarkably similar with his close cropped blonde hair and striking blue eyes gleaming back at him, but the darkness of the mirror accentuated the lines that had begun to crawl across his cheeks.

To the casual observer, he could still pass for late twenties, but he felt much older, as if his insides were crumbling despite leaving a perfect shell. As he was staring into the depths of his own eyes, reliving the various achievements and failures he had experienced since he had started this life, he became aware of a second reflection in the smooth surface. There was somebody standing behind him. Betraying no panic, Altair pivoted to face the newcomer, whilst his mind was a whirlwind of confusion. Usually he could sense every minute change in air pressure. He should have known when the door was opened because there would have been the slightest rush of air as it was pulled into the corridor. As the visitor padded stealthily towards where he was standing, he should have detected the displacement of the molecules, but instead the Air Elemental had perceived nothing.

"Can I help you?" he asked coolly. The other man was tall with a scruff of straightened dark hair. He wore a long black coat, gleaming with buckles and chains that criss-crossed over his chest in a pattern that Altair imagined an old fashioned soldier might wear. He smiled casually at Altair's question, tilting his head to listen to the piano chimes.

"Not me personally," he began smoothly. "But the people I represent will be aided greatly by this... meeting."

"And just who exactly are they?" Altair edged slowly around the coffee table, but the intruder was quick to circle round also.

"You're going to die," he whispered, ignoring the question but pausing to see the effect of his statement. "You might not think you can, but I beg to differ." This riled Altair. Had this man not heard of him? He had been chosen! He was the representative of Air, and could not simply be dispatched at the will of some fancily dressed idiot. He had spent years honing his gifts so that his control over Air was unrivalled.

"You think you can beat me in a fight?" he challenged angrily.

"You think that's vodka you're drinking?" At this, Altair held out the half-drunk glass of vodka and sniffed it. It smelled just like always – the scent of the snowdrop covering the acrid fumes of the heavy spirit. The piano chimes began to clash discordantly as Altair lost his concentration. He raised his hand in an attempt to halt the jilting sound but nothing happened – the air was still filled with musical blows. He tried again, this time flicking his wrist more pronouncedly as the bystander watched with scarcely concealed amusement. Again, nothing happened.

The true horror of what the man had said was now dawning on Altair. Somehow his drink had been poisoned and he could not use his powers. He looked up wide-eyed as he realised that immortal did *not* mean invincible. The unknown man advanced.

"First I'm going to kill you," he sneered. "Then I'm going to hunt down your friends."

"But... but why?" Altair stammered, his voice cracking slightly as he realised his own vulnerability. For countless years now, he had thought that nothing could get at him, because nobody else had the powers he did, and now here he was, reduced to begging for his life.

"Because you shouldn't exist. You can't be allowed to live. Now I have one last question."

"Please don't..."

"Can you fly, Lord of Air?" Before Altair could answer, the other man raised his palm and it felt like a concrete block had hit Altair's stomach. He was lifted off his feet and was only dimly aware of crashing through the plate glass window, then being surrounded by roaring winds whipping at his hair and screaming in his ears.

The next day, Altair was found twisted and broken, lying on a pavement glittering with a thousand shards of glass, and the world began its mourning.

"At the beginning, there was nothing. Nothing until the five Elements decided to create the world. First of all, Ehraifir pulled together all the matter and moulded it into the planet."

The Book Of The Elements

<u>Myst's Call</u>
<u>November 15</u>
<u>19 Years Later</u>

Chapter 1 – The Song Of The Airbrands

Another cloud of smoke billowed into the darkening sky, accompanied by the dull booming of the far off explosion. Myst Waterbrand sat huddled in the shadows, her arms wrapped firmly around her knees. It was all she could do to stop her teeth from chattering - the evening was bitterly cold. As a jet of flame bloomed across the indigo, the scene in front of her lit up momentarily. She was crouched against a wall of mud, her force-musket in her lap. The only company she had was the weapon and the screams of the dying.

The crack of a primitive rifle rang through the air - dangerously close, judging by the clarity of the sound. Myst cast a nervous glance up and down the corridor-like trench, the sodden gouge in the earth curving away on either side of her. It was permeated by the steady humming coming from the mind beacon that had been set up around the next bend, the only constant in a war of ambiguity. The gunfire did not come again.

The thunderheads hanging threateningly in the gloom suddenly broke, adding yet another rumbling cacophony to the atmosphere. As the rain began to fall, Myst held up her hand with a sigh, the tiny droplets of water instantly avoiding her as if she had suddenly become magnetically polarised. The ground around her soon became thick and sludgy with the rain, and Myst snorted to herself. In books and films, this type of weather was called pathetic fallacy, weather that reflected the mood of the characters. Pathetic was exactly how she felt, covered in dirt and grime that was at least a week old. With a sigh, Myst thought back to before the war, when she used to go out and have fun, maybe catching the latest film at the cinema, or drinking with her friends. She remembered being especially proud of her hair, of how she used to wear it up, with two strands hanging down on either side of her face, a jet black frame for a striking portrait. Now, her hair was hastily stuffed beneath a heavy helmet, part of the armour she was wearing. The only part of her skin that was visible was her right shoulder, revealing a small round tattoo. A blue tinted circle with a single wave cresting in the centre identified her as a Waterbrand, a child gifted with the powers of Wonaitohelrai, the Water Element.

Myst took some comfort in the fact that all over the battlefield, her fellow Waterbrands would be shielding themselves from the rain in the same manner as her, and it made her glad that she wasn't a Firebrand. Not that it mattered in the end, she mused. After all, a corpse was still a corpse.

There was the unmistakable sound of feet trudging through the mud and slime, and in an instant, Myst was crouched, her force-musket trained in the direction of the approaching footsteps. It was as if a few frames had been cut from her life and she had simply snapped into her new pose with no transition. As she stopped concentrating on her spiritual umbrella, the rain seeped in and immediately began snaking down her neck. The footsteps slowed down, caution taking hold of whoever possessed them. Could it be an enemy soldier, stumbling into the wrong trench by mistake? Stranger things had happened, thought Myst as she waited, eager for the confrontation to be resolved with either friend or foe, as long as the uncertainty came to an end.

The barrel of a force-musket edged into view, but still Myst did not back down - after all it would have been all too easy for someone to simply pick up one of the special weapons from a dead soldier. As a man appeared, Myst sprang to her feet, catching him off guard.

"Hold it!" she commanded, every cell in her body steeled. The man lowered his force-musket, nothing but a black silhouette beneath the shadows of the towering walls of damp soil.

"Shitting hell!" he exclaimed, breathing deeply. "It's me." Myst instantly relaxed, recognising the voice. It was Riga, an Airbrand and also the flag bearer for her squad. They had been in the same training group all those months ago, and had pretty much stuck together throughout the whole process. It was only at the last minute that she had pulled ahead by a couple of ranks. Riga had become her closest friend since she had joined up, and the two of them could often be found in the early hours of the morning, finishing off a bottle after everyone else had called it a night.

Grinning slyly, Myst did not lower her gun. Unlike when they had first met, the young man's confident side seemed to have faded and now he was jumpy at the best of times - it was fun to scare him.

"Do something anyway Riga, I'm bored," Myst said, deliberately icing her tone to keep the man on edge. It was a simple request, and deep down she knew that Riga appreciated the need for it. It was standard procedure these days to demonstrate your powers when challenged. If you delayed, or did nothing at all then you could easily be mistaken for one of the enemy and killed on the spot.

Riga bowed his head, outstretching his right arm to the sky. The breeze instantly picked up, causing the rain to change direction as it fell to the ground, as if it was somehow confused. There was another crack of rifle fire as a large crow swooped from the inky mass of swirling cloud and perched lightly on Riga's wrist. It eyed Myst silently, as Riga looked up once more.

"That do you?" he asked impatiently, scratching his helmet. Myst sighed with mock disappointment.

"I don't know, it wasn't exactly spectacular," she began. "Make it do something funny." Myst nodded towards the crow. Riga took a step forwards, gently nudging the jet-black bird onto a ledge in the trench wall.

"Later, Captain - I have important news."

It still took Myst a moment to adjust whenever someone called her captain. She was only 25 years old, and had risen quickly through the ranks after volunteering, a recruit that showed some promise. She nodded and then leaned back against the wall as Riga sat beside her, taking off his helmet and rubbing his short brown curls. He was a couple of years younger than she was, and it showed. It was in the way his standard issue armour was a little too big for his slender frame, the way his helmet sometimes wobbled when he walked, but most of all, it was in his eyes. His sandy coloured eyes were fresh and alert - they carried none of the experience that Myst's showed, her life reflected in the depth of her eyes whereas Riga's were clear and bright.

"So what's the news?" she prompted. "If it's the review of tomorrow's plan then I've seen it. I ran into Sylvan this afternoon - he showed me." Tomorrow was the big day, nicknamed The Enforcement by the higher-ups. Tomorrow at sunset was when the Army Of The Elements would leave its trenches and root out the enemy, destroying them one by one. It still made Myst shudder to think of the final move and all the death that would accompany it.

"Then Sylvan told you? I'm surprised they sent me if you already knew…" Riga tapered off into silence as he caught the frown of confusion that Myst was now wearing.

"Knew what?" she questioned, already guessing what the answer would be. The Enforcement was supposed to have happened over a month ago, and by rights the war should have been over by now, but every time the AotE came close to pressing forwards, HQ would back down at the last minute and postpone the charge. Myst presumed they had pulled out yet again. Sometimes it seemed like they almost wanted the enemy to regroup after every surge. This time however, Myst was mistaken.

"You're not going," Riga stated. Myst opened her mouth in outrage.

"What do you mean we aren't going?" she exclaimed, not caring that her voice had risen strongly. "They can't leave us behind, we're one of the top squads in the whole AotE! Without us, the industrial estates would still be under Ghostbrand control."

"I didn't say *we* aren't going," Riga said softly, staring solemnly at his mud-caked boots. Myst still didn't understand what he was getting at - she was blinded by anger at the idea of her whole squad being grounded for The Enforcement. If the war was going to end, she wanted to be a part of it to justify the things she'd had to do.

Once it was clear that she wasn't going to say anything, Riga continued reluctantly. "Me and the others are still going over, it's just you… you've been reassigned." Myst recoiled, the words physically stinging her. "You're to report to the squad command at 0900," he added. That couldn't be right. Sending in a squad without its captain? What had she done to deserve this? She had followed every order, completed every mission and this was how HQ repaid her, by snatching her away before the end? Falling at the final hurdle was bad enough, but being pulled from the race just before it was even worse.

Abandoning all air of command, she folded her arms and shuffled round so her back was facing her comrade. This was no time to sulk, but it seemed to be the only option. If she disobeyed her superiors then she might as well be one of the Ghostbrands awaiting the hunt tomorrow, and there were a lot of soldiers who didn't share her restraint. She heard Riga shift behind her.

"You still want it to do something funny?" he asked tentatively as if walking on extremely thin ice. One wrong word could send him crashing through into Myst's anger. She shook her head stubbornly. "Fine," Riga said. "Will you settle for something beautiful?"

Myst screwed up her face obstinately, adding a childish grunt for the man's benefit. She knew it wasn't Riga's fault, but it still helped having someone close to vent her frustration at. An eerie wailing began, deep and quiet at first, but rising and falling as the notes changed. Within moments, the whole trench was filled with the mysteriously soothing aria, reverberating off the high walls and drifting back into itself, combining a multitude of layers and echoes into an increasingly complex tune. Despite being intent on maintaining her bad mood for the rest of the night, Myst could not help but turn around to see what was going on.

Riga was sitting cross-legged in the centre of the trench, his force-musket laid at his feet. The crow was once more standing on his wrist, and he was stroking it lovingly with his left hand. Myst looked on in awe as she realised that it was the bird that was making the sound - the bird was actually singing. It was as if each caress Riga made somehow coaxed a different note from the creature's throat. Like the beacons of the dark ages, other tunes began to drift up from different parts of the AotE front, mixing into a heavenly orchestra above the battlefields. Riga's fellow Airbrands must have joined in with birds of their own, as Myst could distinctly pick out the calculated shrieks of birds of prey, fleeting bursts of starling song and even the soft bass honking of a regal swan.

Watching Riga, eyes closed as he swayed gently in the bird's thrall, Myst wondered how it must sound to the Ghostbrands, cowering in their makeshift shelters on the other side of the battlefield - the other side of the war. Did they take comfort in the bird music? Or was it a sound of apprehension and fear for them? One thing she was sure of was that the enchanting bolero had given her the chance to dissect her feelings about her reassignment. Myst had reached the core of her issue and it wasn't the fact that she would miss out on the glory if her squad were successful. The true pain was in the realisation that if The Enforcement went wrong, her men would die and she would live on with the guilt of how she left them to do so alone.

A tear welled up in her glistening eye as the haunting tune died down, and she turned to Riga, who was watching her sincerely. She nodded silently to him and settled against the wall, once more hugging her knees to her chest. As Riga straightened up and grabbed his musket, Myst closed her eyes, knowing that as long as he was keeping watch, she could catch a few hours of sleep in safety, trying not to dwell on the parting that would come with morning.

Chapter 2 – Camaraderie

"Next, Ainarai enclosed the planet in a protective shell of gases, and the atmosphere was formed. Ainarai vowed that as long as he was protecting their creation, it would not falter nor sour."

The Book Of The Elements

It was still early when Myst awoke, the sky a pale blue as if morning's pastel had only glanced against its paper. Her feet were numb, as if they had been turned to stone inside her combat boots. She rubbed her eyes, and wondered why Riga had not woken her to change watches. Looking across, she found her answer. The young man was leaning back against the mud, eyes closed as his chest gently rose and fell. His helmet had slipped to an angle, his sideburns blending in with the first signs of stubble along his jaw line.

Normally, Myst would have been duty-bound to discipline a soldier for falling asleep whilst on guard, but instead she found herself watching Riga intently. He was frowning slightly as he slept, and she smiled to herself. In another circumstance she would have given anything to wake up next to Riga and simply watch him sleep until he woke, bleary eyed and tousle haired. Maybe, she mused. When the war was over, she would just be a normal girl. If the AotE asked her to continue serving, she had already settled her mind on declining. *Cut and run*, she thought with a grin.

She reached over and gently nudged Riga's bare shoulder, just beneath his Air tattoo, which was weathered to a tan colour. He moaned softly before slowly opening his eyes and drowsiness was instantly replaced with awful clarity as he realised what he had done.

"Oh gods…" he murmured, grabbing his musket and scrambling to attention. Myst also stood, jabbing him playfully in the back and sending his perfectly learned posture off balance.

"Relax, sleepyhead," she said. "I'm not going to report you, just don't go telling everyone you did it. Careless talk costs lives remember," she chided, repeating the well known phrase that had sprung up near the start of the war. She looked at her watch; she would have to leave soon. "It was close though," she smiled. "If I had slept through my big briefing with command I would have had to kick your ass." Riga blushed and looked down at his boots. Myst took a step forward, waiting for him to once more look her in the eyes. "I should be going…" Riga looked up and Myst jumped in, hugging him as tightly as she could, their armour meshing awkwardly. After a few moments, she broke away, leaving Riga stunned. He tried to speak, but couldn't find his voice, even though Myst knew what he was thinking. "I know, I know, that wasn't exactly professional." The man blushed once more.

"I wish we had more time…" he started, trailing off. He was obviously unsure of what to say to his captain.

"This war won't last forever," Myst said hopefully. "When we win, I'd best get a call or there'll be trouble."

Riga grinned sheepishly. "Do you remember how you felt when you first signed up?"

The young woman thought for a second. She had been so full of anger and duty that she had never thought twice about putting her name on the contract at the volunteer booth in the university quad. The feelings had rapidly faded.

"There's none of that left," she said thoughtfully.

"I know. I just want the war to be over too. Then we can get on with-"

"Whatever we want," she cut in with a curious smile.

"You better be getting off," the young soldier shrugged, and Myst wondered when she would see that youthful lopsided smile again. Riga straightened his back and saluted her.

"You fly that flag high and proud, boy," she said as she repeated the gesture. "And I'll see you on the other side."

"Yes Captain." Riga nodded confidently. Myst turned and picked up her pack from the pool of sludge it was sitting in. She had to use all of her strength not to turn back and give Riga one last smile before she left. The last thing she wanted was for him to walk into battle with distractions in his mind. She had probably given him enough to think about with that hug. Physical contact that didn't result in death was a rarity on the battlefield.

As she left her friend behind, Myst turned her mind to what might be waiting for her when she got to squad command. Some sort of special mission perhaps? Maybe she had done something wrong and was being pulled from the fight as punishment? Although Myst couldn't immediately think of any actual offences that she might have committed, she wouldn't put it past her ruthless employers to have found unofficial fault in some of her actions.

Myst rounded the next corner and passed the mind beacon, the humming reaching its peak. Out of instinct, she reached out and touched it, even though she knew that these special mobile beacons had been limited so no personal messages could be left, only orders for the commanders. After a few more twists in the trench, Myst reached a rusty door set into the mud. She heaved it open and proceeded down the damp steps into the squad command bunker.

There were two men in the bunker, one standing and one sitting at a dusty wooden table. A steady drip of water was beating its way regularly into the ground in one corner of the bunker, and the ceiling was drooping in places, sodden with the night's rainfall. The standing man was obviously a soldier, probably a captain like she was. She glanced at his right shoulder, noticing that he was a Firebrand. As she entered the room she saluted the men, and the Firebrand at least saluted her back. The man sitting at the table however, did nothing except watch with calculating eyes.

He was dressed in an expensive suit, and the look of disdain on his face told her exactly what he thought about being stuck underground with a couple of army grunts. He looked to be in his early forties, his cropped black hair flecked with grey. The briefcase that was on the table in front of him was emblazoned with a silver S inside a purple disc - the logo of Spyrus. Spyrus was one of the biggest companies in the country, which manufactured medicines. The only reason Myst wasn't surprised to see the man there was because she had heard that Spyrus had donated large amounts of money to the war effort. A number of Spyrus facilities in the outskirts were also being used as evacuation centres.

"Ah, Captain," he said in a businesslike tone. "Now that you are both here, we can begin. Two of our associates are currently taking shelter in a special refuge on the outskirts of the city. They must be collected and escorted to the Spyrus tower immediately. Failure to comply will greatly hinder the success of the AotE in this campaign." The man did not seem to pause at all during his speech, as if he was a machine reeling off a pre-recorded message, and Myst took an instant dislike to him. It sounded like he had other things on his mind, as if this was just a formality and he wanted to be somewhere else. Judging by the curling lip of the Firebrand captain, he felt the same way. The suited man rose from his seat and handed them each a photograph before resuming his position at the table, rigid and inhuman.

Myst found herself staring at the face of a young woman. She had startling blue eyes and dirty blonde hair that she wore tied up behind her head. The printed name at the bottom told her that the woman was Seren Airbrand, a name which meant nothing to Myst.

"These people work for Spyrus?" she asked, peering over the top of the photograph. The mysterious man shook his head minutely.

"No, they are associates of the company. He works for the Government." He nodded towards the photograph that the other captain was holding. "Whereas she is a scientist," he finished, inclining his head towards the picture of Seren. "The coordinates of the refuge are at the bottom of your sheets. I suggest you get to the tower before your... comrades make their little march."

"With all due respect," Myst began indignantly, "that *little* march could win us the war."

"And I'll be simply thrilled about that," the man simpered. "But this mission is just as important."

"To us or to you?"

With a wide smile, the man stood up and walked out of the room without saying a word, leaving Myst and the other captain staring bemusedly after him.

A number of things ate away at Myst's consciousness as she and the Firebrand headed towards the jeeps. Why had the man not introduced himself? Did he even have a name? And why had he sounded so nonchalant about The Enforcement? Surely tonight's march would be the biggest news since the fall of the Everrulers over 15 years ago.

Myst's mind was a whirling mass of negativity, but at the heart of it all was the most disturbing thing that she had noticed. The suit that the man from Spyrus was wearing had *two* sleeves, and that was supposed to be against the law. Hiding your brand was not only a mark of disrespect to the Elements, but the brands were a form of identification. Obscuring it was on the same level as faking a passport or driver's license, so why would a member of a respected company like Spyrus walk around in public with his brand hidden?

Chapter 3 – Spoils Of War

"Once the planet was secure in its atmosphere, Wonaitohelrai drenched the parched rock in a storm which lasted over a year, filling the largest and deepest pits to the brim with nurturing water."

The Book Of The Elements

Dust spat up from the tyres of the jeep as Myst steered it through the deserted streets on the outskirts of the city. There was still a lot of activity in the centre, but most people had fled to the depths of the countryside, and the suburbs were practically empty. Still, Myst could understand why the Spyrus associates were holed up out here. With the AotE mobilising, the Ghostbrands would not think to scour the outer reaches.

Now that they were away from the formality of the command bunker, the two captains had started to chat. The Firebrand's name was Talyn, a 28 year old from one of the neighbouring towns. His wife and son had been evacuated at the start of the conflict, and he was desperate for it all to be over so he could see them again. In turn, Myst had explained that she had signed up with the rest of them at the beginning, fuelled by feelings she could no longer muster. She paid particular attention to her bond with Riga. Talyn smiled as she told him of how they had first properly met.

It was Myst's first night off since she had joined the AotE, and her training group had hit some of the local bars hard. It hadn't taken her long to get drunk, and she was soon on her way back to the base. That was when she came across Riga. The young man was stripped down to his shorts, handcuffed to the flagpole. It had been his 23rd birthday, and the others from his lodge had left him there "to see his birthday in." Despite his protests, Myst had sat by his side teasing him until morning when his teammates arrived to cut him free. Although they had seen each other around, and even met once briefly before the war, it was this occasion that formed the foundation of their close friendship.

Now, she and Talyn sat in silence, the jeep racing down an empty main road. The only other vehicles they had seen were burnt out shells, long abandoned. It was like driving through a graveyard, rusted skeletons littering the ground like corpses would later.

The two soldiers lowered their heads as they drove past the statue of the Everrulers in Monument Square, built to commemorate their lives and mourn their deaths. Many times had Myst sat in the shadows of the four bronze men whilst drinking a coffee and waiting for friends, and she knew off by heart the plaque that was engraved on the base of the statue. Four names and four dates that would never be forgotten.

Altair – October 10
Dylan – March 3
Phoenix – April 1
Dexamenas – May 7

Deep down, Myst was relieved that the four statues had survived the devastation that seemed to have engulfed the rest of the city. Obviously, the war had caused its fair share of destruction, but the Eye of Fire, a volcano in the nearby mountains, had recently erupted – although in the two weeks since, it was becoming increasingly harder to tell what the volcano had wrecked and what Ghostbrand bombs had destroyed.

As she kept driving, she noticed Talyn taking some dried herbs out of his side pack, the strong smell of cloves hitting her nostrils. He crushed them in his fingers for a few moments until he was holding a small pile of fine powder in the palm of his hand. With a click of his fingers, the crushed leaves began to smoulder, releasing an overpowering scent into the jeep. A thin trail of smoke wavered in and out of definition before dissipating into nothing. Talyn closed his eyes for a few seconds, letting the flames pick up a little. Myst was surprised that he did not screw up his face in pain as the fire seemed to consume his hand, but then again he was a Firebrand. Myst assumed he had everything under control.

"There is a darkness within the flames," the man muttered, his tone overcast.

"A trap?" Myst queried, taking her eyes off the road briefly to glance at her companion. His dark eyebrows were furrowed, sincerity enhanced by the heavy shadow of the helmet along his brow.

"I'm not sure… but we should be on our guard. We have no idea why Spyrus are interested in this pair. It could be them the darkness refers to."

Myst nodded, turning into a side street and cutting the headlights. She slowed the jeep down until the engine was barely audible, and after a few metres, they were in the shadows of their destination.

Myst gasped softly as she realised where they actually were, even though it looked completely different from the last time she had been there. A set of iron gates lay twisted and broken at the side of the road, leaving the entrance that they had guarded wide open and vulnerable. The two captains stepped forward into a rectangular courtyard, cracked pathways criss-crossing over patches of dirt that had once held grass, soft and inviting. Myst remembered lying there in the summer heat, a can of beer in her hand as she studied for her final exams. Three blackened oaks stood gnarled and blasted in their respective corners of the quad - the warfare had stripped away their finery and essence, leaving petrified remains. The fourth oak tree lay embedded in the side of one of the buildings, a backwards embrace of nature and architecture amidst a layer of broken glass, each minute crystal glittering in the pale sunlight. It looked as if a sparkling snowstorm had hit that one corner only, raining shining blades into the ground. The mournful image was completed by three embossed letters lying in the dust, scuffed and cracked. They were jutting out of the soft mud like tombstones, commemorating the death of the institution they represented, a U, a C and an E - for this was the University of Central England. Talyn turned back to her, a look of curiosity on his face.

"Captain?" he asked. Myst looked at him and shook her head apologetically.

"Sorry," she began. "Just seeing this place. I was a student here before the war you know." Talyn nodded with understanding. "It feels like all this fighting has gone over my memories with a great black brush, and I can't get them back. I can't even remember who's to blame any more." She laughed nervously, hoping Talyn wouldn't think she had gone soft. She had become accustomed to being a soldier first and foremost, but occasionally the young woman still put in an appearance. Talyn put his hand on her armoured shoulder, a reassuring smile on his face.

"Come on, let's just find these two and get the hell out of here." Myst also smiled, relieved by Talyn's informality. It was good to know that she had his support and could still be a person rather than solely a captain. The two of them scanned the quad for any signs of activity, but there were none. The windows were blacked out as per the government's request so it was impossible to tell if anybody was inside. The pockmarks of recent gunfire were accompanied by a number of brazen bullet casings lying in the dirt – Ghostbrand weapons.

Only one of the blocks was in any habitable state, so at least they did not have to search the whole campus. Myst hung behind, staring at a series of scorched lines burned into the mud, while Talyn stepped forward and pushed on the door into the old John Terrence building, the glass crunching as he knocked the last few splinters from the frame. As the door swung inwards, a black rectangle of desolation opened up and the two captains stepped inside.

The interior of UCE was almost as bleak as the outside - much of the glass was shattered and the paint was flaking and chipped. With the windows sealed, it was gloomy and foreboding, with the lingering scent of stale air. With a crackle, Talyn ignited another flame in the palm of his hand to light the way, the other hand firmly holding a force-pistol. His musket was slung over his back. As he walked along the corridor, Myst kicked each door in turn, shining her own flashlight inside and revealing classroom after classroom, deserted and dishevelled. Where was everyone? If UCE was supposed to be the shelter for Spyrus associates then where were they all?

A loud banging interrupted Myst's thoughts. The two of them instantly froze, pistol and musket expertly trained, covering every angle of the hallway. When nothing appeared, Myst and Talyn stalked forward until they reached the first bend. Crouched in front of a vending machine was a thin looking man, dressed in a ragged lab coat. With a grunt of exertion, he lunged forwards and kicked the front of the machine as hard as he could, to no avail. The thick plastic remained unbroken. Talyn coughed loudly and the man spun round, eyes wide with fear behind thick glasses.

"Show us something, now!" Talyn commanded, and the man instantly obliged, clicking his fingers and sending a cascade of sapphire sparks to the cracked floor. Myst let out the breath she was holding without really knowing why. So the man wasn't a Ghostbrand, but surely someone with power was far more dangerous than someone without it?

"Please don't hurt me!" the man stammered. "I'm just hungry." Talyn walked over to the vending machine and rested his hand on the plastic, the heat from his palm instantly melting through. The man eagerly reached through the hole and grabbed a handful of chocolate bars. "Didn't think of that…" he muttered as Myst rolled her eyes. Some people didn't deserve an Element, she thought as she snapped into action, the level of authority rising in her throat like a repressed instinct breaking free.

"We're looking for these people, have you seen them?" She thrust the two photographs into the man's shaking hands. He squinted at them through the gloom before speaking.

"I wondered who Spyrus would choose," he pondered. Myst tutted impatiently - the sooner they found their targets, the sooner they could leave. If Myst was lucky she might even be able to catch up with Riga and her squad before The Enforcement.

"Where are they?" she demanded forcefully. The man jumped slightly as she spoke.

"Up… upstairs," he said weakly, pointing at the ceiling. Myst placed her free hand gently on his back.

"Show us," she said, pushing him forward. Myst was well aware that she was using an innocent man for a shield as she forced him around the corner and into the stairwell, but she had been trained that non-AotE lives were expendable unless stated otherwise. As regrettable as it was, if it came down to this man's life or hers, Talyn's or either of their charges, then unfortunately, the nervous man would be the first to go. When Myst had first been taught this, she had thought it a despicable slight against humanity, but after her first few weeks on the battlefield, survival had triumphed over morality in her priorities. She despised the fact that she had caused and witnessed death as a result of the war, but sometimes it was unavoidable. It was just another example of how war tainted everything, even compassion.

Luckily, the trip up the dark stairs proved uneventful, and they quickly found themselves in another corridor almost exactly the same as the one below. The only notable difference was that the branches of the fallen oak were jutting ominously through the left hand wall, as if they were trying to protect whatever was beyond by lacing the hallway with barriers. Ducking and weaving, the two captains followed the lab worker along the littered corridor until they reached a large foyer area, the usually comfortable chairs piled up against one of the doors.

Huddled in the corner of the large room were about thirty people, all of them dressed differently. Some of them were wearing lab coats like their guide, but others were dressed in suits, and there were even a couple of women that seemed to have been interrupted whilst at a formal occasion, their evening gowns now dusty and tattered around the hems. War could be so inconvenient, Myst thought to herself, the faintest hint of a smile trailing across her face as she took in the bedraggled appearance of the women who had obviously taken hours to prepare for whatever party they should have been enjoying. The nervous man scurried back to his companions as all eyes turned to the two captains.

Without warning, Talyn stepped forwards and placed his hand heavily on the collar of a young woman, literally hoisting her out of the crowd. She remained silent, screwing up her face as the soldier dragged her away and dumped her roughly next to where Myst was standing. She was wearing a lab coat and her face was streaked with dirt. Her hair was stuffed hastily beneath an old cap. The soldier glanced down at the photographs. Talyn had found Seren as simply as that, the young woman's azure eyes unmistakable.

"Are you here to save us?" piped up one of the women in the crowd of refugees. Talyn cast a nervous glance at Myst, obviously unsure of what to say. She set her jaw resolutely.

"No," she stated. "We're looking for Etain Earthbrand. Spyrus has specifically requested that we extract these two immediately." The faces of the crowd fell. "They are coming to collect the rest of you later," she lied as an afterthought, hoping to avoid a confrontation. Someone laughed acidly.

"Right. We all know how this ends." This came from a large man in a police uniform, his bare right arm bulging with thick muscle, the Firebrand clearly tattooed in dark crimson. His side was bandaged, but he stood as he if he was refusing to let it bother him. "Spyrus aren't coming for us; they've chosen their golden quad." He spoke with no hint of being surprised, even though Myst had no idea what he meant by 'golden quad'. Before she could speak, Talyn nodded towards the front of the crowd. A young man in a scuffed shirt and tie was pushing his way through the mass of people. Myst assumed it was Etain.

Suddenly the policeman grabbed him, his rocky arm curving perfectly around the Earthbrand's neck. His eyes widened and he yelped, gasping for air as his captor's arm tightened. In an instant, Myst had raised her force-musket and Talyn was flexing his fingers in anticipation.

"Screw Spyrus," the policeman spat. "And screw you!" With a flick of his wrist, the light bulbs in the ceiling exploded, the gas heating up and bursting into a wall of flame between the soldiers and the refugees. Seren screamed. With one fluid motion, Talyn shoved her to the floor and thrust out his palm, forcing the fire to blossom outwards, the blast of heat threatening to burn the faces of the helpless onlookers. Myst swung the barrel of her musket round and squeezed the trigger. She felt the energy jump out of her as a concentrated stream of ice shards exploded from the gun and javelined through the gap that Talyn had created.

Etain wriggled out of his vice-like prison as the policeman was pummelled by the ice bullets, blood mixing with the rapidly melting shots. Talyn widened the gap in the wall of fire as Myst charged through, snatching Seren's arm and pulling her to the side. With her other hand, she grabbed Etain's shirt and yanked him towards her, heaving him towards the Firebrand Captain. Etain lost his footing and crashed to the concrete. The other refugees were finally beginning to snap into action, overcoming their initial shock at the first attack. Although the entire exchange had lasted a couple of seconds, Myst felt like she had been duelling for hours. She glanced back to where refugees were starting to pour through the hole in the flames and advance threateningly towards Talyn.

"Run!" he shouted, straining against the concentration. Talyn dragged the young man off the floor and lowered his arm, the flames crashing in on themselves, engulfing one of the women who was just stepping through. Her screams pierced the air as the remaining survivors turned their attention to Myst and Seren. With one final thought for Talyn, she sprang into action, hauling her charge away along the corridor.

By the time the two of them reached the next stairwell, Myst was panting loudly. It wasn't easy running in armour that weighed the same as a small person, she thought to herself. Luckily, their pursuers had given up, obviously losing interest once it was apparent that some effort would be involved to catch them. Seren was leaning against the wall, hands resting on her knees, and Myst took the opportunity to look at the other woman. What was special about her? The man from Spyrus had said she was some sort of scientist, but there was still no clue as to why she was chosen. She was absent-mindedly fiddling with a bracelet she was wearing – a thin piece of cord with half a silver heart threaded on. As Myst squinted, she could make out a letter K engraved on the heart charm.

"What does K stand for?" the soldier asked, trying to strike up small talk. It would be far easier to protect this girl if she found she could actually get on with her.

"What?" Seren challenged, immediately on the defensive. She hastily tucked the bracelet into her sleeve. Myst was taken aback by her confrontational manner - after all, hadn't Myst just saved her life?

"Nothing," Myst replied. "I was just admiring your bracelet."

"Well don't."

"We should keep going, I have my orders," Myst grunted, knowing full well that small talk was now completely off the cards. "We need to get to Spyrus tower." Asserting her military superiority made Myst feel slightly better, but Seren's self-possession still grated at her.

"Why aren't they following us?" the other woman asked, obviously trying to change the subject. Myst thought for a second before replying.

"Maybe all the ones that could fight went after Captain Firebrand, or maybe that policeman was the only one who had any talent for combat - after all, going up against soldiers isn't exactly a good idea." Seren nodded, hopefully sensing that Myst wasn't in the mood to hang around. They made their way down the stairs and back out into the ruins of the quad, the air bristling with the tension of the confrontation.

Suddenly, Myst dropped to the ground, pulling Seren with her. She barrelled backwards until she was propped up against the fallen oak tree, eyes wide and alert, straining to confirm what she thought she heard. The sound came again - footsteps. More than one person by the sound of it. She pressed her finger to her lips, as Seren watched her lean cautiously around the splintered bark and twisted roots, clumps of mud helping her form to mingle in with the shadows.

A group of around fifteen men and women were creeping through the quad of UCE, long cloaks floating eerily behind them. Ghostbrands, thought Myst grimly. Each one had an old fashioned rifle slung over a shoulder, jagged knives belted to thighs and calves. It was a raiding party, probably drawn to UCE by the commotion that she and Talyn had caused. She shuddered as the silent figures stalked past her hiding place and headed towards the crumbling entrance, each one of their element tattoos horribly disfigured, long scars slicing through them.

After a few drawn out seconds of cramped crouching, the Ghostbrands were inside the building, and Myst was anxious to leave before the enemy found the people sheltering there. She doubted that they would show them much mercy. She indicated to Seren that it was safe to move once more, then grabbed her arm and led her hurriedly through the wreckage of the university gates.

Myst skidded to a halt at the sight that awaited her through the gates. The jeep she had been relying on to take them to Spyrus lay upturned against a huge bank of soil that looked as if it had been blasted out of the ground. A number of people lay scattered around the vehicle, unconscious or dead, Myst couldn't tell. Behind her, Seren tutted loudly with disgust.

"Stupid Ghostbrands!" she spat viciously. "They don't deserve to live." Myst instantly let go of the other woman's arm, spinning around to face her.

"What?" Myst hissed through gritted teeth. She had rapidly become annoyed, not only because she doubted that the Ghostbrands had wrecked the jeep, but because she knew what was coming word for word. Seren did not back down, her superior attitude almost visible as it waited to pounce from her mouth.

"The Elements fought to give us our power," she stated resolutely. "To allow Ghostbrands is to say that The Elements are imperfect, that they made an error somehow." It was like Seren was reading from an outdated textbook, an opinion that Myst had heard many times before. Furious, she took a step towards Seren until their faces were only a few inches apart. Although Myst stood half a head taller and was bulked out by all her armour, the wiry scientist remained still, her cobalt eyes clear beneath defiant brows.

"Is that really what you believe?" Myst challenged.

"It is… now." The two women stared at one another for a few seconds, before Myst turned and stalked off behind the jeep.

"They're just people, you know," she muttered. "The same as you and me." There was the sound of light footsteps as Seren jogged to her side, hopefully aware of the long walk that lay ahead of them.

"This coming from the captain who has killed more Ghostbrands than any other soldier in the AotE…" Seren said offhandedly, baiting Myst back into the argument. "I've heard of you, Myst Waterbrand. You're something of a hero. An icon of the war, if you will." Myst shrugged off the comparison as she stuck to the shadows.

"Don't believe everything you hear," the soldier muttered. "Every Ghostbrand I've killed would have killed me otherwise."

"And still you defend them?" The scientist sounded incredulous. "Ghostbrands have shot at you, killed your colleagues no doubt. I've seen innocent people die here!"

"Some would say we forced them into it," Myst murmured thoughtfully. "War makes people do desperate things, but I've only killed when I absolutely had to."

"Who was the first?"

"His name was Coen…" That was when things changed, after the first kill. "In a way I resent them for making me shoot first, but I don't hate them because they're-"

"Lower than us?" Seren interjected.

"That isn't true." Myst shook her head, increasing her stride.

"Of course it is!" Seren cried in disbelief. "Can a Ghostbrand do this?" As she finished her sentence, the wind picked up, swirling around and around through the dust until it looked as if the ground was reaching up with twisting tendrils, snatching at the air as it teased. "Or this?" Now the breeze played across the back of Myst's neck, a thousand tiny hairs prickling and tingling. Seren giggled childishly as Myst clenched her fist. The soldier spun around fiercely, breathing deeply.

"Stop it!" she yelled, a tear forming in the corner of her eye. Seren looked taken aback as she noticed the emotion she had stirred.

"I'm sorry," she whispered sincerely. "It must take a lot of courage to justify your actions." Myst sniffed back the tear, turning once more to face the abandoned streets, a look of disgust and pity rapidly being repressed. Once more, the stupid girl had got it wrong. Myst wasn't bothered about killing people. She had squared off with that concept months ago and come out the other side a better soldier. A worse person maybe, but a better soldier, and unfortunately that's what she was at this moment in time. It wasn't this that had upset her. Riga used to playfully harass her with the powers of Air, but when he did it, it was cute and tender. Seren had taken the action and sullied it with her elitist hatred.

With a sigh, Myst glanced at the lights of the small tower in the distance that marked their destination before tightening her helmet and hurrying across the street.

Chapter 4 – Soldier And Scientist

"With solid Earth, protective Air and cool Water, Farinaraiel prepared his contribution. Soaring over the planet, all manner of life sprang from his wake. Plants and animals alike arose from his eternal fires to bask in the glory of their creation."

The Book Of The Elements

The sun had long reached its apex and evening was rapidly approaching as Myst and Seren finally arrived in the cool shadow of Spyrus Tower. Although undamaged, the cold steel and glass looked oddly lifeless, and Myst realised that most of Spyrus' employees must have been evacuated to similar refuges like UCE. Staring upwards, she took in the seemingly endless amount of deserted floors, ending in a cruel metal needle, a shining silver S draped seductively around it, embracing coils poised to pierce the encroaching evening. The mast was the Spyrus mind beacon, the first one to be installed shortly after the last Everruler was killed so many years ago.

As the two women stalked between imposing stanchions, Myst thought back to her childhood and the time she realised that her world would not be as free as those before her. She had been six years old when Dexamenas, the Earth Everruler, was murdered. His fellows had been similarly despatched just months before, yet it was his death that had hit the world the hardest. Dex's murder cemented the fact that humanity was now on its own, a planet alone cut loose from the Elements' watch.

At the time, nobody knew who did it or why, but Spyrus had been quick to act, beating even the government at releasing a defensive measure. Myst supposed the Element Council had been too busy reeling from the tragedy of losing their leaders. Spyrus unleashed its mind beacon, amplifying spiritual energy throughout the city and connecting everyone - except the Ghostbrands, of course. As a scientist, Seren could probably have explained why Ghostbrands registered differently on the mind beacon, but Myst wasn't interested. When it came to fighting, she knew it wouldn't be science that secured the victory.

The beacon soon became precedent for a global network, with the army modifying the design like the mobile beacons back in the trenches. The only contribution the Element Council made was to reluctantly order the identification of all Ghostbrands, 'for their own good.' In under a year, the inevitable road to conflict had been paved, marked and then thrown wide open, although the general public had no idea, of course. To most people, the mind beacon was a convenient method of communication and nothing more. Strangely, it wasn't until a few months ago that the war actually broke out. The Element Council had just been through an election and a few changes had been made. Days later, the country was at war.

Myst shook her head as they came around to the front of the tower, the sleek glass doors pale barriers before them. There was no point dwelling on the past, she thought. So there were many other things she would rather be doing with her life, but she couldn't change that now. She had signed up like everyone else, and not all of them had lived this long. Myst shook her head and realised that Seren was watching her, an odd smile on her face.

"Are you having a moment?" she said sarcastically, before defiantly pushing the glass doors open. She had obviously been inside Spyrus before. Myst jogged after the foolish girl, tutting to herself. If Spyrus left their doors unguarded, anybody could have crept in and the two of them were far from safe. The glass doors led into a cavernous lobby, gloom and shadows chasing away the last of the daylight. A glass version of the Spyrus logo hung eerily in the centre of the room, as if it was floating there of its own accord. Myst strained to see what was holding the structure up, but then figured it was created by Spyrus, so probably *was* hovering by itself. Before Myst could issue any orders, Seren had strolled confidently up to the deserted reception desk and rung the bell, the sound echoing ominously through the foyer. The multitude of glass and crystal seemed to take the sound and project it through every glistening facet, and soon the shrill chime threatened to overwhelm the dusty atmosphere.

Suddenly, a cowering man popped up from behind the desk, and Myst trained her force musket on him instantly. His eyes were wide, his short blonde hair flecked with dust. He looked as if he had been hiding there for a long time, and it took Myst a couple of moments to see why. He was chained to the desk.

"Please…" he stammered pitifully. "Don't shoot." Myst lowered her musket with a frown.

"I'm not going to-" She was cut off as Seren lunged forwards, grabbing the young man by the throat. "Hey!" Myst shouted, running towards the desk, but the other woman ignored her, eyes flashing with malice and arrogance.

"I'm here for The Transcendence Protocol," Seren snarled into the man's face. He gulped, heart racing uncontrollably.

"It… it… it's on…" The poor guy was shaking so hard that he couldn't force the words out.

"Come on!" shouted Seren. Finally, Myst reached her and wrapped her armour bound arms around the smaller woman, pulling her away. With a scowl, Seren released her grip on her captive and he slumped onto the desk to which he was bound, his wrist red and blistered around the iron shackle. Choking back tears, he raised his head, gasping for breath.

"It's on the top floor." He managed to cough the words out more than speak them. Seren smiled darkly.

"Thank you," she said mockingly. The Airbrand pursed her lips and blew the man a kiss, the resultant blast of air whipping the dust around him into a furious storm. As both man and dirt fell to the ground in silence, Seren laughed quietly and walked over to a set of polished wooden doors set at the end of a small corridor, leaving Myst lost for words. Back at UCE Seren had seemed fragile and weak, but here she was more confident. Myst moved around the desk and hoisted the man to his feet, casting her eyes across his body. Through his shirt, she could clearly see deep slashes that had only just healed, as if he had been whipped. His bare shoulder bore a Waterbrand, blue like hers but different, the line cut through the centre unmistakable. The man was a Ghostbrand.

Pity and anger welled up inside Myst, unwilling to imagine what ordeals this man had seen. He was not only a prisoner, but a slave forced to sit at a desk day and night. She raised her force musket.

"Wait…" the man pleaded, his eyes widening even more, shining with tears of inevitability. Myst felt the energy flow through her and into the weapon as she prepared to squeeze the trigger. The young man moaned, turning away from his fate. Myst sent a burst of ice into the chain connecting the man to the desk, first freezing and then shattering the biting metal. The Ghostbrand jumped to his feet, incomprehension tainting his youthful features.

"What's your name?" Myst murmured softly.

"Rayne."

The soldier nodded sorrowfully. "Then go, Rayne," she said. "Run and hide. The AotE will be coming soon, and they aren't all like me." With one last fearful look at the captain, Rayne turned and sprinted stiffly through the glass doors and away from Spyrus forever.

A few moments later and Myst had caught up with Seren, following her into a spacious lift of brass and mirrors. As the lift hummed upwards, Myst watched the scientist stare upwards, back straightened with feigned ignorance, as if she had done nothing wrong. Eventually, Myst could take it no longer.

"Who the hell are you?" she asked, her tone lashed with disbelief. Seren turned to her blankly.

"Seren Airbrand," she stated matter of factly. "I thought you knew that when you came to get me."

Myst shook her head. "You know what I mean. Nobody walks into Spyrus and manhandles the staff." Myst was exasperated. "You knew he was a Ghostbrand, didn't you?"

Seren turned to her, a hungry shine in her eyes. "Did you kill him?"

"No."

"I thought the legendary Captain Waterbrand would want to up her tally."

"As I said," the soldier muttered hotly. "It's not like that. Anyway, he was unarmed and chained to a desk. He wasn't exactly a threat."

"They're all threats," the scientist snorted.

"What's The Transcendence Protocol?" Myst said, changing the subject. If she continued arguing with this woman then she would end up hitting her.

"I can't tell you," Seren sniffed. Gritting her teeth, Myst strode forwards. She'd had enough of the spoiled little rich girl act that Seren was playing and it was time to get serious. Seren had to know that now wasn't the time for games. Something brushed against Myst's armour, soft yet firm and the soldier looked across to where the scientist was backed against the corner. Her hand was outstretched, face creased with concentration as she strove to maintain the barrier of air that kept Myst from her. Foolish girl, Myst thought as she raised her musket. It was obvious that Seren had little combat experience, otherwise she wouldn't have even thought of challenging an AotE captain.

"Do you know what a concentrated jet of water can force its way through?" Myst whispered as she gently tightened her thumb. A serpentine trickle of liquid poured out of the barrel of the musket, hanging in the air, dipping and bowing as if it was being plucked and moulded by invisible hands. Seren raised her eyebrows as she watched the undulating siphon extend towards her. "Not just air…" Myst continued as the stream slipped through the wall of air that Seren was projecting. "Clothes… and skin…" The snaking tendril floated further forwards, looping over itself until it was hanging in front of Seren's left eye. The young woman let out a gasp, the liquid forming into a pinpoint as it edged closer and closer to the soft vulnerability of her eyeball. "And bone." Myst murmured her final words like she was issuing a deadly challenge, causing the scientist to quiver. After less than a second, Seren shrunk down to her usual slender frame, the brief glimmer of power fading from her like a tree's final leaves lost in the onslaught of autumn's bitter rain.

"I don't know exactly," she said hollowly. "It's a generic name given to the procedure when something major occurs." Seren reeled the explanation off in the same manner as the strange man in the bunker, and she must have been repeating exactly what she had been told. What frustrated Myst more was that she could tell Seren was finally being honest. She knew practically nothing.

"Something major?" Myst mused. "Something to do with the war?"

Seren shrugged, thoroughly unhelpful. "It would seem so. In the event of something big, Spyrus chooses representatives for the Transcendence Protocol."

"The golden quad…" Myst muttered to herself, recalling the words the police officer at UCE had used. "Why you?" she challenged, certain there must be more to discover. "What's special about Seren Airbrand?"

The scientist shook her head with a hint of a grin. "I have no idea," she said. "I'm just a researcher. There are lots better than me." Myst looked thoughtful for a second. "But I'm not sorry," Seren added defiantly. "Whatever Spyrus has planned for me, it's got to be better than waiting around at UCE. The only people coming for those others are the Ghostbrands and you know it. I'm glad I was chosen." The young woman finished, straightening her back with an air of superiority.

"But what is it you've been chosen for?" Myst murmured quietly. Before Seren could answer, Myst felt the pressure on her stomach change as the lift slowed to a halt. A metallic chime sounded from somewhere above them and the doors hissed open.

Chapter 5 – The Battle Of Avatars

"Finally, it was Dielunasar's turn to bestow his gift. After careful deliberation, he descended and walked among Farinaraiel's creatures, opening their minds to feeling, emotion, spirit and the power of the craft. Although the five Elements lived together in equality, each with mighty favours, it was Dielunasar who truly brought the world to life."

The Book Of The Elements

The mahogany doors parted onto a rich, lavishly decorated studio. Whilst the rest of the tower was completely devoid of life, this floor shone with wealth, every item seemingly gilded with silver or encrusted with gems. The wall in front of them was made of thick floor-to-ceiling glass, the entire city stretching out below, a band of pitch black beneath an indigo shawl. Beyond the angular silhouettes of houses and offices was the smooth darkness of the battlefield. The more Myst learned about her elusive mission, the more she was willing to wager that she would be safer out on the front than here at the pinnacle of Spyrus tower.

The captain turned away from the looming windows to where a large flat table sat, just off the centre of the room. A bright spotlight shone down onto a scale replica of the battlefield, both sets of trenches impossibly accurate. As Myst got closer, she saw thousands of tiny soldiers arranged in perfect formation, divisions made up of regiments and squads, a flag bearer at the head of each. With a smile, she picked out the one that Riga would be, remembering the layouts and maps she had studied incessantly before she was plucked from the frontlines. The miniscule figure even looked like her friend, synthetic eyes holding the promise of life.

Myst's attention drifted to the opposition, huddled in unfamiliar chaos. Their arrangement seemed to make no sense to her, the squads were not geometric, and rather the Ghostbrands seemed to have just spilled out onto the tiny field and entrenched wherever they landed. Myst had rarely seen the Ghostbrand soldiers at close range, but she guessed that the models had been forged with deadly accuracy. It was odd but, not for the first time, Myst was expecting to see scowls, or red eyes, or some other such propaganda, even though she knew that they were men and women like any others. Instead, the Ghostbrands' reduced expressions showed fear, tiredness and even regret. She could not imagine the effort it must have taken to etch the details on the figures no larger than her thumb. With a shudder, Myst continued to look around the room.

As her eyes roved across the glamorous décor, she saw Seren walk towards a corner that was bare brickwork twinkling with jewels. Leaning forwards, the scientist picked at the stones with her little finger.

"Oh!" she exclaimed with unashamed curiosity. Seren turned to Myst, a bemused frown on her face. "They're growing out of the bricks," she said with disbelief. The soldier and the scientist stared at each other with equal wonder.

The elusive silence was broken by a shrill whistling that seemed to come from both outside and within the room. Seren looked confused, but Myst knew exactly what the whistling signified, as she had been preparing for it for months. The whistles screaming through the trenches marked the start of The Enforcement. When she had first been informed of the signal, she had thought it absurd to herald the AotE's approach, but now she realised it didn't matter if the Ghostbrands knew they were coming or not. This was meant to be the march to end the war.

Eagerly, Myst hurried towards the windows, hoping to catch a glimpse of what she should be leading. The city outside was dark, nominal variance in blacks and greys marking out abandoned streets and crumbling buildings, but beyond was a flock of miniscule lights, an army of fireflies pressing through the darkness on a mission to enlighten the creatures of shadow. She reached up, fondly touching the flashlight mounted on her one shoulder pad. Myst took a deep breath, closing her eyes, envisioning the soldiers moving steadily through the mud. She could hear every stifled breath, every metallic grate of armour and every trudging footfall sinking into soft earth. And then the fighting began. The two armies must have finally collided as the room was suddenly awash with noise. The chattering of rifle fire mixed seamlessly with the various hisses and bangs of force muskets into a single deafening clamour.

Myst opened her eyes and spun round to see the once ordered regiments of the model battlefield now a swarming mass of movement. Each tiny figure must be linked to an actual person on the front, and the captain ran to the table, dropping to her knees in order to spot Riga. She quickly found him on a slope above the trenches, mud splattered across his knees. The soldier's musket was still slung across his back, but he was brandishing his flag like a pike, swinging the long steel pole back and forth, powering into a number of cloaked Ghostbrands. As the table erupted with miniature flashes of light and jets of colour, little Riga shot his hand out, tiny face pure emotion as he lifted a Ghostbrand from the ground and smashed it, arms flailing into the soil, borne by the power of the Airbrand. The avatar turned as a second wave of shrouded assailants crested the hill. The small figure jammed his flag into the ground as he fumbled with his musket, Myst watching with eyes wide and teeth clenched.

Suddenly, the lift chimed and both women looked up as the doors began to move. The young man from UCE stumbled out, a thin trickle of blood running down his forehead. He was alone and Myst noticed that he was wearing an AotE helmet and body armour.

"Where's Captain Firebrand?" Myst asked as she got to her feet, but she didn't hear what Etain said next. She had glanced back at the battle and her world had fallen silent as if she was being held underwater. Riga's flag was lying in the mud, trampled and tattered. The purple emblem was stained with crimson, entangled amidst a pile of bodies, some still twitching from whatever force had slain them. Myst was vaguely aware of someone speaking, but the sound was muffled and deadened. All she could think about was how she had been robbed, the wave of sorrow stinging as it engulfed her. She had turned away for a second and the little Riga was gone, swept away in the flood of war. Myst should have been there with her men – she should have been there to protect Riga.

Gradually, the sound began to feed back into Myst's consciousness, the thick block evaporating.

"What is the Transcendence Protocol?" the young man asked Seren.

"She doesn't know anything," Myst snapped with a sneer. Anger began to boil in the soldier's core. Everything that had happened had been about the stupid protocol. If it hadn't have been for that, she would have been out on the front helping her team. Ignoring the confused looks on the faces of Etain and Seren, Myst slung her force musket and marched towards the lift. Etain was just about to say something when the doors slid softly open and the soldier stepped inside.

When the lift finally reached the ground floor, Myst took a deep breath and waited anxiously for the doors to open once more. As they slid apart inexorably slowly, a suited man rounded the corner and approached the doors, a curious smirk on his ageing features. Myst recognised the man from the bunker. Although it had only been this morning, she felt as if she had not seen him for years. The man stepped forwards, forcing Myst to edge backwards into the lift.

"Going somewhere?" She didn't reply. "And there's no need for that, Captain Waterbrand," the man added, flashing pale eyes towards the musket Myst was clenching. She lowered the gun, but did not release her grip. The man was still not showing an element brand, and as far as Myst was concerned that meant he had something to hide. Even Ghostbrands displayed their mutilated tattoos, she thought.

"You never told us your name," Myst stated icily. "Yet you seem to know all about me."

The man looked pensive. "My name…" he muttered thoughtfully. "My name was lost to me many years ago. For now, however, you may refer to me as Firaire." Myst shook her head slightly, unsure of what she had just heard. It was a word in the language of the Elements, but nobody spoke it now and it wasn't one of the five words she did know - the names of the Elements themselves: Ehraifir, Wonaitohelrai, Ainarai, Farinaraiel and Dielunasar. Come to think of it, Myst remembered, the Spyrus man on the Element Council had a strange name too, but at the time she hadn't recognised it for the ancient language.

"What's the Transcendence Protocol?" Myst asked, refusing to be fobbed off again.

"It's a journey… of sorts," came the reply.

"Well good luck with it," Myst said sarcastically. In truth, the captain could not care less what Spyrus chose to do with its protégés or whatever they were. All she could think about was rushing back across the city and maybe getting to the trenches in time to make a difference. She had done her job hadn't she? Firaire had told them to bring Seren and Etain to the tower, and here they were.

"It's not as simple as that Captain," Firaire said softly as Myst's heart sank so fast she felt it must have been caked in concrete. "Seren and Etain cannot do this alone. We have need of your… skills. Two Captains, two civilians."

Myst gulped, lowering her head. "Captain Firebrand didn't make it. Etain arrived alone."

"Then it seems you have increased in value." Value?? Myst was thunderstruck. Was that all she was, a commodity to be assigned a worth? "Normally of course, we would insist on finding a fourth member to replace him, but well, time is running out. Spyrus needs you to leave now."

"I don't work for Spyrus," she snarled, feeling like a soldier once more. She pointed to the logo on her breastplate. "You see this here? That says I take my orders from the AotE, and nobody else."

"I'm afraid I can't let you leave this building Miss Waterbrand," Firaire scathed, purposefully emphasising the "Miss" as if stripping her of rank verbally would detract from her somehow.

Myst had taken enough shit from Spyrus today, her vessel of anger threatening to overflow with hot rage. "Get bent," she hissed, hoisting her force musket up in the cramped lift until the barrel was inches away from the older man's face. The slightest movement on her part could send a spray of boiling water at him, scarring and burning, yet Firaire did not even move. A sly smile spread across his pale face.

"Please…" he laughed patronisingly. "I'm part of Spyrus, what upper hand could you possibly hope to gain?" He flashed his palm in Myst's direction, and her force musket instantly shattered, hundreds of shards of plastic, white hot metal and rubber gripping clattering against her armour. The soldier only just managed to close her eyes in time before her face was pelted. Myst was stunned at how easily the old man had disarmed her. She sighed in defeat.

"Where is it you want me to go?"

Ardent's Ruin
November 1

Chapter 6 – Transit

"Some species flickered into extinction until eventually humanity emerged. It was apparent that the world was having difficulty controlling its immense power and so the Elements bestowed one final gift before departing back to Elohelmarelnartoh – a gift in the form of four men crafted in the ideal of the Gods. Dexamenas, Altair, Phoenix and Dylan, a representative for each physical aspect of life. They became the Everrulers."

The Book Of The Elements

The bus shook gently as it bounced along the dusty road, the outskirts of the city slipping past as if it was the buildings rushing backwards to escape their inhabitants. The narrow windows of the bus were open, but to those inside, it made no difference. It seemed the air was purposefully avoiding the coach, leaving the atmosphere stale and rank.

21-year-old Ardent sat alone, leaning against the grimy window and lost in thought. He wondered, like everyone else on the packed coach, when he would see the familiar skyline again. Eventually, the houses thinned out, and the vehicle jostled its way onto the main road leading to the motorway. They hadn't been told where they were going - all he knew was that he and a dozen buses full of similarly apprehensive men, women and children were being evacuated because of the war. For their own safety of course. The war had already been going for countless months, but only now had the violence reached the heart of the city. Ardent shook his head minutely, remembering the leaflets that had been posted through every front door when war had first broken out. It had told him to "do his bit" and here he was, slouching into the threadbare upholstery on the hard seat. Not that his journey was without purpose, he had his promise to keep, after all…

Ardent cleared his mind. If what the others were saying was true, then Spyrus had found a way to monitor everybody's thoughts, although he doubted a medicine company would be interested in that sort of thing. He took a moment to glance around at his companions. The woman across the aisle from him was cradling a small child. He watched as she lovingly stroked her daughter's hair, cooing gently with the simple reassurance that as long as they were together, nothing bad could happen. After a few seconds however, the woman became aware of Ardent's gaze, and looked across at him. The hint of a smile instantly faded away as her hazel eyes scanned his appearance, rapidly turning into a look of suppressed disgust. Ardent thought about trying to trick his mind into thinking that perhaps the woman had taken offence to his hairstyle, half spiked, half covering his face, vivid red with black highlights, or maybe she had disapproved of his attire, after all he did look like one of those "street youths" that the high society blamed on rock music. But no, it was obvious that the woman had scrutinised his bare shoulder and seen the mutilated Firebrand that lay on it.

Turning away, Ardent became aware that other passengers were staring at him too, not caring to disguise the fact, even when he stared questioningly back. The young man shrugged inwardly and resumed his position of gazing through the murky glass at the trees that were now zipping past, playfully racing in and out of his field of vision. He had forgotten to check if they were heading North or South. Although his attention was fixed outside of the vehicle, Ardent could still feel the eyes boring into him from every angle. You'd think they'd never seen a Ghostbrand before, he mused, for that was what he was, and surprisingly unashamed of the fact. He had been eleven when his parents had resigned themselves to the fact that Dielunasar's gift was lost on their only son, yet it was he himself who had slashed his brand. *Why hide it?* he thought. It was not like there was a point to keeping his Firebrand intact - he couldn't do any of the things it represented. On the whole, Ardent had lived the last decade of his life just as happily as the decade before that, although sometimes, the briefest hint of disappointment crept into his consciousness. Like now, for instance, he considered how satisfying it would be to burn a few manners into his audience. He could picture the flames leaping from his hands into the faces of the onlookers, even though, he reasoned with a sly grin, if he could have done that, they wouldn't have been staring at him. As it was, he simply ignored them until their grim fascination waned and they returned to monitoring the contents of their own window space.

     Indeterminable hours later, Ardent awoke from a reluctant sleep, his back sore from the cheap fabric he was curled on. The sky outside was turning rosy, the fiery pink one last effort at recognition before the sun begrudgingly gave way to its cold sister. By the looks of the surrounding landscape, the coach had taken them up into the hills, which meant they must be heading North. Ardent made a mental note, as no doubt it would help if he needed to leave.

Suddenly, Ardent was aware of movement out of the corner of his eye. Turning slowly, he saw that the young girl opposite was awake, gently prying herself free from her mother's embrace. She was about eight years old, her blonde hair tied in a plait reaching halfway down her back. The girl sat up and casually surveyed her surroundings. All of the other passengers were sleeping.

"My mum says you're a Ghostbrand," she whispered, leaning forward, sapphire eyes burning with innocent curiosity. In response, Ardent proffered his shoulder so that she could see his damaged brand. Mouth open as she considered this new sight, a tiny flicker of hesitation crossed her small features. "But you don't look bad…" she muttered, unaware that her thoughts were aloud. To his surprise, Ardent found himself smiling. Here was a small child genuinely interested, not because she thought he was a freak, but simply because she sought to know more about the world she lived in. He pulled his legs up and hugged his knees, creating enough space for the child to squeeze onto the seat next to him. She was still eyeing his brand with awe. "Did it hurt?"

Ardent thought for a moment. "Yes," he began. "But it was something I had to do. When you feel that strongly about something, pain doesn't seem so important."

"You did it yourself?" she exclaimed, her high voice ringing with disbelief. "But why? Didn't you want to be a Firebrand anymore?"

The young man paused for a second, trying to find a way of explaining so the child would understand. "It wasn't a case of wanting anything, I'm just not a Firebrand."

"So they branded you by accident?" the girl concluded.

"In a way," said Ardent, trying to keep any hints of resentment out of his voice. He had told himself he was over his issues, and the last thing he wanted to do was rant at a youngster. "People are still very small when they are branded, like I bet you don't remember when yours was done?" She shook her head, clamping her hand protectively over her Airbrand. "Sometimes the clerics make a mistake when they sense your power… sometimes there isn't any power at all."

"And you can't do *anything*?"

"I can do lots of things!" Ardent reprimanded hastily. "My life doesn't have flashes and bangs, but it's still my life. It's just that that's not enough in some people's eyes."

"I'm sorry, I hurt your feelings," she said, looking down into her lap, suddenly withdrawn. Ardent sighed, almost frustrated with the girl's purity. Nothing she said was meant with any intent, yet she was oddly astute in her reasoning.

"Don't worry," he said softly. "You're a lucky girl. Nobody will treat you like dirt, whatever happens."

"I've heard kids at school talk about people like you," the girl said, choosing her words carefully. "They said you started the war, but you can't be that bad. You wouldn't be getting evacuated if nobody cared about you." As she spoke, Ardent resisted the urge to snort sarcastically. The reasons for his evacuation were certainly not because the government cared about him. "I think you're just like us really. With better hair."

Ardent laughed quietly. "Well when we get wherever we're going, I'll show you how to do it up cool ok?" He reached into his pocket and pulled out a single coin and balanced it on his thumb. With a smile, he offered it to his new friend, flicking the coin upwards just as she reached for it. With a wave of his wrist, the coin had vanished, tucked snugly up his sleeve. The girl beamed.

"You *can* do magic!" she exclaimed, eyes roving eagerly trying to discover where Ardent had hidden the metal disc.

"There's no such thing as magic," Ardent muttered, remembering how everyone at school had been taught the maxim of the deceased Everruler, Dexamenas.

Before the girl could reply, the coach turned a sharp corner with a rumble, and began to climb steeply. It looked as if they were finally reaching their destination, the wide, well paved road giving way to a narrow gravelled driveway. Ardent looked down at the girl.

"You best get back to your seat," he said fondly. "I don't want your mother drowning me or something." She grinned as she slid off the seat and turned back to face him, her hand extended.

"I'm Abi."

"Ardent," he nodded.

"Nice to meet you, Ardent Ghostbrand." And with that, she turned and climbed back up next to her formidable mother. Bemused, Ardent turned back to the window. He had never been called that before and technically his surname was still Firebrand, but he kind of liked the idea of being Ardent Ghostbrand. If he ever got back to his friends, he decided, he would get them to call him that. Except his girlfriend, he thought. Eir had always called him Firebrand as a pet name, and he had got used to it as a term of endearment.

The bus slowed to a halt, the crunching of the grit audible over the dying drone of the engine. People throughout the vehicle were beginning to stir, sensing the change in inertia, but Ardent was already on his feet, shouldering his small rucksack. Striding down the aisle, the driver barely acknowledged him as he stepped down into a large circular drive. A number of empty buses were already parked in front of a set of majestic stone steps, while the silhouette of what must have been a stately home loomed up behind, black and sinister against the darkening sky.

Chapter 7 – The Illusion Of Safety

The cool evening air rushed into Ardent's face as his feet crunched onto the gravel. His breath floated eerily into the indigo as he stared apprehensively at the dimly lit manor entrance. He could just make out the faint outlines of armed guards standing either side of the doorway, and as the other refugees filtered past him he could make out brief waves of sound. As he had been warned, the guards were checking evacuation papers to make sure that these people had the right to be there.

Ardent instinctively felt inside his pocket, feeling the lump of the papers he was given before he left. The evacuation warrant did not belong to him and for a moment he fell victim to the notion that the guards might be able to sense that somehow. Having never done even an ounce of craft in all his life, Ardent was still shamefully unaware of its limits. He realised that he was standing alone by the side of the bus, the other evacuees already making their way up the menacing steps and through the doorway, the warm glow of soft light flashing briefly as each one was admitted. It was time to move. His mind was screaming but his feet were rooted with sudden fear. What if the guards found out he wasn't authorised for evacuation? It wasn't that he was afraid of death, for they would shoot him, it was a predominant sense of regret that he would fail in his task, and letting his friends down was one of the worst things that Ardent could imagine. It wasn't too late to turn around and run. The guards hadn't seen him yet, and would be none the wiser if he left, but that would mean lying to Emrys about his family, and he couldn't do that. Not to mention Eir was in there somewhere, having arrived on an earlier bus.

As he mulled over his treacherous thoughts, Ardent's hand slipped onto the other item in his pocket, a small black stone, laced with bright red lines. It was a lump of haematite, which Emrys had given him along with his papers. Ardent had no idea what it was for, but Emrys had said that if he needed protection, he should unwrap the stone. Now seemed like a good time, after all if he couldn't even get inside the building safely, Ardent wouldn't get very far. Casting a glance across the driveway to make sure he wasn't being watched, he crept around the side of the bus and into the shadows of the trees bordering the courtyard. Crouching low next to the still warm tyre, he gently pulled out the velvet wrapped rock and lifted the soft fabric.

At first nothing happened, and Ardent felt embarrassed to be crouching there, staring at the small stone like it was some sort of saviour. Maybe now was not the right time after all - perhaps the stone was intended for something else and it would somehow let him know when the time came. Resignedly, the young Ghostbrand fumbled with the maroon velvet, and that was when his skin brushed against the stone. Maybe it was body heat, friction or something else, but the haematite flashed green. Ardent dropped it with a gasp and watched it curiously as a figure seemed to grow out of the cold black rock.

It looked like Emrys, but different somehow as if this version was a little stronger and more confident. Whilst the image composed itself, Ardent could not help releasing a stifled snigger at his own stupidity. It wasn't Emrys in the stone, it was his brother Etain. Of course Emrys wouldn't have been able to orchestrate this illusion, he was a Ghostbrand just like Ardent. Eyes fixed with concentration, Etain began to speak in little more than a whisper.

"Brave dog, gentle hound

To my journey's end I'm bound
Thee in Ehraifir's name so pure
Walk thou with me to my door
Guard me from harms and all foul act
Bargest, Bargest commend this pact."

Even before Etain finished the incantation, Ardent felt the atmosphere change in his surroundings. The trees seemed a little less oppressive, the grass a little more comforting just out of his reach. The flickering trace of Etain nodded solemnly. "Hopefully this will see you through any trouble. Don't forget to thank him, and take care brother..." With one last glimmer of emerald, Etain was gone, and the haematite was normal again, cold and unyielding.

A twig cracked amidst the gently swaying trees, the mottled shadows hiding a myriad of uncertainties. Cocking his head slightly, Ardent thought he heard soft footsteps padding across the grass, accompanied with light panting but nothing was there when he turned to look. Normally, the young Ghostbrand would have felt the fear seeping through him like a poison, but for some reason he remained calm. It was as if Etain's words had soothed his soul into a state of serenity. The Earthbrand had mentioned some sort of hound, a Bargest, or even *The Bargest*, Ardent wasn't sure which, but he did know that the spell was meant for Emrys, and Etain would never do anything to hurt his brother.

With renewed confidence, Ardent smeared his brand resolutely with dust, then stepped out of the silhouette of the coach and strode across the pebbles towards the concrete steps. His feet fell lightly as he ascended, the hairs around his mauled brand bristling in the cool night. Ardent held in his breath as he approached the guards.

"Papers?" one of the towering men grunted. It was obvious that the guards were bored of their assignment.

Fumbling in his pocket, Ardent proffered his crumpled papers and the guard took them casually glancing at the words. As the man read, the Ghostbrand eyed him carefully, ready to jump back if there was trouble. The guard's armour was emblazoned with the logo of The AotE, the official army of the government, a force musket slung over his shoulder. The soldier on the opposite side of the doorway was tapping his feet impatiently. Ardent was the last evacuee from the coach and the guard appeared to be anxious to head inside.

As Ardent was waiting, something made the first soldier chuckle maliciously. "A Ghostbrand, eh?" he sneered. Ardent snapped his head up, suddenly alert. He was in the middle of nowhere with two soldiers that had been conditioned to hate his kind. Nobody would miss him. "Earthbrand not good enough for this one!" the soldier said, turning to his companion. "Let's have a look at it then." Before Ardent could move, the soldier had his forearm caught in a burning grip. He twisted, forcing Ardent around until his shoulder was inches from the guard's scowling face. Ardent gritted his teeth as his shoulder groaned, threatening to dislocate and incinerate his system with fiery pain. Ardent was sure that the soldier would notice that he had originally had a Firebrand and not an Earthbrand – even with the covering of dust, it was obvious that the colours were different. Before the guard said anything however, a loud wailing howl drifted from the trees.

The guard looked upwards, narrowing his eyes but not releasing his grip on Ardent's arm. Once again, the howling sound pierced the night, louder this time, more ferocious. The two soldiers glanced nervously out across the dark driveway, scanning the front of the manor for any signs of movement. Like a spark flashing from hot steel, a large creature bounded out from the forest and skidded to a halt in the centre of the circular parking area, gravel skittering away as the huge paws trampled it. The beast was covered in sleek fur, black mottled with grey so that as the creature breathed, its body seemed to ripple and shimmer. The soldiers raised their muskets as Ardent was shoved roughly into the wall.

"Bloody wolves..." muttered the soldier closest to the Ghostbrand. Despite two guns being trained on it, the wolf sat on its haunches, tongue hanging out almost cheekily, daring the soldiers to advance. Ardent grimaced as the soldier started to smile. He didn't look like the sort to care for animal rights. With a jolt, his musket shook as he squeezed the trigger, releasing a focused stream of rock shards in the hound's direction. Unable to tear himself away, Ardent saw the wolf bare its yellowed teeth, dripping with saliva as the razor sharp slivers of stone screamed towards it. With a third howl, the creature pivoted and sprung into the air at the same time, vanishing into the darkness as the bullets slammed into the trees, flecks of bark cascading to the cold ground. Ardent stared, wide eyed. Had the wolf been killed? Or had it run away? It happened so fast that he couldn't be sure. One second it was sitting there taunting the guards, and the next it was gone. He squinted, trying desperately to make out the animal's outline in the dappled shadows of the woods, but he could not distinguish anything familiar.

"Alright you, get inside." The guard had turned to face him once more, a slightly curious look on his face as if he himself was unsure as to where the wolf had gone. "It's lucky your brother's some government bod - I wouldn't want to be in some of your mates' shoes right now." With another rough jostle, the guard pushed Ardent towards the door as he and his companion stepped warily down the stairs to investigate the area that was just seconds ago filled with fearsome beast.

Ardent hurried inside, rubbing his shoulder tenderly. The ornate wooden doors opened into a cavernous entrance hall, a highly polished staircase snaking upwards in the centre. Staring upwards, he saw a lofty ceiling, covered in swirling plaster as if the surface was molten, shifting and spiralling as it bubbled. From the noises creeping out from a room to his right, Ardent guessed that the other evacuees had filtered inside. He approached the door, cautiously nudging it until a thin crack of vision was afforded him. The room was some sort of theatre hall, rows of folding chairs set up before a small stage.

As Ardent slid into one of the empty seats, a man in an expensive suit stepped up to a burnished lectern. Both of his shoulders were covered, and Ardent could see shadowy members of the audience whispering and staring in disbelief. The man must be very important, the young Ghostbrand mused, otherwise he would never have been allowed to cover his brand. He waited until he had everyone's attention before clearing his throat.

"Ladies and gentlemen," he began, smiling widely. "I know you are all tired and apprehensive of your new surroundings, but let me assure you that I will personally endeavour to make your stay as comfortable as possible until these difficult times are over." Pausing for dramatic effect, the suited man surveyed the onlookers, eyes glinting almost greedily. "I'm known as Firaire, and I'll be presiding over this little adventure. I want you all to know that if any of you have any queries or issues, please don't hesitate to contact me. We've been taking evacuees here for a couple of weeks now, but they will certainly be asleep now. I'm sure there will be a few reunions in the morning. Before we retire, I'll just go over a few tiny rules that will make things run as smoothly as possible." Ardent frowned, suddenly wary of the man's tone. It sounded as if he was almost happy to have everyone here, turfed out of their homes and running from conflict. "First of all, meals will be served here at eight, one and six every day - make sure you are all here bright and early to get your share. Next, under no circumstances is anybody permitted in the cellar. For your own safety, of course," he said, simpering. "There's a lot of machinery down there, we wouldn't want any unnecessary injuries... Does anybody have any questions?" the man beamed. Ardent glanced around the room, but only one middle aged man had his hand up.

"How long are we going to be here for?" he asked, obviously voicing the thoughts of many. Firaire smiled once more.

"Well you won't be allowed back to the city until the war is over, but as for here," he spread his arms wide like a proud businessman showing off his riches. "Some of you may be transported to other facilities if necessary. We had a bus load transported East just this morning."

Another hand shot up from the crowd. "Can we contact people at other evacuation centres, or home?" This time it was a woman, on the verge of tears. Perhaps she had sons or daughters fighting in the city.

"There will be a mind beacon in the foyer for you to send messages to your loved ones," Firaire said. "We also have a telephone if that method is preferable to you. Now if there are no more queries, I shall bid you good night." As Firaire nodded and stepped down, Ardent shuffled uncomfortably. Was it his imagination, or did the man shoot him a look when mentioning the telephone? Did he know Ardent was a Ghostbrand?

The young man shook his head slightly as people began filtering out of the hall. Suddenly, all Ardent could think of was sinking into the warm embrace of a soft mattress. He would start searching tomorrow - after all, he had been stuck on a stuffy coach all day. He shouldered his backpack and joined the slow moving stream of evacuees as they shuffled up the grand staircase and into a long corridor, heavily polished wooden doors set at regular intervals. In small groups, the others began separating off into these rooms, leaving Ardent standing in front of one of the few remaining unclaimed doors. He wearily pushed the dark wood and entered the room, before halting completely, eyes wide with fear. The wolf was crouching in the centre of the room.

The rasping breath of the wolf was the only sound as the door gently swung shut behind the Ghostbrand. Trying not to make any sudden movements, Ardent edged to the side and lowered his rucksack, the wolf's eyes never leaving him for a second.

"Um..?" Ardent gulped. The wolf watched him carefully, eyes focused with extreme dedication. Out of nowhere, a guttural voice sounded in Ardent's head, rough and unkempt just like the shaggy creature that sat before him.

"You summoned Ehraifir's hound, human! The Bargest has done your bidding, what say you?" Although the wolf remained still, Ardent was sure that the voice belonged to the animal. He frowned briefly before remembering what Etain had said in his projection. Maintaining eye contact, Ardent made a small bow, holding his palm out sheepishly.

"Thank you great spirit, for protecting me and helping me pass through safely." With that, the Bargest gave a light nod, padding over to affectionately lick Ardent's hand. The young man smiled as the rough tongue tickled his palm. Suddenly, the Bargest yelped loudly, causing the human to jump back in fright. The wolf was now glaring at him menacingly.

"Unclean!" the voice barked sharply. "You do not have the gift! How is this possible?" Ardent looked down at his palm, then realised what the Bargest was talking about. The wolf must have sensed that he was a Ghostbrand. Ardent held out his hand hopefully once more, but the creature leapt forwards snapping violently and falling a hair's breadth short of crunching Ardent's wrist. The young man began to panic, edging towards the door.

"It… it was a friend of mine," he stammered. "He recorded the incantation in haematite."

"Fools! You contrived to trick the Bargest! A regrettable mistake." The motionless animal's ethereal voice roared with the malice of a forest fire. "I shall not help you or your kind again…" With a final howl, the Bargest sprung from the floor and launched itself at Ardent, teeth bared…

Chapter 8 – Detrimental Vision

It wasn't until early afternoon that the sun's rays crept
through the thin glass and gently kissed the sleeping man's
cheek. Hazel eyes flickered open, immediately creasing in
the brightness as Ardent sat up shakily. His head felt like he
had collapsed after a night of severely heavy drinking, and
the young Ghostbrand cast a bleary eyed glance around the
room, half expecting to see a number of empty bottles.
Rubbing his forehead, Ardent suddenly remembered what
had happened. The Bargest had pounced and then
vanished, only millimetres from his face, leaving Ardent
unsure as to whether he had blacked out through the
power of the great wolf, or through fright alone.

The back of Ardent's neck was starting to get hot,
and he shifted along the bed, moving out of the glare. Even
though the sun was millions of miles away, it was amazing
how it could warm a person in a matter of seconds. Ardent
closed his eyes and thrust his arm into the beam of heat,
imagining all of his cells revelling in the warmth, basking in
a carefree ocean of fiery lava. Ruefully, Ardent opened his
eyes and sat up. That was the most fire-related fun he was
ever likely to have, sly grins at the images contained within
the furnace of his imagination. He looked at his watch, the
chrome reflecting on the wall, a miniature porthole looking
out into the depths of peeling rose wallpaper. Ardent
frowned when he realised that he had missed breakfast and
most of lunch. If Firaire's speech was accurate then the
next meal wouldn't be for another four hours. That left
plenty of time to investigate the mansion.

The first thing Ardent noticed when he reached the
ground floor were two guards standing at the foot of the
stairs. Both of them were armed, and when Ardent hurried
past them, he noted that they were not the men who had

tried to rough him up the night before. That meant there were at least four soldiers here, probably more. He sidled along the corridor, pretending to look at the lavish artwork that hung from the walls, but all the time he was creating a mental map of the house in his mind. As he wandered along, subtly trying each locked door as he went, he eventually found one that clicked open.

The smooth door opened into a large gallery with a number of ageing paintings hanging from the walls. A particular image caught his eye. Mounted in an ornate gilded frame, the picture hung at the far end of the room, staring along its length as if watching over it. The painting was entitled "The Arrival Of The Everrulers" and showed the four Elementals in their first moments on earth. Dexamenas was standing proudly on a rocky outcrop as he surveyed the new world. He looked stern, his bluebell eyes poised with thought. Next to him, Phoenix was crouching, wreathed in flames. It looked to Ardent as if the Fire Everruler was staring right at him, the flames of his undiscovered fire radiating from him, almost daring Ardent to find his own power. Behind Phoenix, Altair and Dylan were falling from the sky, nothing more than brightly coloured, vaguely man-shaped comets borne straight from the palace of Elohelmarelmartoh.

"Ardent?" It was a girl's voice. The young Ghostbrand spun round and saw a teenage girl hovering in the doorway. Her emerald eyes were unmistakable as Emrys and Etain's sister. Ardent ran across the gallery and hugged her tightly, conveying his relief and affection through the contact.

"Eir! Are you all right?"

"What are you doing here?" Eir said, her eyes wide with sheer surprise at seeing him. She wrapped her arms around him, snaking her hands into his shirt and up his back, and he longed to kiss those soft lips.

"Not here," he whispered. "Come up to my room before-" He was interrupted by a shrill calling, and moments later a middle aged woman came bustling into the room. The two of them sprang apart as she immediately began to fuss over Eir.

"There you are!" she reprimanded. "I told you not to wander off."

"Mum!" Eir complained. "I'm eighteen, I think I can wander around a house by myself. You wouldn't care before the war." Eir's mother only stopped fussing when she finally noticed Ardent standing there, an awkward look on his face. He had secretly been dreading this moment, even though this was why he had come here.

"Ardent? But how did…" she said, trailing off. Ardent knew she was stopping herself from asking how a Ghostbrand got himself evacuated, after all the only reason why Emrys had papers was because Etain worked for the government. The Earthbrands' mother quickly changed tack. "Where's Emrys? Why didn't he find us last night?" She cast her eyes around the room just in case her son was hiding somewhere. Ardent noticed her expression fall and took a deep breath.

"Emrys isn't here, Mrs Earthbrand. He… he gave me his papers instead," he said sheepishly. The woman looked stunned, as if Ardent's words had slapped her in the face.

"But??" she stammered, trying to find the right words. "Why would he give them away? Doesn't he want to be safe? There's a war on, you know!"

"He sent me to make sure you and Eir were safe," Ardent said, raising his hands defensively at Mrs Earthbrand's look of fierce indignation. "He said he had something to do, but he wouldn't say what." The woman seemed to deflate, sinking into the soles of her shoes as if she had given up. It was obvious that she couldn't talk her son into appearing, and her eyes began to shine with tears, which she made no effort to brush away. Eir gently put an arm around her.

"Something to do?" she muttered half-heartedly through her sobs. "What could be more important than evacuation?" Eir looked questioningly at Ardent, but the young man could only shrug apologetically. Emrys had been purposefully vague when handing over his papers, and perhaps even he himself had been unsure of what lay before him. When he gave no answer, Eir guided her mother towards the door, casting a glance over her shoulder and mouthing the words "Wait here", then the two of them were gone, leaving Ardent alone with his guilt.

Sitting on a highly ornate wooden chair, knees tucked under folded arms, Ardent felt even more out of place perched on the gilded throne when it should have been Emrys here, happily reunited with his family. Mrs Earthbrand would have cried tears of relief and happiness, and the three would have at least been able to enjoy each other's company whilst the war was fought in the distant cities, a world apart from the refuge of the mansion. Should Ardent have refused to help his friend? Perhaps he should have forced Emrys to come here instead? Would Mrs Earthbrand tell Firaire that he was not supposed to be here? All of these questions smouldered in the back of the Ghostbrand's consciousness as he eyed the door warily, waiting silently for the embers of dissent to cool.

It was over an hour before Eir finally reappeared, panting slightly as she jogged into the room, blushing apologetic roses.

"I'm sorry, I sat with mum and must have just dropped off," she said as Ardent gave her the 'what took you so long' face. "I've been getting really tired since we got here, but breakfast hit me like I'd stayed up all night." Ardent shrugged, thinking that he would probably be asleep too if it wasn't for the guilt he was feeling.

"Where's your dad?" he asked.

"He got transferred somewhere else. They needed men to help build something or move something at one of the other centres. He volunteered, you know how he is." Ardent nodded, remembering what Firaire had said the night before about people already being moved on. He also realised why Mrs Earthbrand had reacted the way she had. She had just been separated from her husband and now found that her son would not be here either. There was an awkward silence as the two of them stared thoughtfully at their own respective patches of floor, but it was Eir who spoke first. "So what's the real reason Emrys isn't here?" she asked, an obvious lump in her throat. "He isn't...."

"He's fine," the young man said, hoping it was true. He tried to make his eyes blaze with sincerity so that Eir would believe it too. "But I wasn't lying when I said he didn't tell me what he was up to."

Eir's eyes widened pleadingly, anxious for even the smallest grain of information. "What do you think he's doing, Ardent?"

The Ghostbrand thought for a second. There were any number of possibilities, but Ardent had remembered the ferocity in Emrys' emerald eyes and he knew that he was going to do something big. He didn't have the heart to tell Eir that he had seen her brother sneaking off with Ghostbrand rebels so he did the only thing he could do. He lied.

"It's Emrys." He tried to smile. "He probably didn't want to leave without Etain. I bet you he's waiting for Etain right now and the two of them will turn up any day now." Eir did not look satisfied, her brow creasing as she considered Ardent's explanation.

"But how would he get here? He gave his evacuation papers to you, and I'm not even going to ask how you managed to get past the security checks." Ardent glanced away, hoping Eir wouldn't notice him shifting nervously. The face of the Bargest was still hauntingly fresh in his mind. "And anyway," Eir continued. "Etain isn't coming here and you know it. They'll probably need the government employees in the city to sort things out with the war." Ardent looked blank.

"Well that's the best I've got, ok?" he sighed, exasperated and wishing he could be of more help. The two of them should be making proper use of their unexpected time together rather than steaming towards an argument. "You asked me what I thought and I told you. I can't help it that Emrys gave me his papers when by rights I should have been left in the city to get blown up or shot." Eir opened her mouth to speak, but Ardent waved her attempts aside. "Don't you think I'm feeling bad enough? If anything happens to him I'll never forgive myself. He's my best friend you know, so don't think you've got the monopoly on wanting him safe." As Ardent finished, he could feel his face getting hot, the raw emotion scalding its way to the surface. Tears were welling up in the corner of Eir's eyes, and with one final shake of her head she turned, almost crashing into the suited Spyrus man as she did so. Firaire gave a muffled yelp of surprise as the young girl hurried past him, then stepped forwards, hands clasped in front of his jacket.

"I thought you'd be asleep by now," he said disapprovingly. Ardent frowned.

"Why do you say that?" Ardent said, the backlash of his outburst turning his words into a challenge. The man from Spyrus shrugged, grinning a large fake smile. It was the kind of expression that was probably taught at Spyrus training sessions, Ardent thought.

"No reason. Most people like to take a nap after lunch."

"Yeah, well I'm not tired," Ardent snapped.

"Fair enough," Firaire simpered. "There are plenty of things to keep you occupied. There's the mind beacon… but I'd say that's not your thing." Was this corporate drone mocking him? Ardent set his jaw defiantly.

"You don't know me."

"There's only one Ghostbrand here and that's you, Emrys," Firaire stated matter of factly.

"At least I show my brand, scarred or not." Ardent spat, indicating the sleeve covering the spot where Firaire's brand should be. The older man smirked knowingly, like a lion teasing a mouse.

"Although you're not like your mother and sister are you?" he said tauntingly. "Different coloured eyes, and I'd swear you're a little too hot-headed for an Earthbrand." The pit of Ardent's stomach dropped, and he instinctively slammed his palm over his brand. This man somehow knew, had known all along that he wasn't Emrys. He thought back to the other night when Firaire had seemed to look right at him when mentioning the telephone.

"I… I was on the cusp of Fire," Ardent stammered, too shocked to think of a stronger argument. He folded his arms and shuffled into the corridor, feeling the man's steeled gaze dancing infernos across his shoulders. As soon as he was out of view, the young Ghostbrand broke into a run, desperation fuelling his limbs. Ardent skidded around the corner, almost crashing into a small desk and upsetting a vase of wilting snapdragons. The two guards stationed at the foot of the staircase advanced, immediately sensing trouble. The nearest soldier was a typical grunt, wide shouldered with thick-set features, a couple of days' beard sprawling across his jaw line. He raised his palms and Ardent instinctively ducked down, fearing an imminent blast of power. When no scorching flames engulfed him, Ardent looked up through cautious eyes. The two soldiers were side by side now, exchanging sly grins.

"Easy there, little man," the first guard said. Ardent snorted quietly - this guy was only a couple of years older than him at the most. "Where are you going so fast?"

"I need to send a letter." Ardent spoke as defiantly as he could, hoping his attitude would deflect any unwanted questions. He had also swiftly decided that a letter would be the best method of contacting Emrys. Obviously, neither of them could use a mind beacon, and a telephone call could easily be tapped. At least in a letter, Ardent could write in some sort of code and hope Emrys understood what it meant. The soldier looked as if he was about to speak, and Ardent could picture the miniature cogs inside his head turning. For some reason, he also imagined them to be rusty and unused. Before the soldier could speak however, his companion nudged him gently and tilted his head, indicating Ardent's bare shoulder. The first soldier nodded a hugely exaggerated expression of understanding and then chuckled.

"The study's down this way on your left."

The Ghostbrand rolled his eyes and elbowed his way past the heavily armoured men, ignoring their stifled whispers that reminded Ardent so much of secondary school. Except this time the bullies had force-muskets.

The study was as typical as the rest of the mansion. The walls were panelled in dark oak, with tall bookshelves rising up at regular intervals. The room could have easily passed as a small library, and the additions that Spyrus had obviously made before letting the evacuees in were stark and ugly. There were a number of modern looking desks arranged in the centre of the room, with stacks of paper, envelopes and stationery. Nailed crudely to the wall was a hook upon which hung a wire basket. There were already a few letters in there, waiting to be sent away to other evacuation centres, or perhaps even into the heart of the war itself.

Ardent snatched up a sheet of paper and sat at the nearest desk, twirling a pen between his fingers. Now that he had the chance to take stock of his situation, his mind was completely blank - the fires of his previous necessity had burnt to ashes.

"Emrys," No, even that first word was shit, Ardent damned himself as he scribbled it out. He was pretty sure that Firaire knew Emrys wasn't here, but what if the guards didn't? Writing a letter to himself would definitely arouse suspicions. Ardent screwed up the paper and thought for a second before beginning to write once more.

"E – The papers are lost - the host smells fire. He will probably look for earth to extinguish – A
PS. Ladies are safe, Dad elsewhere."

It wasn't very inventive, but it was the best Ardent could do. Hopefully it was simple enough for Emrys to understand, but cryptic enough so that when it was read - Ardent was sure that the letters would be checked before they were sent - it would just be seen as idle chat. Reading it through one final time, Ardent folded the paper into a

small square and stuffed it into an envelope. He was careful
not to write a name above the address. As an afterthought,
Ardent scribbled a tiny design in the corner of the
envelope. It was the secret symbol of the Ghostbrand
resistance, a circle with a line through it which represented
the disregard of the elemental brand. Still unsure if Emrys
was involved with the freedom fighters or not, at least that
symbol would add importance should anyone from the
resistance see it first. The young Ghostbrand dropped the
letter into the wire rack, and took a final sweeping glance
around the musty room. A book was left open on a desk in
the corner, and curiosity leaped and sparked in Ardent's
mind. Anything to distract him from the awful predicament
he potentially faced.

The book was aged and worn, the cracked leather
that bound it might once have been green, but had now
faded to a forlorn grey. It had no name, but it looked like
some sort of encyclopaedia. It was open at a page of
simplistic phrases, translated rudimentarily into the old
script.

"Giareretohinargiasar – Greetings," he read quietly.
"Maryoh naraimarel inasar – My name is, Ina lohinavirel
aitoh – I live at." Seeing the words laid out before him,
Ardent began to recognise similarities between the two
languages, certain letters and patterns that repeated.

Curiously, Ardent flicked back through the book
until he rested on a page imbued with a sketch of a large
black wolf, shaggy and wild. His eyes took in the
information hungrily.

*After Farinaraiel flew over the land and forged all creatures,
so enamoured with his efforts were the other Elements, that he granted
each of them a familiar. All were loved and respected, but none more
so than Ehraifir's hound, which he named Bargest. When the wolf*

eventually passed, Ehraifir enlisted the help of Dielunasar to ensure that Bargest's spirit would endure. Faithful and honourable as in life, the spirit of the Bargest could still be invoked, even after the departure of the Elements. It was Ehraifir's wish that those who needed help, guidance and protection would not be ignored, and would be cared for as he was by his trusted companion.

Unless they were a Ghostbrand, he thought acidly. He left the room, the initial fear he had felt when speaking to Firaire staved off, temporarily at least. It was amazing how much lighter he felt, knowing that soon Emrys would realise his friend was in trouble. Maybe right at this moment, Emrys was leading an army to free them? Without meaning to, Ardent smiled. He could just picture his best friend, short and awkward looking, standing at the helm of a vast armed force. Not likely. But at least he would know to keep out of sight just in case Firaire did start looking for him for whatever reason. Perhaps Emrys could get in touch with Etain somehow?

As Ardent rounded the corner into the main hall, he saw a thin gangly man carry the wire rack out of the study and take it down a set of concrete steps that must lead to the basement. Ardent checked his watch. It was early evening, but much too late for a postal collection. Perhaps the letters would be sorted and screened the night before? It didn't matter now, he mused. The letter was out of his hands, all he could do was wait and see what happened. He ascended to the first floor, ignoring the guards at the foot of the stairs that still seemed to be sniggering at him, and made his way to his bedroom at the end of the corridor. Had he done the right thing? Firaire definitely knew he was an impostor, but how much trouble was he really in? Hastily rummaging in his rucksack, Ardent pulled out a stick of incense, jammed it into a gap in the floorboards and lit it with a match. The mixture of cinnamon and cloves was supposed to be good for dreaming and visions, and Ardent hoped for a hint that he had made the best decision. Throwing himself down onto the bed, Ardent closed his eyes and wished for time to pass as quickly as possible…

A man was running along a dark road, rubble and wreckage littering the way before him. Flames blossomed in the navy sky as the war raged throughout the city like a forest blaze, immolating all it touched. Rifles and force muskets chattered, accompanied by screams and choking breaths. Ardent found himself in the centre of the pitted street, a burnt out car by his side, glinting rusty grins in the muzzle flares. He watched the figure running towards him, ducking and weaving as buildings fell either side, their battle sadly over. As he drew nearer, Ardent could see he was not armoured like an AotE soldier, nor was he cloaked like a Ghostbrand fighter. The only thing of note was that he was clutching a small envelope in his left hand, the paper crumpling as he gripped with fierce importance.

Ardent tried to take a step forward but found that he was rooted to the spot. He attempted to speak, but again was foiled by whatever rules were governing him. All he could do was pivot as the mysterious man barrelled past him, panting with exertion. The young Ghostbrand was vaguely aware of the heat rising, the air beginning to shimmer with mirage haze, and the running figure seemed to notice it too. He drew to a halt just ahead of where Ardent was fixed and turned back, eyes wide with apprehension. For a brief second, it was as if the man was staring right into Ardent's soul, a look of resignation on his face, but Ardent soon realised that he was not staring at him, but through him. As Ardent spun to see what had caused the running man's despair, another mysterious figure dropped from one of the shattered rooftops. He was wearing a long coat, buckled in shining silver across his chest, which fanned majestically as he landed in a perfect crouch. Rising slowly, the man took a step forwards, cruel pleasure glinting in his stony eyes.

"I didn't think you'd make it this far," he taunted casually. "Usually I'm sent after much larger prey, but you gave me a good run."

"Please…" the running man stammered, seeming to shrink in size with every step his pursuer made towards him. The agile hunter radiated power, physically forcing the smaller being backwards. "This doesn't concern you, just let me go." The two men looked at each other with fond hatred, and Ardent suspected that their chase had been ongoing for a long time. Now it would draw to an end.

The heat became unbearable as the hunter stepped forward and grabbed his prey by the throat. Surely they must feel it? *thought the young Ghostbrand desperately as he watched the second man place his palm over his captive's heart. Ardent willed himself to jump forwards and break the two apart. The smaller man immediately began screaming, a guttural cry aching with pain and fear. Ardent closed his eyes, unwilling to watch the murder before him but unable to move away from it. Suddenly, a triumphant crack reverberated throughout the street, its only applause the tinkling of glass from the windows that the sound had smashed. Ardent didn't want to imagine what had been done to the running man to cause such a noise, but opened his eyes anyway. Surely the truth could not possibly be as grim as something his mind could dream up. To his surprise, both men were still alive and equally as confused by the cracking as Ardent was. The hunter had dropped his victim, who knelt panting at his feet, tears in his crystal eyes. Both men were looking fearfully towards the distant mountains, the tallest of which was spewing dark plumes of smoke and spouting gouts of orange. The Eye of Fire was erupting.*

Without warning, the tarmac itself split, a gaping maw widening with jagged rubble teeth, spewing forth jets of steam. The shells of buildings groaned objectionably as the ground shifted, the red glow of a deep fire tinting the derelict strongholds. With the faintest gurgling sound, a wave of molten rock, fluid neon, erupted from the chasm, spitting forth onto the road from a gulf of black smoke. More tarmac collapsed into the lava, and the two men trapped in the centre of this new hell began to scramble for safety, their battle forgotten. With another eruption, the flames swallowed them both, the screams drowned out by the fire's own primitive grating as it raged past its cage of rock and tar. Horrified, Ardent stared as a slip of paper floated gently down to his feet. It was the letter that the running man had been clutching so protectively, the envelope burned away and the corners blackened. Ardent didn't bother to pick it up, his soul extinguishing hollowly as he read the words gazing up at him.

"E – The papers are lost - the host smells fire. He will probably look for earth to extinguish – A
PS. Ladies are safe, Dad elsewhere."

With a shout, Ardent sat up, chest heaving, his fringe plastered to his forehead with hot sweat. Blinking steadily, he cast his eyes warily around his room. The stub of the incense stick had long gone cold. It was dark outside and the moon was high in the sky's velvet blanket, cushioned amidst a foreboding body of black cloud that hung over the mountains. *Definitely after midnight*, he reasoned. Rolling onto his feet, he began to take stock of what he had just witnessed. Dream or premonition, it was clear that sending that letter was a big mistake. Ardent had to get it back.

Chapter 9 – Suppression Elixir

The young Ghostbrand took a deep breath as he hovered barefoot at the top of the steps to the basement of the manor. He had taken his boots off and left them tucked under his bed, wanting his footsteps to be as quiet as possible as he snuck into the forbidden part of the house. In the same vein, he had also removed the chains and rings he wore in his clothes for fear of them signalling his whereabouts.

On his way down from the upper floor he had not encountered anybody, and figured they must all be asleep. It seemed like Eir wasn't the only person that was feeling exhausted lately. Even the guards at the main staircase were gone, but Ardent wasn't sure whether this was a blessing or a curse. At least if they were at their posts, Ardent would know where they were, but now they could be anywhere, waiting to shoot hot death his way. Steeling his resolve by picturing the fiery departure of the two figures in his dream, Ardent began the long descent into darkness.

The soft carpet of the main hall rapidly gave way to the unrelenting granite of the basement, the cool stones caressing the soles of the young man's feet. The gentle touch lulled Ardent into a feeling of ease. It was the middle of the night, he reasoned hopefully. Nobody would be about - he could just find the letter and sneak back to his room, simple as that. After a few moments, he felt the pressure lift slightly and he reached the bottom of the staircase. He blinked anxiously, waiting for his eyes to adjust to the gloom of the sterile corridor he now found himself in. Ardent could make out a number of doors, none haloed with the rectangle light of inhabitants. To his dismay, the doors did not have any signs indicating what lay within. It looked as if he would just have to try every door until he found what he was looking for.

The young Ghostbrand took a breath before tiptoeing to the nearest doorway. Tentatively pressing his pierced ear against the smooth wood, he could hear nothing.

"Here goes..." he muttered to himself, slowly easing the door inwards. It was some sort of storage room, tall stacks of containers towering up the ceiling, each one bearing the silver Spyrus insignia. Across the logo was stencilled a single word: 'Airtox'. Ardent searched his mind, but couldn't remember seeing that particular product on Spyrus' medicine list – maybe it was some sort of cleaning product instead? Firaire had mentioned that the company owned the manor, perhaps it doubled as some sort of storage facility? Whatever it was, this room definitely did not hold Ardent's fateful note, so he stepped cautiously back into the hallway.

As he made his way stealthily from shady room to shady room, Ardent saw a multitude of offices and cupboards, a kitchen and even what looked like a small scientific laboratory, the test tubes and softly humming apparatus reinforcing the clinical atmosphere of the lower floor. At this point, Ardent realised two things. Firstly, there was more to this house than everybody upstairs knew, and secondly, finding his damn letter was going to be much harder than he thought.

Something rustled in the gloom behind him and Ardent wheeled around, suddenly alert. Nothing. The corridor was empty, shadows shifting ominous and oppressive. Was he imagining things?

Ardent's resolve began to bow as paranoia seeped into his mind. He hovered nervously, mid step, internally duelling with his conscience. Stay or go? A second noise cemented the decision for him, the undeniable sound of hushed voices approaching through the gloom. A spark of panic ignited the kindling of unease and Ardent sprang towards the nearest door, his toes bounding lightly and silently across the cool stone, dancing gracefully on heels of terror. Without pausing to let his eyes pick out the features of his sanctuary, the young man felt his way cautiously across the large room, a wayward ember floating away from scorching flames. As the voices grew louder, Ardent wedged himself into a dark corner behind a counter of some sort.

Don't come in here, don't come in here, don't come in here, Ardent willed, forcing his mind to prevent the voices from coming any closer. If only he wasn't a Ghostbrand, he could have at least melted the door lock and fused it shut. The voices approached, drawing inevitably towards the room.

"I expect to see no evidence…" That was definitely Firaire. So what was the Spyrus associate talking about?

"I think you'll find the system adequate." Ardent couldn't place this second voice, but his intrigue was baited. He drew a sharp breath and tucked his knees in just as the lights flicked on. The transition from complete darkness to harsh sterility was jarring, and the young man fervently tried to blink the glare away.

"Are all the test subjects disposed of?" Firaire asked matter of factly. Ardent turned his head awkwardly and craned his neck as far as he could without being seen to look around the room. There were four counters that looked more like workbenches than anything else. Long black sacks lay on top of the benches, protective rubber gleaming in the cold light. Shelves of bottles and jars, each containing a different coloured substance, lined the walls and in the far corner of the room stood a large metal furnace, blackened and coppered with soot and rust. A carpet of ash emanated from the furnace, overthrowing the clinical void of the floor tiles. Even the air seemed to be permeated with the idea of incinerating, as if taunting the Ghostbrand.

"When can we proceed to the next stage?" Firaire asked impatiently. Ardent had missed the reply to Firaire's first question, but judging by the older man's tone, it had not been satisfactory.

"We've been dosing them since they arrived." Despite being unable to see, Ardent could sense the second man's pride, accompanied with the sickening image of him beaming with pleasure. "They are sleeping most of the time now, but I would advise waiting at least till tomorrow afternoon. Lunch will give them a final hit to ensure everything runs… smoothly." Ardent's eyes widened. Didn't Eir say she had been feeling tired ever since she arrived at the manor? They were putting something in the food! Some sort of Spyrus drug. Ardent remembered the stacks of chemical drums he saw earlier and shuddered.

"Tomorrow afternoon it is, then," said Firaire coldly. "Tomorrow marks the beginning of unquestionable victory. They couldn't manage it with the factories, but we will help them into destruction." There was the sound of shuffling footsteps as the two men paced around the room.

"I want all of these done tonight," Firaire said, flicking his hand casually over the counters. Ardent pressed his back firmly against the counter as the men passed by, subconsciously sucking his stomach in, making himself as small as possible. "And these?" he continued. "What are these?" Ardent glanced around the side of the table. Firaire was pointing to a small shelf laden with watches, jewellery, and even a complete soldier's uniform. Hanging over the edge of the box was a small pendant that looked very similar to the one Mr Earthbrand wore. The other man, who was slightly older and wearing a white lab coat, looked sheepish as his superior glared at him.

"Waste not..." he muttered nervously. He spoke as if he was expecting retribution, but instead, Firaire just sighed.

"Get rid of it." The scientist nodded and hastily scooped the items into a box as Firaire made for the door. As Ardent crouched in the shadows, he heard the scientist fiddling with something over in the corner, and within moments the temperature soared as the incinerator growled into life.

"Oh, sir?" the scientist asked. Firaire paused in the doorway. "Just out of curiosity, what are you going to do with the Ghostbrand?" Ardent's blood froze whilst Firaire deliberated.

"Well if the suppression elixir is as effective as you claim, Lakin, nobody in this building will be able to use Deus' gift. He will not be so different tomorrow, and he will die with the rest of them, whoever he is." There was a moment of silence in which Ardent's entire consciousness was forced into an ashen void. He was marked for death, along with almost a hundred other evacuees at the facility. "Although," Firaire began again wryly. "He did have the nerve to come here and parade about like he were a normal person. Yes, I do need a little entertainment, especially now that we've had the phone call from the other side. The host will be here soon." Firaire seemed to have forgotten his company for a second, drifting into his own thoughts before snapping back. "But as for the Ghostbrand, I'm going to march into his room, wake him up gently, and then give his worthless carcass all the fire he should have been born with."

Ardent felt sick as Firaire swept out of the room. He was paralysed, pressed into the corner with his arms wrapped around his knees. As the incinerator made the room stifling, Ardent's insides were frozen – with Firaire's death sentence, he felt as if his time was already slipping away. His eyes were squeezed tightly shut, as if he could open them up again and somehow be safely back at home, the war over or never started. Even as Lakin started heaving the sacks into the furnace, Ardent was fixed in place, trembling with fright. Only when the rank odour of the burning seared his nostrils did he finally open his eyes. It smelled like a roast meal but with rotten meat, and with grim realisation, Ardent worked out what the scientist was burning. Test subjects? Personal belongings? Suppression elixir? He knew exactly what kind of evidence Firaire was referring to. Spyrus had tested their elixir on people, and even one of the soldiers had fallen victim to their twisted experiments. Then he remembered the pendant in the box. People had already been transferred? An excuse to explain away missing evacuees. And that meant Mr Earthbrand…

Surging anger rushed through Ardent's body, fuelled by sheer dread and the knowledge that he was in mortal danger. Without thinking, the young Ghostbrand leapt to his feet and reached for the nearest bottle from the wall. Yelling fiercely, he hurled the vial at Lakin, shards of glass and dull coppery powder exploding over the scientist's back as he hunched over the furnace. The older man shrieked in surprise and then vanished in a magnesium flash.

The smell of ozone was punctuated by a crackling sound that seemed to echo around the room as Ardent blinked the spots from his eyes. There was nothing but a blasted silhouette to mark the spot where Lakin had stood just seconds before. Ardent was unsure what had happened to him, but he decided that he didn't care. It was them or him now, he reasoned as he hastily stuffed as many random bottles into his pockets as he could.

As he turned, he realised that the incinerator was still on, the last of the corpses charring in the cinder tray, the air waving invitingly in the heat. Ardent stared into the embers, an idea forming in his mind. *Out of the ashes*, he thought to himself with a small grin. It was the only way Ardent could see to get all of the evacuees together in one place so that he could warn them.

Scanning the shelves briefly with hopeful eyes, Ardent quickly spotted the biggest glass container. The jar, which was bigger than his head and filled with a powder that resembled iron filings, took all of his strength to lift, but after much panting and straining, Ardent had it resting on the furnace's feeder tray. The Ghostbrand took a moment to step back and consider himself. Only a short time ago, he had spent his days lounging in the sun, revelling in the heat of the world, his biggest concern being what part of him to pierce next, and now he was perching on the brink of arson and probably murder. *War changes everything*, he thought with a melancholy sigh.

Ardent pictured what his navel would look like with a bar through it, every muscle in his slender frame tensing to run once he'd raised his foot and firmly pushed the jar into the flames.

Chapter 10 – The Wolf's Betrayal

The indigo canvas of sky was just beginning to consider the idea of dawn as Ardent crouched behind an elaborately sculpted bay tree. It was shaped into a coiling serpent, and his breath ascended in frosty bursts through its poised fangs.

It had been over five minutes since the young Ghostbrand had left the incinerator room and squeezed through a painfully narrow window, clawing his way up a coal chute until he had flopped gracelessly onto a blanket of dewdrops. He wondered what was taking so long. He had only assumed that the Spyrus chemicals were volatile enough, but what if the contents of the jar weren't flammable at all?

As if solely to quell Ardent's worry, there was a deep rumble as the powder ignited in the underbelly of the house. After that, a number of things happened. Firstly, a majority of the ground floor windows cracked as the force of the explosion rippled upwards. Next came the inevitable influx of lights flickering into existence and raised voices, followed by the sound Ardent had been desperately hoping for. Alarm bells.

Within a minute, a startled crowd was pouring onto the grass, bewildered eyes and gaping mouths surveying the chaos, searching for the slightest shred of comprehension. Smoke was billowing from the lower windows now, forcing the crowd of evacuees further and further from the building. Ardent stared apologetically as yet another blast rocked the foundations, the once noble manor shuddering in protest as the fire ravaged underneath. The evacuees were close, with a middle aged man wrapped in a fraying dressing gown standing within an arm's reach of Ardent's hiding place. Where was Eir? He was about to step out and mingle with the throngs of confusion, spreading the hushed message of warning, when something caught his eye.

In a shadowy corner, partially hidden by the overhang of ornate balustrades, Firaire was talking pointedly with an AotE guard. Ardent retreated into the refuge of his bay tree, and watched as the soldier nodded his understanding and strode confidently towards the evacuees, leaving Firaire wearing a sickening smile. The guard clapped his hands and began issuing orders, more troops emerging from the gloom to support him. Together, they began to shepherd the civilians across the lawn and into the trees, Ardent following apprehensively a couple of steps behind, trying unsuccessfully to catch a hint of what was happening. After a few metres, Ardent found himself staring into a natural amphitheatre, a bowl of emerald velvet sinking below the gnarled trunks, roots twisting over the lip like coiled serpents, the morning's dew forming saliva of anticipation.

The evacuees were huddled in the centre of the dip, their breath rising as if the bowl was steaming. The soldiers had produced clipboards from somewhere and were reading out names to make sure that everybody was there. Ardent wasn't sure what they would do when they realised he was missing. He severely doubted that anybody would run back into a burning building for a Ghostbrand, even if there was no war. Halfway through the list, the guards faltered as a group of shadowy figures approached through the trees. As they got closer, Ardent could see that it was Firaire, this time accompanied by more suited Spyrus men. Even the soldiers turned around and looked up expectantly at the newcomers, the sloping ground putting a metre between the two groups.

Each Spyrus official wore the same inhuman expression, as if their faces were hewn from lifeless rock, and with a terrible burning in his gut, Ardent watched, immobile and silent. For what seemed like minutes, nobody uttered a word, the woodland silent out of respect or caution. The silence became palpable, the people in the pit shuffling awkwardly whilst the onlookers stared down at them. Firaire tilted his head to one side, a cat looking curiously at oblivious prey. As one, the five suited men raised their right hands, grim understanding dawning on the faces of those at the front. In the blink of an eye, five streams of energy shot into the amphitheatre, and a large section of the crowd erupted in flashes of violet and fell twitching to the ground. Not even the AotE guards could act as the blast enclosed them, cracking armour and bone alike. The forest burst into chaos, screams piercing the air, driving needlepoints into Ardent's ears. Those standing to the rear of the group turned and began to scramble up the mossy slope, reduced to all fours only to be cut down by a second wave of amethyst as it tore into their backs. Ardent recognised the man that had spoken up on the first night, saw him explode in a burst of fire. It was smouldering, disfigured lumps that fell back into the pit. The remaining survivors thrust out their palms, faces straining with concentration though tears polished their raw flesh. Of course, nothing happened - the suppression elixir had done its job and the evacuees were unable to create even the smallest burst of sparks. The young Ghostbrand turned away as the last of the evacuees were executed mercilessly, the screams instantly muted as if the world had had enough of this torture and simply switched it off. Lives extinguished by the very men who were ordered to protect them, but why? What did Spyrus have to gain by doing this? Murdering innocent civilians was way beyond the territory of a simple pharmaceutical company.

Eir's face kept floating in front of Ardent's eyes, but now the fresh, gleaming expression he last saw was replaced by a charred and brutalised hulk of flesh that was barely recognisable. Choking as he pictured the shattered emeralds of his girlfriend's eyes, Ardent thought how he would never touch the girl's smooth flesh again, how he would never hear her laugh at one of his jokes, and feel her hands across his chest. He could not help but let out an audible sob, but froze instantly as he did so, sucking back the next burst of scalding sorrow. There was no sound coming from behind him, the whole of the forest pulled into an empty void of silence. Slowly, Ardent edged himself around the gnarled trunk, only to see one of the murderers staring right at him.

There was a brief moment where neither man stirred, cold and unblinking, then like pure ignition, they both jolted into action, Ardent pivoting in the damp leaves.

"Here!" the man cried as he darted forwards, his fingers snapping barely an inch from the trailing straps on the Ghostbrand's jeans. Ardent held his breath, weaving snakelike between pillars of cold bark. It would only be a matter of seconds before he was reduced to the same crimson pulp as the rest of the evacuees. Completely powerless. *Not completely*, he remembered as he jammed his hand wildly into his pocket. As he lowered his head, a jet of violet energy soared over him, crackling malevolently as it skimmed his hair. A boulder in front of the fleeing Ghostbrand shattered, small chunks of rock pelting his skin, and he cursed, trying for purchase on one of the many bottles he had stolen from the labs.

The first bottle missed, the rainbow elixir inside swirling into an orb of pearl as the bottle spun through the tinted mist. Ducking and diving, Ardent could see the verdant lawn approaching, so risked a glance behind at his pursuer. The first man was frantically leaping over fallen branches and clumps of bracken, wildly sending bolts of violet in all directions. As Ardent stared, the scene appeared to slow down, until he could focus on every minute detail. Twigs and leaves floated gracefully from the canopy in a rain of brilliant sparks, smoke rose from burnt foliage, and the young man could even make out the forms of two more figures barrelling through the woodland. Calmly, he pulled another random vial from his pocket, this one filled with a vibrant, almost neon red liquid. Ardent jumped back as another jet rocketed over his shoulder, took aim with a squint, and hurled the container towards the Spyrus man's face. The weight of the bottle caused it to veer away to the left, and Ardent was about to turn and run when the glass splintered against a towering pine. The liquid within latched onto the bark like a mountaineer, clawing for purchase and spreading over the tree with alarming sentience until the whole plant was glowing vermilion. The suited hunter raced closer, paying no heed to Ardent's efforts when the evergreen suddenly lost all structure, collapsing in on itself in a fiery surge of liquid flame. Pounding into the forest floor, droplets of the molten conflagration cascaded into the nearby greenery, in turn setting it alight. Ardent paused just long enough to see the men stumble to a halt behind the inferno barrier before spinning on his heel and sprinting back towards the mansion.

In the shadows of the manor house, Ardent did not afford himself a moment's rest. The pervasive odour of charcoal bloomed from fissures in the floorboards, amidst wreaths of smoke.

The young Ghostbrand sprinted up the stairs, the polished wood shifting uneasily under his weight. As he emerged onto the upper landing, Ardent was instantly drawn to his dorm room, hoping that Spyrus would not risk coming back into the burning building, no matter how much they seemed to hate him.

The bedroom had been ransacked. What few possessions he had brought with him now lay in pieces strewn across the carpet, tattered strips of clothes adding tangled veins to the fragments of his life. Ardent remembered Firaire saying he was going to wake him up and kill him first, so perhaps he had destroyed the room in anger upon finding it unoccupied. The young man sat down on the remains of the bed, now viciously snapped into a sloping valley of mattress, and emptied his pockets, the remaining bottles spilling out and rolling onto the floor. Now that he was stationary, Ardent could finally consider the gravity of what he had witnessed. Mass murder. That was the only word for it. Firaire and his men had butchered everyone at the facility, even the guards who were under their employ. Ardent thought once more about Emrys' family. What would he say to his friend if he ever saw him again? That he saw his family murdered but failed to help them? Ardent's mind was in conflict. He had been trying to help the evacuees when he started the fire, but instead he had brought them all together for an easy kill. Did that make him equally culpable?

The young man's remorse was interrupted by the dread sounds of footsteps in the once grand hall, echoing oddly on the singed rug. Panicking, he began to scramble around the room, casting roving glances into every shadow, searching for anything that could help him escape. His eyes fell on the velvet wrapped haematite and he snatched it up, hoping that he could somehow convince The Bargest to help.

Once again, the shimmering mineral veins rippled as skin touched stone. Etain appeared, flickering in the smoky air, recited the incantation and vanished. When The Bargest silently padded into the room, its eyes narrowed with recognition, teeth bared angrily.

"You!" the creature growled, the husky voice burning into Ardent's consciousness. "Are you simple in some way?" The young man stepped back, affronted by the insult. "I told you that I would not aid you again. Dare you to presume I won't hold my word?" The emphasis in the hound's tone stabbed the man's mind with every syllable.

"I know, but you don't understand," Ardent stammered, hastily raising his palms as the wolf emitted a low snarl. "There are men after me. They're going to kill me, you have to help!" The Bargest remained motionless at his pleas. Abandoning his attempt for sympathy, Ardent changed tack. "Do you know Spyrus?"

The Bargest's citrine eyes glinted. "I am aware of that group."

"Well there's a war on," Ardent continued. "Spyrus are supposed to be in charge of evacuation, but they've just murdered all the innocent people here. I... I saw it. Now I'm the only one left and they're coming for me."

The wolf tilted its head curiously. "Your conflicts are no concern of mine, Ghostbrand." The creature turned to leave before Ardent blurted out.

"I know what you are!" The Bargest glared back over its tufted shoulder, powerful muscles tensing as it squared its back. "You were Ehraifir's hound, an Element's companion. Doesn't that mean anything? Ehraifir wouldn't want this war, and I can help stop it. If..." he paused, "you help me survive."

"What my master wants, I would not know," the psychic voice boomed. The Bargest was obviously becoming angry. "When he and the others flew home to Elohelmarelnartoh, I could not follow, and so I was abandoned to aid those in need for all eternity. There is no respite, for I cannot die again, but I do have pride and standards. I shall not help you, unclean one."

"Fine," retorted the man provocatively. "I should have known better than to seek help from a bitter, lonely old pet." He immediately knew that he had gone too far, as The Bargest stiffened, its shaggy mane bristling with fury.

"We shall see," the wolf whispered coldly. It tilted back its head and released a telepathic howl so loud that the polished wood panels shook and rattled. Amidst the painful wailing, Ardent could pick out faint words calling the men downstairs towards him.

"No!" he shouted, lunging forwards, but The Bargest had vanished, the haunting sound immediately replaced by the creaking of the stairway. "Shit, shit shit!" cursed the Ghostbrand, hastily grabbing one of his bottles and trying desperately to dredge up what else he had learned from the library. He had just enough time to hide the vial behind his back and take a breath before the first suited assassin appeared in the doorway. "Ina aimar Airaidielnartoh Farinaraielbarainardia, ainardia ina haroylohdia giaraiehtoh paroywonelrai!" Ardent bellowed, mustering as much command as he could. As he had hoped, the Spyrus man was startled by his use of the forgotten language, pausing long enough for the Ghostbrand to whip his arm forwards and heave the small glass bottle towards the man's face. He dodged to the side, but too slowly, the container exploding against his left shoulder. The bottle must have held some sort of acid, the man's suit and then skin rapidly beginning to smoulder and burn as the sickly yellow liquid splashed over him.

Screams and noxious fumes permeated the thick atmosphere as the man stumbled backwards, knocking into one of his colleagues who had just arrived panting in the corridor. The new assailant took in the scene and instantly raised his palm, brows meeting as anger contorted his features.

"Wait!" The palm was lowered as Firaire stepped into view. He considered the injured man with frosty disinterest and stepped past his slumped form. "You have caused us much intrigue, Ghostbrand." He lunged forwards with a speed contrary to his age and punched Ardent forcefully in the jaw. The young man fell to his knees, face throbbing. "Are you a freedom fighter?"

"No," Ardent managed shakily. He was facing destruction - terror engulfed his entire being and he desperately tried to hold in the sobs that were threatening to burst free. "I came here to find my friends. Friends that you murdered."

"Then it appears you were in the wrong place at the wrong time. It comforts me to know that it was nothing more." Firaire leaned closer. "But I still have to kill you."

"Please!" Ardent begged. "I need time… you killed my friends. Innocent people."

"Aww hush now," Firaire cooed mockingly, leaning down to cup the younger man's cheek. "I'm sure you'll see them again in the next world." In a single fluid motion, the Spyrus associate slid his hand upwards, his palm covering Ardent's face. The Ghostbrand could not move, his energy sapped by the reality of his doom. His world was enveloped in a sweltering rose. Ardent could feel Firaire's pulse through the ageing skin and he was forced to close his eyes, swallowing back the urge to retch. "If your kind go there, that is."

Ardent screamed helplessly as Firaire's heated palm burned through his face.

The Fall Of Peace
October 15

Chapter 11 – The Useless Twin

"Did you even ask them about me?" Emrys Earthbrand stood on a patch of reedgrass, the common rolling away down the hillside. It was early evening, the sun hanging low in the sky and gilding the heather that cut radiant swathes across the bushland. On a clear day, you could see all the way across to the mountains, but this late, the horizon shimmered into an intangible haze seemingly only a couple of miles away. The Earthbrand couldn't even see the top of the Eye of Fire, the highest mountain in the country, and a dormant volcano.

Emrys turned around to face his brother Etain, his mirror image. The two of them were twins, and had been inseparable throughout their twenty-six years. They had been put in almost all the same classes at school, had the same friends, and even the same untidy scruff of a hairstyle, but now Emrys felt he couldn't be further from his brother.

Behind Etain, the city sprawled wide and prosperous. The four oaks of UCE bloomed above the rooftops in the centre. In the western section of the metropolis, the Temple of Branding sat upon its raised mound, spires and crenellations breaking the skyline. A thousand sunsets reflected in the quicksilver windows of the Spyrus tower, easily the tallest building there, and Emrys often thought that it looked as if Spyrus and the Temple of Branding were constantly at odds with each other, commanding and glaring up and down at one another across the city. The vision was completed by the motorway and the river lacing out of the corner, two lifelines pulsating from the urban heart.

The brothers had been coming to the wasteland for years, watching the city shift and grow. It wouldn't be the same alone.

"Well?" Emrys demanded hotly. His brother looked surprised.

"Come on Emrys!" he snorted accidentally. "You know people like you can't do a job like that, it's demanding."

"People like me?" Emrys turned away angrily, stepping out of reach as Etain made a grab for his shoulder.

"Ah, I'm sorry…" he said softly. "I didn't mean it like that, just… you know, we aren't the same, Emrys." Emrys swallowed awkwardly, waiting for his brother to say it. "On the outside, sure, but there are some things that I can do and you can't. And vice versa."

"Name one thing I can do that you can't!" Emrys snapped.

"Um…" Etain thought for a second. "Play the violin?" Emrys shook his head as his brother chuckled to himself. Stepping away, Emrys seated himself on the dusty grass stalks, feeling betrayed. While he contemplated the root of his annoyance, he noticed the dirt shifting around his feet. Within seconds, the small rocks had spelled the word Sorry, the tail of the y curling elegantly around a sprouting dandelion.

Etain stood waiting for a reaction, the evening breeze ruffling his hair and making his skin tingle. He knew he shouldn't have said what he did, but his brother couldn't keep relying on him forever. When Emrys still didn't move,

Etain gingerly stepped forward and sat beside his twin, suddenly aware of how fragile his brother looked sitting in the coppery grime in his faded jeans and worn shirt. He patted Emrys reassuringly on the back, feeling tense muscles.

"Emrys…" Etain continued to nudge his brother, hoping at least to annoy him into nudging back, but Emrys remained motionless, arms firmly locked around his knees, closed off.

"Beer's up!" Etain looked round to see the brothers' best friend, Ardent, strolling towards them, a six-pack of beer in his raised hand. Ardent was a Firebrand but, like Emrys, he could not use his power. Unlike Emrys however, the younger man did not seem to care about it. It seemed that Ardent was comfortable with what he was.

The Firebrand half fell roughly onto the dirt next to Emrys before reaching across him to pass a can to Etain.

"Don't worry," he began with a nod towards Emrys. "I got you some cider for your refined tastebuds." He fished another can from one of his many pockets and set it next to his friend's feet. Before he could ask why Emrys looked so miserable, Etain began pointing to his ear.

"When did you get that?" the Earthbrand asked incredulously. Ardent couldn't resist, beaming and tilting his head so that Etain could get a look at the scaffold bar running through his ear.

"Yesterday!" Ardent said proudly. "It's Jade, supposed to attract love and prosperity." Etain looked thoughtfully at the polished green spike.

"Does that kind of stuff work for you guys?" he asked. Emrys shifted his feet awkwardly and reached for his drink.

"Of course," Ardent reasoned. "I can still have effects done to me, even if I can't do it myself, right Em?"

The young Earthbrand still remained silent. "Ok seriously, what is wrong with you tonight? You haven't said a word."

"Ask him..." came the frosty reply. Ardent looked questioningly at Etain, who shrugged apologetically.

"I got the job," Etain said quietly, not wanting his friend to make a big fuss about it. To his dismay, however, Ardent jumped to his feet and ran over, punching Etain firmly on the shoulder.

"Well done mate!" he roared. "Etain Earthbrand, government man! I knew you'd get it." As Ardent continued his congratulations, Emrys clambered up, dusted himself off and stalked away, leaving the cider barely touched. Ardent turned and made to chase after his friend, but Etain held him back, firmly gripping his arm.

"Leave him," the Earthbrand said. "He'll deal with it, it's just hard for him, you know?" Ardent watched the diminishing figure disappear behind a rise in the common, before leaning back and opening another can.

The two of them drank and talked until the sun had vanished beneath the horizon and the stars had peppered the sky with diamond fragments. Etain lay on his back, haloed by the glow of the city's lights. He was thinking about how different his life would be now he worked for the government. True, it was only as an aide to one of the ministers, little more than a manservant, but who could say where it would lead? He had been a rural boy all his life, but now a world of promise and opportunity awaited him. It was no wonder his brother felt upset - Emrys had every right to be, cheated by genetics as he had been.

Ardent laughed, shaking Etain from his thoughts. The young Firebrand had spotted a set of stars that formed a rude pattern and was treating it like the funniest thing he had ever seen. Smiling, Etain got to his feet, for a second wishing his brother could be more like Ardent. Nothing ever seemed to get the Firebrand down - his mood was invincible whereas Emrys tended to dwell on even the smallest of issues. His feeling immediately became guilt and shame as he saw his brother's face in his mind. Emrys was a part of him, indeed for the first part of their existence, they had been one. Whatever made Emrys the way he was, Etain was certain that it affected him too, and to change Emrys would change him profoundly also. Shying away from the potential deepness, Etain tapped Ardent lightly on the shoulder and began to walk through the darkness.

Less than an hour later, the two of them were strolling up the rough gravelled driveway that led to the farmhouse where the Earthbrands lived. The lights of the city were nothing more than a simple change of hue cresting over the hill the two friends had just crossed. Behind the farmhouse stretched an infinite plain of black velvet, the thin horizon defining the sliver of farmland from the acres of sky lost in the night. To Ardent it was freedom, but Etain couldn't wait for the noise and the rush of urban life to bloom and thrive around him.

As soon as he pushed open the heavy oak door, Etain's nostrils were bombarded with the smells of cooking. There was a large cast iron pot of bubbling stew, and sprigs of various herbs hung from the solid beams, each one sending a mouth watering aroma dancing around the large kitchen. Etain's mother was standing at the sink, elbow deep in soapsuds. Wisps of foam drifted lazily into the air every time she shook her arms in the bubble clouds. Only when Ardent closed the door loudly did she turn around, her rosy cheeks and ruddy complexion complementing her beaming expression. She rushed forwards and wrapped her arms around her son, leaving a pair of soapy arm prints on his back as she quickly kissed him on the forehead.

"I'm so proud of you," she gushed. "We're eating outside tonight to celebrate. Hello Ardent dear." She turned her attention to the Firebrand, giving him a quick hug then stepping back to look him up and down. "I see you've stuck another bolt though yourself. Has your father seen it yet?" Ardent shook his head as the woman chuckled with acceptance. "Well you wouldn't be you without them, I suppose. You'll stay for dinner? There's plenty of food."

"Cheers Mrs E!" Ardent said gleefully.

"Etain, go out to the garden and help dad will you? Ardent, you can peel those potatoes and pop them in the stew." The two young men nodded as Mrs Earthbrand turned back to scrubbing the cutlery.

Etain's father looked up as his son stepped off the decking that surrounded the house and into the walled off section of field that they called the garden. The tall greying man was resting one of his stocky arms on a young sapling in the centre of the grass.

"Give me a hand with this table, lad," he called. "Can't seem to get it level."

"You're getting old, dad." Etain laughed as he too set his palm on the springy tree. Within seconds, the whip like plant was curving and bending, almost flowing as it stretched into shape. It wasn't long before the two men were standing next to a perfectly formed table with four sturdy legs rooted into the soil and a top of interlaced branches, woven into a surface of smooth bark. After the meal, Etain would return the tree to its natural position but it would serve its purpose without objection until then.

In the kitchen, Ardent was busy stirring the stew, fervently keeping up with the twins' mother as she flitted about the room adding a pinch of this and a dash of that. There was only a lull in the torrent of culinary excellence when Eir emerged from upstairs. Hearing footsteps on the chunkily rustic staircase set into the far wall, the young man turned, his heart skipping a beat. He had been seeing Etain's sister for almost six months, but her parents did not know, and it was all the two youngsters could do to keep their secret. Ardent remembered when the twins had found out and he had endured the typical big brother threats about how he would be dismembered if he ever hurt her. The two held a lingering gaze, burning with the passion of their hidden relationship, before Eir's mother bustled between them holding a large stack of plates.

"Don't just stand there gawping at each other! Carry some of this out, it's ready." Once again press-ganged into kitchen service, Ardent broke the stare with the hint of a smile.

The meal flew by in a gust of light chat and great food, despite Emrys turning up half way through and sitting mutinously silent for the duration. Eir gave him a scowl before turning back to the conversation that was now in full swing as the remaining bottles of wine were poured out. Her parents were discussing who everyone would be voting for in the election next week. Apparently, one of Spyrus' top men was running to be on the Element Council and with all the work Spyrus had done for the world of medicine, he was tipped to win. Eir sighed, and not wishing to be bored to death by politics, she raised her glass.

"To Etain's new job!" she cut in loudly. The impromptu toast had the desired effect and now her parents were simultaneously praising Etain, and grilling Ardent on what he was going to do with his life. Luckily they had had the sense to realise that Emrys wasn't in the mood to talk this evening.

As the Firebrand was explaining his plan to open up a tattoo and piercing business, Eir studied his face with disguised interest. He had a twitch when he spoke – his head would occasionally flick to the side, but his eyes blazed sincerity and unwavering belief in the words coming from his lips which were perfectly formed despite the chrome ring through the lower one. The thought of man and metal excited her, and she knew he had other piercings... *Wasn't the conversation done yet?* She thought desperately. Eir extended her leg under the table to where Ardent sat opposite, pushing her foot between his shins. The young man paused and shifted mid sentence but managed to maintain his composure as he finished his description of 'Ardent Style'. Finally, he flashed Eir a questioning look to which she retaliated with teasing raised eyebrows of her own. Understanding crept onto Ardent's face as Eir got to her feet.

"Everything ok, dear?" asked her mother.

"Yeah, we're just going upstairs to check the mind beacon," Eir replied, again nodding towards her boyfriend. With an awkward smile, Ardent left the table and the two of them went inside.

"Aww..." cooed Mrs Earthbrand as she watched them fondly. "They're such close friends, it'll be a shame when Eir gets a boyfriend." Etain snorted laughter into his wine as the woman watched with confusion. He couldn't believe that his mother was so blind to the romance blossoming right in front of her, but he figured she wouldn't even consider the possibility of Eir and Ardent together.

Upstairs, the mind beacon lay forgotten as the two young people were rapidly racing towards becoming one. In the last six months, it was Ardent that had felt the need for restraint, uncomfortably aware of how their pairing could destroy his friendship with the entire family, but now, overwhelmed by the tremors of desire pulsating from the frail form he held in his arms, he surrendered to her emotions.

And so they stood, a pillar of flesh amidst a desert of discarded clothing, his arms enfolding her, her left hand resting tenderly on his chest, the other with fingers hooked under the waistline of his boxers, waiting for the final nod of acquiescence.

"I love you, Firebrand," she whispered as they sank onto the bed.

In the garden, the last of the wine had been drained and the talk had petered out. Mr and Mrs Earthbrand were clearing everything into the house and Etain was focusing on returning the makeshift table back to its original state.

"You should talk to your brother," Mrs Earthbrand said sagely as she scooped another armful of cutlery. Emrys was sitting alone on the wall at the end of the garden, facing the open fields with his back to his family.

"He won't speak to me."

Mrs Earthbrand rolled her eyes at her son's ineptitude. "He's sulking, I know," she began. "And probably the last thing you feel like doing is venturing into his misery, but there's no time to just let this blow over by itself. You leave in two days, and if you go without smoothing this out then he might not get through it. It's you he needs right now, Etain." The young man sighed. She was right of course, but that wouldn't make this any easier.

From his perch, Emrys heard footsteps approaching and hastily wiped his sleeve across his face, hoping that whoever it was wouldn't see the streaks of reflected moonlight his tears had painted. It was probably only his mother telling him to come inside anyway. To his surprise, it was his brother that climbed over the crumbling bricks and sat beside him, the two of them silent sentries of the velvet countryside. Neither spoke for a long time, but Emrys was internally willing his twin to just get on with it. Eventually, Etain plucked up his courage.

"I'm sorry about the job, all right?" he tried. Emrys clenched his fists tightly, outraged. How could his brother be so wrong? Was he really that petty? Sometimes it seemed like Etain got all the craft but none of the brains.

"I'm not bothered about the job," Emrys snapped. "I couldn't give two shits about the job."

"Then what?" Poor Etain was obviously confused.

"The first day of high school," began Emrys. "When Kale Airbrand pushed me in the mud and made me cry, you were the one that picked me up. Do you remember what you said?" Etain remained silent. "When they wouldn't let the Ghostbrands sit with the others at graduation, you were the one that argued and got me in. You said it then too."

Etain lowered his eyes. "I said I would always stick with you..." he murmured remorsefully.

"Don't you get it? It's you, Etain. When you're gone, what will I be? Who'll fight for me? I'm useless without you."

"You stupid, stupid arse!" Etain cursed exasperatedly. "Have I ever once called you useless? You don't need me for everything, you're a grown man and things are different now. You fight for yourself, Emrys. Then you'll know what you'll be. If I hang around forever, you'll carry on depending on me and that's not fair on either of us."

"But what if I can't?"

"Will you know if you don't try?" Etain's temper was rising now. "I don't want to hear you say you can't, Em. Not ever. That's not who we are. Remember, you fight." Emrys stared resolutely into his brother's steeled eyes. He could tell that Etain believed what he was saying, and by looking at himself reflected in the eyes of a face so similar, he began to believe it too. He nodded and the two of them jumped down from the wall and headed into the house.

Chapter 12 – Election Day

The city was oddly quiet, the hush of anticipation muting all sound like a thick blanket. From the balcony of her father's villa, Llyr Airbrand could see that every public area was packed with people, all standing in silent expectancy. A large screen had been set up in the market square and over a thousand citizens were in front of it, a congregation of raised heads. The light breeze was ruffling the banners that seemed to hang from every building and post, making the smiling faces they bore twist and contract grotesquely. The structures surrounding Llyr's home all fluttered the same image of a greying yet friendly looking woman, the twinkle in her eyes making it impossible to dislike her. Anise Earthbrand had been the chairwoman of the Element Council for the last thirty years and had done great work for the city, the country, and even the world. She was a figure of strength and democracy, and had survived the last three elections in landslide victories, but now she had lost a number of key members of her council, and she was up against serious competition.

Llyr looked further out across the city, to the other side of the market square where the banners gradually changed to purple, this face stern and calculating. The trail of decorations culminated in a large version of the face, covering twenty floors of the Spyrus tower. The man known only as Tohelnar had an important role in the Spyrus medicine company, and now was running for councillor based on some sort of amazing air purification system he had pioneered. Since the world was currently embroiled in debates about pollution and global warming, Tohelnar might well get voted in.

Months of campaigning and canvassing had all led to this – Election Day. One person would be victorious, the other would have wasted time and money - but none of it mattered to the young Airbrand. Llyr would still be rich and comfortable whoever won the stupid election.

"Miss?" Llyr took one final glance across the city before turning round slowly. The butler was standing before her, immaculately dressed and grey hair combed to perfection. He had served her family for longer than she had been alive, but he was a Ghostbrand so Llyr had never bothered to get to know him properly.

"Well?" she snapped impatiently.

"Mr Airbrand has asked for you, Miss." The Ghostbrand bowed and left silently. Llyr took a deep breath as she stepped in from the balcony and walked across the hallway with its highly polished floor. The door to her father's room was closed, but she didn't knock before pushing the extravagant oak open. Although she had been inside before, entering the room always made her gasp slightly. The bed was in the centre of the room, her father lying unmoving. A television mounted on the wall was showing quiet coverage of the election proceedings. Around the edge stood a number of different machines: a respirator, heart monitor, drip. All supplied by Spyrus, of course, but they hadn't been able to cure him completely of the disease that was eating away at his organs. Mr Airbrand had been a key member of the Element Council, but had been forced to retire as a result of his illness. Amongst others, it was his departure that had led to the election that would be announcing its results very soon. Each extra day brought by the machinery was another chance to experience something for the last time. The man did not move.

"The butler sent me…" Llyr said as she stepped forward tentatively. There was still no reaction. "Dad?"

After what seemed like hours, Mr Airbrand tilted his head towards the sound.

"His name is Colt." It took the young woman a few seconds to realise that her father was talking about the butler. "Have you spoken to the doctor?" the old man continued. Llyr shook her head. "He says I'm very close to… the end. Before I go, I have to tell you something." Now, Llyr leaned forward eagerly. She knew it was wrong to be thinking of inheritance, but surely she would be getting most of the family's assets? "Where do you think all our money comes from?" he asked.

"From your job on the council?"

To Llyr's surprise, her father laughed a hoarse croaking chuckle. "If the council paid twice as much," he said. "It still wouldn't be enough for all this." He tried to wave his arm, indicating the riches that adorned the walls, but he was too weak to lift it. "Our lives have been paid for by Spyrus." The aging man paused for the look of surprise he knew his daughter would display. "To explain properly, I'll have to go back twenty years or so, to when the Everrulers were killed. Dark days they were - you won't remember it, you were so small. On the day Dex went, you were with your mother, and I was at work. In a meeting with the thirteen heads of Spyrus." Llyr raised an eyebrow. She never realised her father had had such influential dealings. "Thirteen there were, and thirteen there always will be, though I'm not sure how many of them are the same today," Mr Airbrand continued. "Anyway, during this meeting, one of the Spyrus men was missing. They were all on edge about something and wouldn't rest until their man returned. I knew then that this Spyrus man was somehow responsible for killing the Everrulers."

"That's hardly proof, father. It was probably the Ghostbrands," Llyr interjected.

"The fact that Spyrus paid me this long to keep their secret is proof enough," the man replied. "The Ghostbrands are innocent."

"It doesn't matter, I still despise them," Llyr stated coldly.

"You know, sometimes I regret sending you to that school. If I'd known the price of your education included your morality, I would have sent you somewhere else."

"If Spyrus did kill the Everrulers, what stopped them from killing you?" Llyr changed the subject hastily, not wanting to sully the remaining time the two of them had together with an argument about the treatment of Ghostbrands.

"I have my theories," Mr Airbrand said gruffly. The strain of the conversation was obviously taking its toll on his fragile health, but he would not relent. "The meeting I was in all those years ago was because Spyrus wanted a man on the Council. I turned them down. When the Everrulers formed the Element Council, they worked together to place extremely strong protection spells on its members."

"Your pentagram tattoo?" Llyr had always wondered about the electric blue star her father had on his chest. Mr Airbrand nodded.

"It is a pity the Everrulers did not think to do the same for themselves, although not many could have bettered their power. But Spyrus found a way. However, the spells that protected me remained intact. Now imagine if a member of Spyrus was elected onto the Element Council?"

"They would get the spell and-"

"Be impervious to harm, yes."

"But what about the election?" Llyr exclaimed.

"Tohelnar is probably going to win."

Her father nodded. "That's why I've told you now," he continued. "Things are going to get a lot worse. Who knows what will happen if Spyrus get into the Council. But you know their secret now. You can use it when I'm gone."

"How?"

"If anything major ever happens, Spyrus have an action called the Transcendence Protocol, and they pick four people to do it." Llyr looked at him questioningly. "I know this because in the interview, they said they would include the Council in this protocol if they were allowed in, but that's all I know. Look at me, Llyr." He stared at his daughter with failing vision and saw her staring back with intense dedication to his words. "Something major *will* happen if Tohelnar wins this election. Spyrus own the research company you work for, extremely high up, but that's probably your chance. You have to do anything you can to get on this Transcendence Protocol. Knowing that they killed the Everrulers could help. Make them take you - it will be the only way to survive." Mr Airbrand lay back into his pillow and closed his eyes as Llyr took in the weighty information she had just received. She would have to piss a lot of people off if she wanted to succeed, but she could live with that.

"I'll do it, dad." He did not acknowledge her. "Dad?" Had it taken this long before? "Daddy?" The desperation began to creep into her voice as she stepped forward and grabbed her father's hand. Nothing. The heart monitor started its high pitched monotone, and at the same time, the reporter on the news announced that Tohelnar had just won the election. A deep cheer boomed in from the city outside, accompanied by the frenzied celebrations on the screen and the cold unfeeling beeping, and for the first time in eight years, Llyr Airbrand cried.

Chapter 13 – Exponential Outbreak

It didn't take long for the election buzz to die down, not that the wave of voting hysteria had really managed to seep into the life of UCE anyway. The age where students were actively political was long gone. So what if the Element Council changed a few faces? Myst Waterbrand comfortably allowed the politics to pass her by as she lay on the grass in the quad after a particularly boring lecture on art through the ages. After a rough childhood that had delayed her going to university for a few years, she deserved to be blasé about matters that didn't concern her now she was finally living her own life. How could it possibly affect her, lounging in the shadow of the mighty oak, young enough and carefree? The changes were subtle at first…

The next day, Myst's Classical Sculpture class was cancelled. She arrived huffing and puffing, only to find a hastily scribbled note on the door telling the class to go to the main lecture theatre. Intrigued, Myst made her way to the John Terrence building, joining an ever-increasing stream of students whose lessons had also been disrupted.

In the foyer, the campus security team were marshalling the younger generation left and right, separating male from female. The boys were being led upstairs to the second lecture theatre, whilst the girls were being shown into the larger auditorium. As she passed the nearest campus security guard, Myst noticed that the entire team had been given new uniforms. The cheap dusty grey jackets were now sleek, fitted black coats making them look more like bouncers than anything else. The man had a small purple pin badge on his left breast pocket, and a silver chain at his waist, shaped like a snake at the join. Very swish, Myst thought as she passed into the lecture theatre and jammed herself gracelessly into one of the cramped folding seats.

The clamour of curiosity became a subdued hush as one of the lecturers took to the podium. Myst had seen the man around campus, but was not taught by him and she didn't know his name.

"Good morning, ladies," the lecturer began unenthusiastically. "I apologise for the disruption to your timetables, but thanks to a new initiative by the Element Council, you all have to sit through a seminar on self defence." From the poor man's tone of voice, it was obvious that he did not care for this intrusion on academic learning, and Myst pricked her ears up. If something had rattled the Uni staff, then she felt she should know what it was just in case the student body could capitalize on it somehow. The lecturer introduced some sort of specialist. The extent of the safety training Myst had received so far was a brief talk with the Senior Residents in halls, which amounted to 'don't go through this car park at night because you might get mugged.' Nothing like that had ever happened to her, or anybody she knew, so why they had suddenly chosen now to teach everyone how to break somebody's nose with the palm of their hand was a mystery. Still, Myst listened with interest for the next couple of hours until she was finally released, unaware of how much knowledge she had actually absorbed.

The next day, the student's lesson was also cancelled, the vague explanation of 'premises inspections' being cited as the reason on the mind beacon message she had received that morning. She had no idea how the Ghostbrand students were expected to know about it though. Perhaps they would have simply turned up and found out first hand.

By the time the Waterbrand next made it onto campus, everything seemed back to normal. Lectures were still boring, the popular girls were still a set of bitches, and Myst was slowly creeping towards a degree and life itself. But she couldn't worry about that now, she had to maintain some sort of social life, and tonight was one of the must-attend events of the academic year.

That evening, the atmosphere was charged with excitement as Myst and her roommate Briar joined the steady flow of eager students moving towards the UCE arena. An Earthbrand, Briar was wearing a deep viridian gypsy skirt and a white top with a ruffled sleeve. The other shoulder was bare, brand proudly on display. Her hair and neck were adorned with wooden beads. Myst had decided to keep it relatively simple with a pair of jeans and a skinny t-shirt. Of course, she had her hair in her favourite style, swept back with two loose strands across her ears, but she had also spent an extra hour defining her blue Waterbrand with phosphorous ink so that it glittered and shone as the final fragments of sunlight hit it.

The two young women flashed their tickets at the stony-faced security guard then picked their way through the crowd towards the edge of the pitch. Myst rarely took an interest in sports, but the Varsity Chargeball final was always worth watching. The blend of craft, running, throwing, catching, tackling and usually acrobatics was so enthralling that even the Ghostbrands had developed their own non-craft version, which they had lovingly named 'Cropper-Soccer'. The moniker was apt, as the games often resembled a union of ball sports and wrestling.

Another reason that the Varsity matches were so popular was that the final represented the culmination of the sports rivalry between UCE and the neighbouring British Midland University, and whilst the feud was always light-hearted and friendly for the most part, there was always the chance of a ruck at the final. Not to mention

BMU had thrashed UCE last year and the home team were gunning for victory.

The crowd cheered excitedly as the players jogged out onto the padded game-space. The UCE Falcons were in white sleeveless vests, with navy shorts, the various knee pads and shoulder braces criss-crossing over toned muscles. On the opposite side of the pitch, the Wolves of BMU were huddled in a circle, for a final pep talk from their captain as they checked the buckles on their formidable black uniforms. White versus Black, Myst thought. Good versus Evil. Two tribes suited up for an hour of serious war before heading to the clubs in a swarm of jovial drinkers, rivalry forgotten until next year's Varsity contest began.

Myst noticed that BMU were playing four Firebrands up front, which was risky considering the two Waterbrands in the frontline of the home team. Perhaps UCE were in with a chance this year.

The two captains stepped forward, resolutely glaring at each other with stolid game-faces. The crowd hushed once more as the referee wedged himself between the towering leaders. He was clutching the Chargeball against his chest, its crystalline finish glimmering in the spotlights, all trained on the centre of the arena with halogenic expectancy. Seconds passed before the referee seemingly tossed the ball into the air in impossibly slow motion then retreated from the pitch as the tinted orb arced upwards.

Slam! Everything jumped forwards, the action catching up on itself as Fen, the UCE Captain, shot from the ground and snatched the ball, turning it a forest green with Earth charge. The opposing Firebrand Captain barrelled into Fen's torso, the ball slipping from the Earthbrand's grip. Half the arena erupted in outrage as the Chargeball skittered across the pitch, the other players scrambling for it. Fen got to his feet, angrily shoving the other captain with both hands.

One of the BMU players got his hand to the Chargeball, successfully neutralising Fen's Earth charge, replacing it with his own Air force. Whilst the majority of the attention was now focused on the fist-fight that was rapidly developing between the two captains, the BMU Airbrand scooped the ball to his chest and began to sprint towards the opposite score-line. If he made it past, then he would earn ten points for UCE's rivals. Myst found herself watching him as he ran unchallenged, closer and closer to the first score of the match. He was younger than her, a first year maybe, his closely cropped brown curls adding further youthfulness to his appearance. There was something about him that the Waterbrand felt compelled to root for, though she couldn't place it. Perhaps it was the idea of one single person taking a stand and making a move for something important, she reasoned. Whilst everyone else was distracted by the testosterone showdown at the other end of the pitch, this guy was still focused on the goal. As she watched, Myst liked to think that she would display the same qualities of dedication.

Unfortunately for the young Airbrand, his unchecked progress was drawing to an end. First, the UCE defender tore his gaze away from his captain, eyes widening furiously as he saw how close his encroaching opponent was. Panicking, the defender sent a frenzied blast of water droplets from his palm, but the Airbrand had been expecting it. The charging BMU player lowered his own palm parallel to the floor and catapulted himself from the ground, using the air like a cannon. He spun in the nothingness, his body twisting and rippling as he flipped over the Waterbrand defender's efforts. Airbrands always did the best stunts, Myst thought as she watched with glee.

The noise of the crowd rose to fever pitch at this aerial display, and the other UCE members finally became aware of the situation. Five separate waves of energy surged towards the Airbrand as he hit the ground running. Sensing defeat, he heaved the Chargeball to one of his team-mates just as the collection of force blasted him back into the air and then smashed him into the protective barriers that surrounded the arena. Myst felt a hint of guilt as the young man crumpled, but she always felt that way at the beginning of a match. Once she got used to the serial attacking and shooting she could handle it, and anyway, Chargeball arenas were strictly monitored for power usage. If anybody 'shot to kill' as it were, the energy would be nullified before it hit.

And so began the furious hour of the Varsity Chargeball final. As Myst had expected, the obligatory streaker ran across at half-time just as the BMU cheerleaders were performing their routine. The roars of mirth from the crowd drowned out the disgusted shrieks of the girls as the high-spirited young man was apprehended by security guards who rolled their eyes, thoroughly unimpressed.

The second half of the game was equally as exciting as the first, and BMU, who were twenty points behind, were beginning to show signs of frustration. It was as the clock was on the final countdown that the Captain truly gave in to defeat. He hurled the fire-charged ball from the halfway line, turning away angrily before he saw the result. A Waterbrand and an Earthbrand reached the shimmering scarlet orb at exactly the same moment, neither of them anticipating the other's charge. The resultant collision of the three elemental forces was enough to flatten all the players on the pitch as it radiated from the ball. Luckily for the crowd, the elemental dampeners kicked in before anybody caught the blast, although from her position in the front row, Myst felt the rush of energy surge towards her before the machines hummed into action.

The clock chimed and the crowd exploded simultaneously with cheers and commiserations as the players scrambled to their feet and dusted themselves off. The UCE team converged into a massive group hug whereas their defeated opponents trudged back to the changing rooms, trying to avoid the criticising glares of their fans.

Before long, the tide that had swept the masses into the arena had turned, the lure of alcohol and loud music pulling them once more into the open air. Myst and Briar hung back, letting the majority of the crowd flow past them as they took in the last of the celebrations on the pitch. The Varsity games always left the young Waterbrand speechless, her ears ringing with the excited din, but Briar liked to ask lots of inane questions such as 'wasn't it great when…?' or 'how about that Firebrand?' As they joined the end of the steady procession, Myst resigned herself to giving a series of nods and murmurs until the adrenaline coursed out of her system.

"Did you see that?" Briar asked.

"Mmm-hmm."

"No Myst, look." The Waterbrand detected a note of concern in her companion's voice, so she stopped to look where her friend was pointing, brow furrowed with curiosity. Up ahead, the crowd was surging forward, forming a circle around something that had got them all excited. Pushing her way through the jostling onlookers, she frowned as she took in the scene before her. A group of lads were kicking a curled form that cowered on the verge by the side of the path. It was a boy, and the closer she got, the younger he looked. Sixteen? Fifteen? His thin frame trembled as blow after blow rained down on him.

What had he done wrong? Why wasn't he retaliating or defending himself? Briar arrived at Myst's side just as the bullies stepped back from their prey with a feigned hush of remorse. The boy uncurled and stared at his attackers, eyes glistening and chest heaving as he held back sobs. Tentatively, he braced his shoulders and hauled himself to his knees. One of the others immediately jabbed his fist upwards, the dirt beneath the poor lad mimicking the action, a jutting pinnacle of earth thrusting up and sending him crashing onto his back once more.

That was when Myst realised the truth. The young boy was a Ghostbrand, and that explained everything. As the tormentors continued their malicious campaign, she looked around at the crowd. Most had shamefully moved on, but a few sick members remained, voyeurs to perverse destruction.

The Waterbrand decided she had seen enough of this terrible display as she stepped forwards, palm raised angrily. Eyes flickering slightly, she trained in on the moisture in the cooling night air and lowered the temperature even more. Ice crystals began to hang like a curtain of stars around the fragile child. The individual shards solidified into a temporary shield just as a rock was flung at the boy's ribs. The ice cracked, but the stone did not pass through.

"That's enough!" the Waterbrand shouted, suddenly feeling a lot braver than she had a few moments ago. The attackers turned to face her, expressions of surprise rapidly becoming sneers of contempt when they saw the vigilante before them. Behind the pack of wolf-like marauders the boy squirmed, nothing more than a silhouette behind the wall of ice.

"Standing up for Ghostbrands, eh?" the lead figure snarled cockily. He advanced until his nose was inches away from Myst's. She stood resolutely against his intimidating leer, a single figure in a tide of malice. "Soon, that sort of behaviour will get you into trouble…" The Waterbrand had no idea what the miscreant was talking about, and hoped he was just trying to frighten her. Then a number of things happened.

The tormenting youth shoved her roughly backwards in a successfully cheap shot. Myst stumbled into Briar, who was just arriving out of breath behind her, and spun off her friend's shoulder. The Waterbrand toppled through the imbalance and cracked the back of her head on the kerb as she landed awkwardly on the unyielding concrete.

Her brain was sent into chaos. Her ears rang with a dull echo and everything sounded muted as if she had plunged under water. Fluorescent blobs jellyfished across her vision and nothing would transmit to her limbs, as though her body was buried in her misfortune. Myst was dimly aware of her ice handiwork shattering into diamond slivers as her concentration faded, before a multitude of angry yells deafened her pounding senses like crashing waves. She saw bodies flying impossibly through the air, again creating the impression that perhaps they were all now swimming under water, but then she felt hands scraping at her as she frantically tried to blink the spots from her eyes.

Myst awoke with a gasp – one of her blinks had turned into a blackout. Her head was throbbing, but at least she could see and hear properly once more. She was also relieved to find that despite the confusion, she was still on dry land. Briar was cradling her, puffy-eyed and makeup streaked, but when she saw her friend was awake, she blew out a relieved breath.

"Thank the Elements you're all right!" she gushed, pulling Myst into a tighter embrace. Two figures were standing in the road, the smaller of which must have been the boy that had been attacked. As she strained her eyes, she recognised the other as the courageous Airbrand from the BMU Chargeball team. That explained the flying people, she thought. Using Briar for support, Myst hauled herself to her feet, pausing unsteadily while her brain caught up with the rest of her body. The two men noticed the movement and moved towards her. The Airbrand's eyes were brimming with concern, and Myst thought she noticed the hint of a smile as he drew closer.

"Are you ok?" he asked. "You took quite a hit." Although Myst appreciated the question, she wasn't used to being fussed over, especially by men, so she hastily changed the subject.

"How long was I down there?"

"Only a few minutes," chipped in Briar. "Riga got rid of those creeps."

Myst turned towards the Airbrand. "Then I owe you some thanks." He nodded silently as she looked at the boy, a cut on his lip oozing blood across his chin.

"Thank you for stepping in," he began timidly. "They wouldn't have stopped, not for a Ghostbrand." As he said the damning word, he looked at the three of them intently, as if waiting for their reaction. When nobody flinched or spat in disgust, he continued. "I'm Coen."

"Do you need a doctor?" asked Briar, taking in the cuts, bruises and stains that covered the child like camouflage. He patted himself down gently, testing the extent of his injuries with a sniff.

"Nothing broken…"

"Did you know those guys?" Riga asked.

"No, I was just on my way home from a friend's when…" Coen swallowed, trying not to let the others hear his voice cracking. "My mum will be worried about me." At this, Myst realised she must have been pretty close when guessing his age.

"Where do you live? We'll walk you." He inclined his head up the street, and the four of them turned to leave.

"Hold it, traitor!" A jerky figure stepped out from behind a car at the side of the road. Coen immediately sprang backwards behind Riga, one hand on his shoulder as he peered round. As the figure stepped into the halo of the street lamp, Myst saw that it was the leader of the bullies. He was reluctantly accompanied by one of his friends, who was hanging back, massaging his ribs with a pained grimace. Riga's work, she thought.

"Come on Kier, just leave it," the henchman muttered. He could obviously sense the defeat that his ringleader couldn't.

"Shut up!" Kier spat before focusing his attention on the huddled gang in front of him. "Look at you, swarming around that scum like it actually matters. Like it's one of us?" Nobody moved. The hooligan changed his reasoning. "Do you know how many of their kind I've sorted?" he said, a grin forming on his lips. Myst didn't want to imagine what 'sorted' actually meant, but she felt an intense hatred for this man boiling up inside. He began to laugh coldly, and Riga raised his palm threateningly, but the Waterbrand placed an arm across his chest to hold him back as she stepped torwards the bully. With a solid crunch, she jammed her palm into his face, a perfect imitation of what she had learned in the self-defence class. She levelled him instantly in a bloody crash and his companion spun on his heels and fled.

"That's for knocking me down, you dick," Myst said curtly before turning back to her friends.

"Wow…" breathed Riga admiringly.

Almost an hour later, the two young women shuffled into their flat, after it took Briar what seemed like twenty minutes fumbling with the keys. Once they had dropped Coen off with his extremely grateful mother, Riga had gone his own way. Myst's head was awash with thoughts, all underpinned with the concussive throbbing, which had only slightly lessened. It was obvious that Kier and his thugs had only attacked the helpless boy because he was a Ghostbrand, but some of the things the bully had said had disturbed her. All the talk about traitors, and 'sorting their kind'? Attacks on, and even murders of Ghostbrands weren't unheard of, but they weren't a frequent occurrence. Not for a long time now, but the young man still presented a problem. If there were people trooping around the city taking matters into their own hands, then law and justice could not survive.

Myst took a deep breath, and was suddenly filled with an incomparable rage and a desire to fight all wrongs everywhere, superhero style. The thought that people like Kier still existed was disgusting to her. Her reverie of righteousness was interrupted as Briar sidled up to her, proffering a steaming mug of hot chocolate.

"Sleepy time?"

"In a minute," the Waterbrand replied casually. "I'm gonna check the mind beacon first, maybe listen to a bit of music. If I go to bed now, I won't sleep. My head's too full of storms… and pain."

"Ok," Briar laughed tenderly. "Don't stay up too late." With her long skirt, it looked like the Earthbrand glided up the stairs, leaving Myst soaking cocoa through her system. She moved into the living room, which was a

constant battleground between the opposing forces of
student laziness and female tidiness, and picked her way
over to where the mind beacon stood humming quietly in
the corner. *Student laziness seems to be winning tonight,* she
thought with a smile, but her highly efficient and slightly
neurotic flatmate would clean it up tomorrow, no doubt.

Myst slid her hand onto the cool, highly polished
contact plate and cleared her mind. It took a certain degree
of concentration to access the beacon, and for a second,
she was unsure if she would be able to with all the
confusion brewing in her head, but soon enough she felt
the familiar sensation of her mind almost lifting out of her
skull and becoming free, floating in a void of pleasant
warmth. If there were any messages, they would float out
to her undulating consciousness and impart their contents
before she closed her mind to the channels of information.

After a moment, a sinew of glowing iridescence
snaked out towards her, just visible like a projection on the
inside of her eyelids. As the message reached her, an official
sounding voice slowly faded in. Myst vaguely recognised
the voice as belonging to the man who had just been
elected onto the Element Council, though she couldn't
remember his name.

"Ladies and Gentlemen, an era of shadows is
drawing to an end. We stand now on the brink of an era of
greatness. Yet before change there must come conflict.

Evidence has finally come to the light that
Ghostbrands were indeed responsible for murdering the
Everrulers twenty years ago. Phoenix, Dexamenas, Altair
and Dylan, the protectors of all, were savagely and
unexpectedly cut down one after the other. As a result, we
as representatives of humanity have had to act without
their guidance and wisdom for so long. It has not been easy
and my esteemed colleagues on the Council have been

forced to make a number of difficult decisions in this period of confusion. Believe me when I say that in the first week of my tenure as an Element Councillor, no choices have been as hard as the one I am here to announce. Take some comfort first in the knowledge that the perpetrators of this terrible crime that shook the very foundations of our society are finally about to be brought to justice. A gang of militant Ghostbrands were responsible for the planning and execution of a campaign to eliminate the Everrulers.

Earlier today, the police apprehended the ringleaders of the organisation who have since confessed to the murders. In accordance with the statute laid down by the Element Council immediately following the tragedy, any persons found responsible were to be immediately sentenced to death. As such, the Ghostbrands will be put before the firing squad tomorrow at noon.

Already since the issuing of this report, threats have emerged against the Council, and indeed all of the Encrafted. Suffice it to say that actions have had to be taken, and it is with a heavy heart that I announce that the Council's only option was to declare war on this rising faction of Ghostbrands. That's right, Ladies and Gentlemen, we are now a nation at war.

Thankfully, the Army of the Elements is ready to mobilise against such uprisings, however we urge any and all of you to do what you can. Take a deep a breath and take the plunge for your rights, your country and your craft.

Furthermore, in order to prevent conditions from deteriorating, the following Ghostbrand statutes are temporarily suspended. The right to assembly – suspended. The right to vote – suspended. The right to a free trial…"

At this point, the Waterbrand pulled her hand from the beacon, the words thundering into her consciousness.

War. The country was at war with the Ghostbrands. Out of nowhere. War. The Army, the AotE, was already moving.

She took a deep breath and felt the strange sensation of anger and righteousness once more flooding her lungs. Tomorrow, Myst Waterbrand would be at war.

Chapter 14 – Five Minutes To Noon

The whole city - and country no doubt, was blanketed in silence as all attention was focused on three men and two women. The Ghostbrands were huddled together in the centre of a crude wooden stage that had been set up in the middle of the packed square. Around the perimeter, five spires of unrelenting black metal pierced the midday sun, releasing the faintest fragrance of dill and peony into the cloying air. They were ceremonial versions of the dampeners found at Chargeball arenas, but these hadn't been seen in public for over fifty years, when executions were abolished. Even when the council announced their special exception reserved for the Everrulers' murderers, nobody actually believed it would happen. Until now. Four minutes to noon.

As a light zephyr wove its way through the gathered masses, the white flags that topped each dampener rustled cacophonous thunder across the silent crowd. The sun blazed down on the people, burning the backs of their necks but nobody moved. Such awful rapture that even the burning orb would not relent its gaze elsewhere.

Myst and Briar stood shoulder to shoulder in the uncomfortable heat. They had just come from the volunteer rally at UCE – Myst would be starting her training within a week, whereas Briar had been chosen to work in the Planning and Organisation Division. Already the appeal was wearing off, Myst thought, as she stared into the eyes of the Ghostbrand nearest to her. Rather than glaring defiantly like a cold-hearted killer, the poor man shuffled awkwardly in vain attempts to keep his eyes out of the sun. His legs were shaking and he kept muttering quietly to himself. Some final prayer maybe? Although Myst had no idea to exactly what a Ghostbrand might pray.

The woman next to him was crying and rocking back and forth, and the Waterbrand had no doubt that the three Ghostbrands that she couldn't see were in a similar situation. For a second, Myst found herself thinking of Riga, wondering if he was here too. Parts of her wished that he wasn't here to witness this public display of justice.

Three minutes to noon. Across the square, Etain and Eir watched nervously as four hooded figures stalked solemnly into the arena of death. Neither Earthbrand had noticed where they had come from, but both knew their purpose. The Ghostbrands on the platform straightened as they observed their executioners. The anonymous citizens seemed to float towards their compass points, and Etain could not help but fantasise about the people beneath the hoods. Had they volunteered for this? Or was it perhaps a job they had been specifically chosen for? Maybe it was like Jury duty, and everybody would get a turn eventually? This of course led the young man to consider if he would be able to do it. He narrowed his eyes as he thought about it, coming to the conclusion that he might be able to summon the courage to take a life if the convicts definitely deserved it like this group did. What if his new job required him to? Etain banished that thought as quickly as it had come. He was going to be a simple admin assistant, not a government wet-worker. Two minutes to noon.

From a café across the street, Llyr stood anxiously glaring at the clock mounted on the yellowing wall. The sooner this was over and done with, the sooner she could get back to shopping. She had to look her best for her father's funeral, after all. Of course she wanted to see the world get rid of a few more skulking Ghostbrands, but seriously, why the need for all the pomp and circumstance? As she pictured in her mind how she would have done this, quickly and easily in a dark pit somewhere where they could scream as loud as they wanted and nobody would hear, one of the executioners began reading the last rights to the guilty party. She couldn't make out exactly what was being said, but she hoped it made the Ghostbrands feel even worse for what they had done. She had only briefly considered what her father had said about the Ghostbrands' innocence, and her mind was resisting the idea in a hurricane of conflict. On the one hand, she had thirteen years of private education, where she was tucked away at a boarding school in the hills – a veritable fortress of anti-Ghostbrand future socialites. On the other hand however, her father – the man who had raised her, and that she loved and trusted more than anybody in the world – had said the Ghostbrands were innocent. She was certainly sure that *he* believed it, but he had been on his deathbed – was his mind entirely reliable at that point? Regardless of what her father thought, she had made her mind up many years ago.

One minute to noon. The formal tone of the speaker faded to silence, and Llyr craned her neck to see through the café window. The dispensers of justice had raised their right hands. One of the Ghostbrands opened his mouth.

"We are inn-"

A couple of miles away, Ardent and Emrys sat eyeing each other anxiously. Mrs Earthbrand had insisted that they stayed out of the city, and so they were bundled away into the hayloft of the barn, away from any forms of information or contact. Ardent understood the woman's desire to protect them. Both he and Emrys knew what today meant for people like them. He shifted uncomfortably in the scratchy straw, then froze. There was a brief flash, followed by a rumbling sound like a distant storm, then silence. Noon.

Llyr's Determination
November 13

Chapter 15 – Inheritance

The city had changed. The last time Llyr Airbrand had
stood on the balcony of her father's luxury villa, the streets
were awash with coloured banners and excitement, but
now all she saw was apprehension and fear. There were the
obvious cracks and burns from the volcanic eruption, but
also a number of smaller signs that suggested a shift in
atmosphere. A lot of the restaurants had stopped opening,
and some buildings were boarded up completely. The few
establishments that had belonged to Ghostbrands had been
abandoned and ransacked, though not necessarily in that
order, and the solitary citizens that were in the echoing
streets hurried past the gaping windows and graffiti without
a second glance. For some people, these broken facades
were a testament to the decline of morals and fraternity,
but for Llyr it was progress. It was about time something
was done about the Ghostbrands, and indeed, her first act
of the war was to sack the butler.

Her father warned her that something major would
happen if Spyrus became part of the Element Council, and
now they were at war. How convenient. Not that the
conflict was a bad thing, Llyr thought wryly. Ghostbrands
were like a sickness, a disability, and this was the cure.

Turning towards the large bay window, she stepped
inside and moved along the lavish hallway. She paused
briefly at the door to her father's room – the one they had

both been in when he had died – before heading to the far end of the landing.

It was a study, but large enough to hold a small conference, with an immaculately polished mahogany table in the centre, surrounded by expensive leather chairs. The walls were lined with bookcases, shelves carrying strange twisting sculptures, and one wall was occupied with a projector screen.

"Sorry to keep you waiting," she said unconvincingly to the suited man who sat at the table. His briefcase was already open, a sheaf of papers in his hand. Upon seeing the young woman, he stood up and offered his free hand, which she did not shake. The man was the family lawyer, but Llyr had only seen him a few times at the villa before. This was the first time she had met him as the family representative.

"Miss Airbrand," he began. "As you know, your father had a long and distinguished career with the Element Council, and as such-"

"Just get on with it," the girl sighed, waving her hand impatiently. The lawyer looked taken aback, obviously used to a certain degree of decorum when dealing with such matters. After a slight pause, he continued.

"Mr Airbrand left one hundred thousand pounds to the Council fund, and a further twenty five thousand to a number of local charities." Llyr rolled her eyes. "The rest of his assets he left to you, including this place." At this, the girl's eyes lit up even though she had known that the outcome would be something like this.

"Where do I sign?" she asked casually. The lawyer pushed a sheet of paper and a pen towards her, and she swept it up eagerly.

"Oh," the man remembered. "There was an envelope as well." Llyr didn't even look at him as she waved her hand dismissively once more and signed the paper.

After the lawyer had packed away his things and been ushered impatiently from the building, Llyr retreated to her bedroom and sat cross-legged on the bed twirling her fingers through her hair. She turned the envelope over and over, but there was only her name written in perfectly curled script on the front. It was her father's writing. With a deep breath, she tore the envelope open and a number of items spilled out onto the baby pink duvet. There was a card, a letter and some sort of necklace.

The small rectangle of card was gilded in gold leaf, with a shield made up of the four element symbols - the logo of the Element Council. In immaculate print was an invitation to the annual Council ball, but it was addressed to her and not her father. She had been a few times before, but only as his guest – she had never had an invitation of her own. Only for an instant did it strike her as surprising that the ball was still going ahead despite the war – after all, none of the social elite would be fighting – why shouldn't they let their hair down?

Next, she unfolded the letter. As she did so, the unmistakable scent of her father drifted out and filled her nostrils with memory. So many times had she sat in the study when she was little, playing with pony figures or writing in her diary as he worked at the desk. Her eyes flickered as she read.

My dear daughter, by now you will have received the decisions I laid out in my last will and testament. I hope this comes as some comfort, as I know you will be doing all you can with regard to our final conversation. I hope your efforts are proving fruitful, but there is one last thing I can do for you. The talisman included with this letter is specifically charged with your protection. Wear it at all times and if

Spyrus moves against you, the stone will crack. I hope it does not come to that however, because unlike lightning, Spyrus will continue to strike once they sense you are a threat. It is my only hope that you make the Transcendence Protocol before they act, as it will be the only way you will be truly safe from them.

I managed to secure the invitation for you as the daughter of one of the longest serving council members. You may not feel like attending, but the Council Ball will be full of very influential people, and now that Spyrus are undoubtedly on the committee, there may well be a number of the Spyrus heads there. Use this chance to get as much information as you can.

Go well Llyr, my summer breeze.

Full of curiosity, the young woman picked up the pendant and rolled it between her slender fingers. It was a small, squarish lump of shining black stone, highly polished so she could see faint traces of her topaz eyes reflected in the well of darkness. It might have been jet or obsidian, she wasn't sure. Wrapped around the stone was a thin wire of copper, somehow burnished onto the rock so that it looked as if the two substances had grown together as one. The wire rose up at the top to form a loop, through which a fine silver chain was threaded.

Llyr had to admit, it was a finely crafted piece of jewellery, but she couldn't help thinking that her father had been overreacting when he had written the letter. So what if they were at war? It wouldn't affect her in the slightest. She wasn't a fighter – she certainly had no compulsion to sign up like the unwashed masses. Of course the AotE would conquer the slimy craftless monsters and the world would be back to normal, a cleaner and better place. The Transcendence Protocol was probably something designed to protect the most important members of Spyrus so that if all was lost, at least they alone could continue the company's work. But that was impossible. There was no way that the Ghostbrands could win this conflict and so Llyr would not need protecting.

As far as Spyrus was concerned, their secret had died with Llyr's father. There was no reason to suspect that he would have passed the information on, and what would he possibly have to gain from doing so? Yes, the young Airbrand thought. It would be a lot better all round if she forgot the whole thing. Besides, she considered, the necklace didn't really go with any of her outfits. But she would of course still attend the Council Ball. She had to be seen to be coping with her father's death like a strong independent woman, and nothing said that louder than turning up in a room full of stuffy old councillors wearing a slinky black number and raising some heart rates.

Chapter 16 – Whispers On The Wind

The limousine pulled up to the Grand Union Hotel and a footman held the door as the radiant woman stepped out. Llyr was wearing the most expensive dress she could buy, a one off from a highly esteemed French designer. She barely had to flash her ticket to the attendant at the entrance, the man nodding in recognition even though she had no idea who he was. She had been expecting this, of course. There would be many of her father's old friends at the ball, and Llyr was all too aware of the fact that she was about to be swept away in a gust of condolences and sympathy. The sooner she got to the bar, the better, as it would at least distract her from everybody projecting their sorrow onto her. Passing a number of men in dinner jackets – one-sleeved, of course, but with a black velvet forearm brace over the bare side – the Airbrand saw a tray of high champagne flutes bobbing along above the heads of the crowd. Within seconds she had swept over to the servant and snatched two glasses from his shining platter. She knocked the first drink back in one inelegant gulp, then began to sip the second as she stalked across the room, trying to avoid the sorrowful eyes that seemed to be following her around. Why couldn't they just stop staring? Couldn't they tell she was coping just fine? She heard the sound of laughter pulsing out from a secluded corner, and fought her way towards it as she drained the remnants of the second drink.

Huddled together was a group of people all around the same age as Llyr. They had obviously been dragged along by their important parents, and she recognised quite a few of them as children of the councillors. There was one young man that she had not seen before, and the others were all listening to him with rapt attention. She edged closer just as he was finishing an anecdote. Everybody laughed once more as she ingratiated herself into the group.

"Ah," one of the boys exclaimed cheerfully. "Another forlorn council brat, hi Llyr."

She nodded in his direction. "Couldn't escape then?"

The boy shook his head with a wistful grin. He turned to the unknown young man. "This is Kier," he began. "Tohelnar's son." Kier stepped forwards and held out his hand. She took it and looked into his face. He was handsome, but the good looks were offset by a hint of bruising across his nose, which had a crick in the centre as if it had been broken. It was like a beautiful vase ruined by the tiniest of hairline cracks.

"I was just telling the others about some of the Ghostbrands I've sorted out," he said as he flexed his hands. He grabbed another glass from the nearest waiter and offered it to her. Llyr took the drink and drained it in one. For some reason, she was feeling the need to drink more and more. Normally she would have relished in hearing tales of Ghostbrand humiliation, and would have definitely fallen for Kier's confidence, but she kept looking at the bruise he wore like a badge of failure. He had obviously been careless enough to let someone take a shot at him – and that spoke volumes.

"Looks like one of them sorted *you*," she retorted spitefully. Kier blinked for a second, but obviously hadn't picked up on her hostility.

"Ha, no. That was someone else. We could go somewhere quieter and I could give you a recap?" Did he just wink at her?

"No thanks," she snapped. "I don't go for damaged goods." Before the young man could reply, she turned on her heels and ran to the bathroom. Luckily, nobody tried to stop her as she forced her way past the queue and jammed herself into a cubicle. She sat, head in her hands, taking deep breaths and not fully understanding what was happening to her. She had drunk champagne lots of times before, but never so quickly. She was trying to show everybody that she was dealing with her situation. Wasn't she? Llyr shuddered, her head following a few milliseconds behind like an echo. No more drinks tonight, she thought. The young woman had finally realised that the best way to show how strong she was was to just face all the questions and sympathy and get it out of the way rather than hiding behind alcohol. Hopefully, she would be able to regain her composure and go modulating before anybody noticed her behaviour. While it would be painful to force herself through endless gusts of well-wishers, that was the true way to show she was coping, by seeing it through. *Although, I could cheat a little*, she thought as she sniffed lightly.

Leaning back, Llyr closed her eyes and took a deep breath. She felt the air pulsing across the room from the conditioning unit in the corner. There was the aroma of the cheap perfume of whoever had been in before her, intertwined with the fragrance emanating from the vase of lilies that stood on the marble counter by the sink. As she had closed her eyes, next she made a conscious effort to close her mind to the sense of smell. With each sense that she numbed, the more heightened her hearing became. Eventually, she could pick out faint wisps of conversation echoing as vibrations in the air, growing louder all the time as she refined her senses. After a few moments, she could almost see a schematic type plan of the bathroom and the dancehall beyond, glowing in a faint citrus yellow. As footsteps and words created ripples in the air, she felt it and mapped it into her subconscious image. Llyr's world became a dissonance of voices as she made the final internal adjustments.

140

"-terrible isn't it? I mean nobody-"

"-they are rather good aren't they? I especially like the little prawn ones-"

"-bastard hairdryer-" *Does this phrase seem familiar? :)*

Llyr chuckled quietly to herself as she sifted through the mundane snippets of people's lives. An invisible network of baggage that collided and bruised anybody that was unlucky enough to walk across its path.

"-haven't seen her in a while-"

"-looked a state though, poor thing. Obviously still upset about her father-"

Stay away from that corner, the young Airbrand thought to herself. If she could just work out who she needed to steer clear of, it would make the evening go a lot more smoothly. She continued to scout for any signs of the mourning sympathy.

"-a vodka chaser please-"

"-protocol is simple. You have to-"

Llyr's eyes snapped open and she held her palm against the cubicle wall. Protocol. Could it be? She hurried to her feet, straightening her dress as she slammed the door open and marched out into the fray of suits and sophistication. She knew exactly where she was heading, for the voice had belonged to Kier.

The young woman wove her way through the immaculate crowds until she reached the corner of the younger generation. They were all still exactly as they had been, with new drinks of course. She waited politely until one of the girls had finished speaking before announcing her presence with a curt cough.

"How about that recap?" she said, keeping her eyes directly on Kier. The councillor's son lit up as he saw the eager expression she was wearing, and gave a sly grin to the other young men as he sauntered towards her, cocky and sure. *Bingo,* Llyr thought, recognizing the signs of attraction. If she could charm him into talking quickly, she wouldn't have to kiss him. Llyr grabbed his hand and led him a twisting path through dancing couples and groups of casual chatters until they reached a quiet alcove under a carved floral awning. Kier leaned in towards her shoulder, his breath warm and teasing against her branded skin.

"I knew you'd change your mind," he murmured softly. He pressed against her, and she could feel him straining beneath his clothes. As he gripped her, she could feel the desire rising within him, and she began to move as if to break free of his grasp.

"This isn't exactly what I…" Llyr murmured as she struggled against his arms.

"Shh…" Kier began clawing at her back, forcefully searching for the straps that would release her to him. The young man buried his head into her shoulder whilst leaning into her so fiercely that her back was chafing against the cold marble wall. Llyr squirmed, suddenly afraid that her plan would backfire and take her somewhere she had no desire to go. *Time to get back in control,* Llyr thought to herself.

With one swift motion, Llyr shot her hand forward, fingers extended like hawk's talons, and pinioned Kier's crotch in a vice grip. As she did so, she used her shoulder to force his body around and into the wall, and in that half a second, she had the young man incapacitated.

"Easy, tiger," Llyr hissed. Kier managed to force a high-pitched yelp through his clenched jaws and she felt his yearning fade in her hand. "What's the Transcendence Protocol?"

"How do you kn-" The young man was cut off as the Airbrand dug her fingers in sharply. "It's an emergency thing that Spyrus have," he squealed.

"And?"

"I don't know…when something big happens, the company pick four people for it. That's all, I swear."

"Who did they pick?"

Kier looked confused as he thought about the question. "It hasn't happened yet…"

"What do you mean?" Llyr snapped. "What about the war?" As she clenched, she felt him writhing in her grip. She looked into the man's face and realised he was laughing through the pain.

"War isn't big enough to warrant Transcendence," he smirked as he shifted awkwardly. "And trust me, the war is no surprise to Spyrus. Why would they use the last resort when victory has been certain since before it began?" Stunned, Llyr released her grasp and took a step back. Panting, Kier reached down to check the damage. He was muttering under his breath, but the young woman wasn't listening. She had been wrong. The Transcendence Protocol had nothing to do with the war, and that meant there was still some possibility of a major event, one that Spyrus might not have anticipated. But what could be that bad?

Her mind became a gale of questions, and the party seemed to lose all appeal in the winds of uncertainty. Every face seemed to be staring at her with malicious intent, and even the string quartet aria that had been drifting lazily around the hall now grated and stung as it passed the young Airbrand's ears. It was definitely time to leave.

She spun around and came face to flustered face with the newest member of the Element Council, Tohelnar.

"Miss Airbrand," the hawkish man muttered. "How sorry I was to hear of your father's untimely passing."

"Thank you," she managed awkwardly.

"I understand you were with him at the time?" An oddly personal question, considering her father and this man had only met once, Llyr thought defensively. She feigned a smile and watched as the man stared at her with searching eyes.

"Yes, he was asleep," she lied. "He was very peaceful."

"No last minute gems of information then?" Tohelnar asked with a casual air. Llyr froze, even her chest seizing up as her lungs suddenly refused to take oxygen. Everything her father had told her had been true and now the Spyrus head was trying to ascertain if she knew their secret. She forced the air through her throat as she spoke.

"I'm afraid not. As I said, he was sleeping." Immediately, the oppressive choking sensation that had engulfed the room seemed to lift as Tohelnar cracked a wry smile.

"Pity," he commented. "Well once again, I'm sorry for your loss. I'll let you get back to my son." He cast a glance past Llyr towards where Kier was still leaning against the wall, a flushed look across his smooth cheeks. The young Airbrand stared straight into the inquisitive eyes of the older man.

"We're done," she said icily before slipping past him and heading for the door, back straight and head held high. However, as soon as the fresh air teased her bare arms, she broke into a run, heels tapping a rhythm of panic on the unyielding pavement. As she ran, she couldn't help feeling like she had well and truly blown it. So what if she had lied to Tohelnar about her father? As soon as the man spoke to his creep of a son, he would find out that she had been asking about the Transcendence Protocol, and who else could she have heard about that from? If she hadn't been so desperate to find out even the smallest snippet of information, she could have waited to speak to someone less risky.

As she neared the space where her driver was diligently waiting, Llyr vowed that the first thing she would do when she got home was put on the necklace her father had left her. For she was now convinced she would need it.

Chapter 17 – The Criminal Shroud

The next couple of days Llyr spent languishing in the late
Mr Airbrand's study, surrounded by ever-increasing stacks
of paperwork and rapidly cooling cups of coffee. If only
she had been as dedicated with her A Levels, Llyr mused,
she might have been a career girl by now, but in those days
she had lived under the misconception that Daddy would
be there forever to pay her way. Llyr had resigned herself to
laboriously sifting through every document her father had
kept on the off chance that she might come across
something useful. So far she had been disappointed. It
seemed that the council man had decided to leave no
evidence that he had ever crossed paths with Spyrus, save
for his final words with his daughter. The only positive was
that although she had immediately donned the protective
necklace, it had not cracked yet.

Only after the last manuscript had been discarded
did Llyr decide to turn to her craft for inspiration. She had
hoped that she would be able to find something concrete in
writing rather than rely on the often sketchy interpretations
that she got from divining, but now it seemed she had no
choice. With a sigh, the young Airbrand closed the study
door on the memories of her father and headed along the
corridor to her own room. The villa echoed with loneliness
since she had fired all the Ghostbrand staff, but Llyr was
not disconcerted. Independence was all part of her coping
image.

As she entered her bedroom, she was once more
struck by the feeling of isolation, and a sudden image of her
younger self popped into her mind. Whenever she had
been lonely when she was growing up, Llyr always used to
scribble her feelings down in her diary. Once she had left
school, Llyr had often snorted derisively at the thought,

finding the idea that a child could find solace in a diary ridiculous, although she knew at the time why she had done it. It felt like she was never truly alone as long as she had the scented pages to confide in.

Llyr knealt down next to the bed and pushed around underneath the overhanging sheets, her hand closing around the corner of an old shoebox. When she had lifted the lid, Llyr was looking down at a collection of notebooks, some decorated with ponies and butterflies, others with bright pink and yellow flowers. For a moment, she simply stuck her hands into the box, feeling the glossy covers and the softer paper within, until at last she drew the nearest diary out and flicked to an empty page. She was half tempted to snatch up a pen and begin writing once more, pouring her feelings between the hardback covers, but she resisted. Instead she thumbed backwards to a random page and began to read…

"July 18
I've literally spent the whole day with Kyan – we snuck out after morning registration and went exploring in the woods outside school. Everything feels so different when we're together and I swear we almost kissed… next time, definitely. I know people tease him for being a Ghostbrand, but it doesn't matter really. If anything, it makes him more resourceful - stronger than us. He's a good guy and that's what counts. I can't wait to bring him home and-"

Angrily, Llyr slammed the diary shut, dropping the book back into the scuffed shoebox. *Of all the pages to pick,* she thought with distaste. She glared at the box for a second before grabbing the whole thing and dumping it into the bin by her desk. It was foolish to have kept it for so long – memories of a time when she was weak and emotional. Her hand instinctively shot to her opposite wrist, where the last vestige of that time hung, hovering millimeters away from the bracelet she was wearing. *But no,* she told herself. *It's just a trinket – it can stay.* Crisis over, the young Airbrand took a deep breath and thought once more about what she was actually meant to be doing.

Walking over to a small alcove where she kept her tools, Llyr pulled back the rosy netting and was immediately assailed with the scent of incense long burnt out. She reached out for a row of brightly coloured candles, took them down one by one and set them in a circle on the carpet. There were eight in total, and each of the Scrying Candles represented a different aspect of life. Llyr lit the candles and stared intently as the flames took hold. She had no idea what chemical was on the wicks of the candles, but the trails of smoke that came from each one were the same colour as the candle itself.

At first, all Llyr saw was eight vertical tendrils of smoke, fading into invisibility as they reached the ceiling. The smoke was supposed to mix and form patterns that could be interpreted, but so far there was nothing. Perhaps her mind wasn't clear enough? Taking a deep breath, the young woman strained to focus her mind on what she wanted to know. How could she get on the Transcendence Protocol? Before she'd even formulated the question, the lines of smoke began to waver like strings being plucked in the air.

With a spluttering gasp, six of the Scrying Candles flickered then died, leaving only the purple and white trails of smoke, which were now entangled with each other, dancing a twisting waltz across the centre of the room. In front of her eyes, the violet strand widened and flattened while the white smoke stretched and curved around it. In seconds, it had become a purple circle with an S shape across it – the logo of Spyrus. So that was the answer?

Obviously the key lay in the depths of the chrome tower, but Llyr couldn't see any way to get at it. Once more, she lit the candles and focused her mind. How to get the information from Spyrus?

As the young woman stared, the smoke seemed to ripple as an unseen breeze snaked through it. This time, it was the blue and orange trails that dominated, representing mood and education. The blue band of mood was strong and thick, so Llyr took that to mean that she had to be strong willed. Perhaps the knowledge and education would come in time? She watched for a few seconds more, but the image did not change.

Llyr snuffed the candles and thought resolutely. If it was a question of dedication, she was unfazed. When it came to getting what she wanted, Llyr had grown up with the knowledge that all she had to do was take it.

The next morning at nine o'clock precisely, the glass doors of Spyrus tower slid open with a faint hiss to admit the smartly dressed and highly confident Llyr Airbrand. In the early hours, she had ransacked her wardrobe and dug out the most professional looking suit she could find. Her hair was pulled back tightly, and she had retrieved an old pair of glasses from her father's desk. She had no doubt that she would be able to stroll around the lower levels freely, but if she made it to the upper floors, the chances of her being recognised would increase severely. As it was, nobody gave her a second glance as she purposefully strode over to the front desk.

She leaned over the counter where a man sat typing at a screen. He had blonde hair, freshly cut short and looked every bit the dutiful receptionist except for his eyes. He watched the monitor in front of him with a distant expression as if he didn't understand or care about what he was doing. It was a few moments before he looked up.

"I've been called about the Transcendence Protocol," Llyr stated, leaving no space for the man to question her. "Tohelnar himself requested that I come." As she had hoped, the blatant name drop had the desired effect. The man began typing once more, this time with a flash of vigour. Whilst she waited, Llyr glanced around the lofty foyer, a cavern of glass and steel that housed countless hundreds of workers going about their business beneath the giant crystal Spyrus logo like a colony of single-minded ants.

She turned her attention to the receptionist, looking him up and down as he fished information from the database. He was reasonably attractive, and Llyr scanned across to his arms where a Waterbrand was nestled on his bare shoulder. A Waterbrand with a scar across it. Before she could stop herself, the young woman spoke.

"I didn't know Spyrus employed Ghostbrands?"

"It's hardly employment," the man muttered as, without taking his eyes from the screen, he held up his wrist to show her the cruel tag that kept him at his station. Llyr couldn't believe it! He was now chatting to her like they were equals!

"I wasn't asking for your opinion," she snapped. "Now which floor am I going to?" The receptionist looked at her with a patronising smile. He clicked the monitor off, and Llyr realised her mistake. He had the power here. Ghostbrand or not, she couldn't exactly make him let her through – she was right in the middle of Spyrus after all.

"I'm sorry," he said unconvincingly. "I'm not getting any reply from Level 5 Archiving. Without that, I'm afraid I can't let you in." Llyr stared furiously, willing the man to crumble under her gaze. If this were any other situation, she would have given him something to cry about but she couldn't risk it now.

"When Tohelnar hears about this, he will make sure you're punished," she lied as she turned to leave.

"I'm sure he will, Miss. Have a nice day." The man flashed her a smile once more before turning back to his work.

Fuming, Llyr marched back onto the street, cursing all Ghostbrands everywhere. She vowed that if she ever saw the receptionist again, she would make him suffer – after all it was his fault that she had lost her temper, and she was sure that this was the reason he had made up the story about the clearance from Archiving. But, she thought, at least one positive thing had come from the conversation. She now knew where she had to go. Level 5 and the Archiving Department.

When Llyr arrived back at the villa, she had formed a rudimentary plan in her mind. It was a ritual that she had last used when she had been at school. The Criminal Shroud rendered the user immune to being caught by any law enforcers, but at the time, she and her friends had only used the ritual to create mischief around the school, never for anything actually illegal. *How she had grown*, she mused. Luckily, she still had the ingredients required for the task.

She checked and double-checked the process as she waited for night to fall. The shroud wouldn't make her invisible so she still had to wait until she was sure everybody would be out of Spyrus.

When the last lights in the tower had faded to black and the sounds of the few remaining citizens had died down, Llyr began the ritual. She was already dressed in dark leggings and a black roll neck and had everything set out on a mat before her. First, she anointed a wide candle that she had roughly carved into the shape of a skull with a mixture of oils. Lighting the flame, the Airbrand took a deep breath and inhaled the scents of hydrangea and asafoetida. As the aromas danced their way through her senses, Llyr suspected that half of their effect was simply to relax the caster enough so they could actually bring themselves to commit whatever act they had planned.

Next, Llyr took a scrap of paper and a pen, pausing briefly before she wrote. This was the tricky part, as she had to be as exact as possible when describing what she intended to do. She remembered the first time that she had used the shroud at college. The gang of girls had decided to steal their report cards and change some of the grades before they were sent out. Beforehand however, they had simply written "break into the school" on the required slip of paper. Entering the building proved no problem, but as soon as they took the actual report cards from the principal's office, they were apprehended by campus security. Only after they had all been severely reprimanded by staff and parents alike did they realise that stealing the report cards had been classed as a separate crime that they had not mentioned during the ritual.

After working out exactly what she wanted to achieve, Llyr finally put pen to paper.

Break into Spyrus Tower. Find the Transcendence Protocol information on Level 5 Archiving. Leave Spyrus Tower

The young woman was half tempted to add something about the Ghostbrand receptionist, but she was planning to enter the tower through a side door to avoid the main foyer. With a final check, she held the paper into the candle's flame and swiftly tucked the ashes into a small pouch along with fennel seeds and crabgrass. She slid the velvet bag into her pocket and took one last glance at the candle as it slowly burned time away. Once the wick reached its end, the Criminal Shroud would be lifted and

Llyr would once again be vulnerable to capture. She had to be in and out before that happened. The young woman took a deep breath and opened the door.

What seemed like an age later, the young Airbrand stood in the shadows of a Spyrus corridor. Getting in had been easier than she had expected, the side entrance she had selected was mercifully surrounded by other looming buildings, and her forced entry was completely swathed in the inky darkness. Up ahead, she could see the faint glow of the lift floor indicator. From what she had gathered last time she was in the building, the corridor would curve to the left up ahead and open into the vast crystalline foyer.

Llyr slid over to the lift and thumbed the number five. Naturally, she was wearing gloves as she wasn't sure if the Criminal Shroud covered such details as fingerprints. Within seconds, the machinery gave a slight hum and the doors glided open, waiting eagerly to carry her to Level 5. The young woman's stomach lurched as the confined cubicle began to ascend. She afforded herself a moment's rest, leaning against one of the highly polished mirrors that attempted to make the lift look a lot larger than it was. She figured that she had been away from the villa for about an hour, and the candle would perhaps be about a third of the way down by now. That left her two hours maximum to find what she was looking for and get out of the building.

The lift slowed to a halt and the annoying familiarity of a bell ringing heralded the smooth opening of the doors. Llyr pushed herself away from the mirror and gasped. There was a man staring at her.

"Um?" she gasped awkwardly. The man was dressed in a navy zip up and combats, with the Spyrus logo on his chest. He was definitely security and Llyr was in big trouble.

"Working late, miss?" Llyr took a step back, the man's words stunning her. Was he joking? After a moment, she realised how stupid she must look to him and took a deep breath before speaking shakily.

"Yes?"

The man nodded. "No worries. Just let me know if you need anything."

"No… I'm fine." Without another word, the security guard nodded once more and turned on his heels, walking back up the corridor. As his footsteps got softer with distance, Llyr exhaled with relief. Her ritual was obviously more effective than she had given herself credit for. It didn't matter that she wasn't invisible, it seemed that she could convince people that she was supposed to be there. She faced the dark corridor ahead of her, expression falling as the shadowy passage seemed to stretch out before her eyes. With stark resignation, the Airbrand realised that she had no idea where to go from here, and her potential guide was slowly walking away. She was on a time limit after all. "Wait!" she called exasperatedly, already wondering if she had just sold herself to discovery and punishment. Up ahead, the security guard paused, checking his watch while she caught up. As the young woman arrived, flushed with what she hoped looked like embarrassment, the man raised his eyebrows questioningly.

"Change your mind?" he asked musingly.

"I've been asked to do some work on the Transcendence Protocol," Llyr began hopefully. "Trouble is, I don't usually come this far along. Rather than be stuck here all night, I hoped you would be able to show me where it is?" Just for safety, she batted her eyelids but the guard was already motioning for her to follow him up the corridor.

After what seemed like an endless journey of twisting and turning corridors, in which Llyr was sure that they must have crossed over and gone back on themselves at least twice, the two of them were standing outside a plain door with no window or label of any kind. The only thing that set the door apart from the wall was a gleaming panel the size of her palm, and as she looked closely, she realised that it was in fact a palm reader. Nobody outside of Spyrus would be able to open the door, regardless of what rituals they were currently using.

Betraying as little emotion as possible, Llyr made a lengthy show of removing her gloves, pulling on each finger separately and rolling the fabric over her nails carefully. Next, she pretended that one of her nails was caught, and lifted her hand to her face to scrutinise the situation more closely. Come on, come on!

"Here, let me." The guard leaned forward, placing his palm against the panel. The machine beeped loudly in the silence, and the door swung open. Llyr nodded her thanks and stepped inside, kicking the door shut behind her. Gentlemen were so predictable, she thought. Even the ones who had no manners still hated to be kept waiting, so either way she couldn't have lost. She placed her ear to the door and heard the satisfying sound of footsteps heading away round the next corner. With another deep breath she squinted in the darkness and surveyed the home of the Transcendence Protocol.

The first thing she noticed was the stale air. Closing her eyes, she could picture thousands and thousands of dormant particles, each one a miniscule yellow pinprick star against the velvet space of her mind. The yellow was dull, lethargic and tired, not the vibrant energy that air should be. As a test, the Airbrand waved her hand in front of her face, the particles she brushed against flaring into life once more as they interacted. The air began to dance, invigorated by her presence and attention. Llyr opened her eyes.

The room was empty except for a single large filing cabinet, again unlabelled. Llyr couldn't help but feel disappointed. With all the importance her father had placed on the mysterious protocol, she was expecting something a little grander. Spyrus weren't the company to skimp on extravagance, so where were the banners and flags? The plinths, pedestals and mood lighting? Instead, the room looked like an old cupboard where the junk was kept. The room where things with no place were left to rot. Suddenly Llyr shuddered, checking back to make sure that the door had a handle on the inside and that she hadn't sealed herself in. Who knew how long it would actually be until the protocol was used for real? A brief image flittered through the woman's mind, a desolate butterfly of lost hope. She saw herself as a rotting corpse, a sliver of light across a sunken face when somebody finally opened the door to the hidden room. Stretching her hand through the void of darkness, Llyr felt the comforting smoothness of the metal handle she had pinned her survival on. Now that she was sure she was able to get out, she turned her attention back to the filing cabinet itself.

There were three drawers, and the layer of dust that covered the entire structure told Llyr that it had not been opened in a number of months. She gently blew the dust away, whipping up a miniature tornado of swirling grey clumps that twisted and fell slowly onto the tiled floor. As she pulled open the top drawer, the Airbrand was once more disappointed by what she found. There were only two faded paper wallets tucked against the very back of the container. One was labelled "Protocol Events" and the other "Participants". As much as she was intrigued by what Protocol Events could mean, Llyr was fully aware that her time was bound to be running out by now, so she reached for the "Participants" folder. As she prised open the crumbling cover, a single sheet of paper with a list of names greeted her. Most of the names had been crossed out and in hastily scrawled pen there was a list of reasons why the names had been removed. Llyr frowned distastefully as she saw that apart from a couple of people who had been "promoted", all of the others read "deceased". The last four names were marked as "current" – Etain Earthbrand, Seren Airbrand, Myst Waterbrand and Talyn Firebrand. *So these were the ones Spyrus had chosen?* the Airbrand thought idly. By the side of Etain and Seren's names was written "Evacuated to UCE" and the other two names were labelled with "Active in AotE".

    Underneath the list was a set of pictures, the Earthbrand's on top. He was handsome in a messy sort of way, with hair that just wouldn't stay down no matter what. He wore a shirt and tie, but looked like he would be more comfortable in a t-shirt. Obvious country boy. Underneath was the picture of Seren. She had blue eyes the same as Llyr's but her hair was blonde verging on brown - nothing like the burnished red that coursed down onto Llyr's shoulders in ruby rivulets. In fact, if it wasn't for the hair, the two of them looked quite similar. And that was when Llyr formed her plan. She was going to go to UCE, pretend to be Seren and get herself on the Transcendence Potocol.

    Llyr had all she needed so she put the folder back and slipped out. The building was silent, and the only change was the hue of the sky. The indigo blanket that had fallen over the city when she left her home was now a shawl of pitch, dotted by the occasional star. She hurried to the lift, jabbed the ground floor button and let the machinery carry her to freedom.

Chapter 18 - Serenity

It was unusually cold as Llyr stood at the gates of UCE and the raw night air would have bitten into the young Airbrand's skin in seconds, if she had not perfected the skill of changing the air pressure around her so she that was constantly surrounded by a pleasantly warm aura. Getting cold was for common people. The wind that was bowing the surrounding undergrowth playfully swirled away from her at the last moment, teasing and free.

She looked up at the buildings beyond, uninviting and foreboding. It certainly didn't look like anywhere she would like to be evacuated to. Would Spyrus really have sent their chosen ones to this dump? Well, the young woman thought. She had come this far, and even if it was merely to prolong the trek back home, she was going to have a look around.

Reaching lightly for the bolt, Llyr pulled as slowly as she could, managing to keep the noise to a minimal clanging. Light footed, she padded catlike across the quad, flitting from shadow to moonlight as she passed the towering oak trees. When she reached the nearest window, she pressed her face against it, trying to divine the contents of the room. All she could see was a haunting representation of her own face, ruddy cheeks on a pastel portrait. In a split second, half of Llyr's face was cast into a rosy glow. Blinking, she looked across the quad to where a light had just come on in the opposite building. So there were people here! Hefting the bag of clothes she had thrown together, she stalked over to the glass doors of the John Terrence block and pushed them open, the dust catcher unbearably loud as it scraped across the debris-laden tiles.

Before Llyr could move, echoing footfalls were pounding down a nearby staircase. She heard boots crunching on broken glass before a cascade of figures blustered into view. There were three of them, two men and a woman, but they weren't military. Llyr could tell from the way that they were standing that they had no training. These were just ordinary people. The woman was dressed in a full-length gown of deep burgundy, looking like she had been pulled out of a world of sophistication and refinery, only to be dumped in this wreck of a university.

The wind picked up, rattling the windows threateningly as the four stared at each other. It was clear to the Airbrand that the three evacuees were scared, and she began to wonder what had happened to them. What horrors had they seen? She decided to play it weak and needy for now, after all she would get a lot further if she could ingratiate herself with these people.

"Please," she began. "I just need some shelter. The other evacuation centres are full. They told me to come here and it looks like you have space?" Without a word, one of the men nodded and they turned back to the stairs. Taking this as a signal of acceptance, Llyr followed them.

A couple of floors up, the stairwell opened up into a small foyer area with numerous doors leading off. The Airbrand assumed that before the war, these would have been classrooms and lecture halls, bright and welcoming, although now everything was covered in a layer of grime like a parasite leeching out all the positivity that had made UCE what it was. A number of figures huddled in the dirt, all dressed in various different outfits. Llyr saw a number of people dressed formally like the woman she was with, a man that looked like a doctor and even a monk from the Temple of Branding. It seemed as if none of them had had the time nor forewarning to pack a change of clothes. As such, the room was permeated with the rank odour of sweat and the air was thick with the depression and anguish of those it smothered. Subconsciously, the young woman maintained her barrier of air currents because despite the temperature now being tolerable, the thought of mingling with the festering smog repulsed her.

They weaved through the withdrawn figures until they reached the far wall, where a man was standing, tall and commanding. He was wearing a policeman's uniform, and of all the people at UCE, he alone looked capable of dealing with the dire situation they had all been cast into.

"Another new arrival." The woman spoke to the policeman with a certain degree of reverence. It seemed that the evacuees had appointed him their leader. He turned, the Firebrand visible on his muscle-corded shoulder.

"I suppose I better give you the tour," he grunted. He didn't sound friendly, but he wasn't hostile. More resigned, Llyr decided.

The policeman introduced himself as Achaniel, before leading the Airbrand around the confines of UCE. Despite the size of the campus, it was only this block that offered any vestige of protection and even then, many of the doors that led from the foyer opened into uninhabitable rooms of concrete chunks and cracked tiles. In all, the evacuees had access to the foyer, two classrooms, a pokey student toilet and a small kitchen that had been a simple refreshment station. There was also the ground floor corridor, and a fire escape that led to the roof. It was cramped and uncomfortable, a fact that was apparent on everyone's faces. Despite the lack of training, Achaniel had managed to organise the evacuees so that they were now running foraging parties and keeping watch in shifts.

After the tour, they returned to the foyer. Some of the evacuees had gathered around a small fire of random debris – mostly broken furniture salvaged from the rest of the building. Achaniel explained that the heating hadn't worked since they had got there. They were lucky that the water was still connected. The two of them joined the group and sat as a bottle of whiskey was passed around. From the snippets of conversation, Llyr gleaned that they all of the evacuees had some connection to Spyrus, although none of them were employed in the upper echelons of the network. At last, the various different conversations died down, and the evacuees sat staring into the dancing flames, the silence punctuated only when the wood cracked and spat flurries of sparks to the ceiling.

"So what happened here?" Llyr asked casually. When nobody answered, she continued. "I mean, it doesn't seem to be an ideal place to keep people safe? UCE isn't exactly out of the war zone." At this, some of the others looked away awkwardly, but Achaniel didn't bother to hide his anger.

"We've been left here," he spat acidly. "While they were hauling us out of our homes, telling our families that they'd see us again soon, Spyrus said that UCE was like a holding centre – just a temporary place until we could be moved to one of the evacuation centres out in the mountains or somewhere. That was a fortnight ago."

"So they just sent you here with no security? No heat or facilities?" Llyr couldn't believe that one of the world's leading companies for medicine would just abandon its employees in this worthless shell.

"Oh no," piped up one of the women. "Spyrus didn't know that UCE had been attacked until we actually arrived. That's when they left us here." The look on her face said all that her words could not. The lines of resentment and anger were scratched deep into these people and the feelings would take many years to heal.

"So all this happened before you got here?" the Airbrand said with a wave of her arm.

"Most of it. We don't know if it got hit accidentally, or the Ghostbrands found out it was going to be an evacuation centre and wrecked it on purpose. After that, there was the volcano. We're still in the shit."

The woman turned away, another jaded soul created through neglect and mistrust. Llyr felt awkward inside. She had never experienced hardship in her life, because she had known that her family would always be there to back her up. These people had been mistreated and cast aside like old scraps, and the young woman found herself with an odd swelling in her gut after forcing herself to listen to their story. Was this sympathy? She had never spent much time on other people's feelings. Always out for herself, she couldn't afford to get dragged down by deadweight problems that didn't concern her, and yes, she was well aware that she had a reputation of being selfish and rude but what did it matter? In the end, she was still sitting here in the dust waiting for something to happen. Llyr Airbrand, stuck with the commoners in a ransacked university, huddled round a fire of splintered desks.

But of course she could just go home, back to the life of comfort and luxury, couldn't she? But what about the Transcendence Protocol? If her father was right, then if she didn't get on it she would be as good as dead. And this brought her back to her current situation. She couldn't just abandon her search and jump in a warm bubble bath, she had as little choice as everyone else here, and that must have been what she was empathising with – the complete lack of freedom.

Llyr was snapped from her crisis of consternation by a shout from above. Achaniel leaped to his feet as a woman in a lab coat appeared from the roof stairwell.

"We've spotted a group of Ghostbrands heading this way," the woman said anxiously. "I think they've already spotted the light from the fire."

The policeman stared thoughtfully for a brief moment. "Thanks Seren," he muttered. "Right. Anybody who thinks they might be able to offer some defence cover, get up to the roof." Llyr barely registered the words, she was lost in her own thoughts. She'd found Seren Airbrand but now she'd also found herself on the verge of a Ghostbrand attack. All she needed was a moment alone with the scientist to learn what she could about the Transcendence Protocol and then be on her way. She didn't much care what happened after that. As she flicked back into the here and now, Llyr realised that Achaniel was looking at her quizzically.

"Um?" she managed.

"Well?" the policeman asked. "Are you going up?" He shook his head towards the stairs. Llyr nodded and ran after the scientist.

The stairwell opened up onto a wide expanse of flat concrete. From up here, there was no indication that the rest of the building, or indeed campus, was a ruin. The wind whipped through Llyr's hair, angry serpents writhing in the gusts. To the East, the sky was beginning to phase from black to indigo as the sun contemplated appearing, although nobody would have blamed the resplendent orb for shunning the war torn city completely.

A line of evacuees stood resolutely before the raised lip that protected them from the sheer drop to the cold ground below. The Airbrand guessed that these were the only people that had any experience. She wondered why

Achaniel wasn't up here too, but perhaps he was preparing something on the lower floors. Llyr sauntered forwards, picking out Seren from the line and moving to stand by her side. The scientist's lab coat was blowing majestically behind her, although the image chillingly reminded Llyr of a Ghostbrand cloak. Neither woman spoke although there was so much that the Airbrand wanted to say, she was well aware that now was not the time. She peered over the edge, her entire world swirling as her stomach lurched, the ground stretching away yet rushing towards her at the same instant.

Like a swarm of beetles, the evacuees saw the group of Ghostbrands spill through a gap between two of the blocks and into the quad. Their cloaks rippled constantly, giving them a liquid quality as they spread like ink across the pool of murky grass and churned mud. As the ghastly soldiers fanned out, one of them stepped forward. There was nothing that distinguished him from the rest, but like Achaniel, Llyr could instantly tell that he was in charge. He stared up at the building, taking in the positions of the evacuees on the roof and no doubt checking the surrounding windows for entrenched evacuees. When he spoke, his eyes were fixed on one of the middle floors, and the Airbrand guessed that some of the others had presented themselves.

"Don't be afraid, Encrafted," the Ghostbrand shouted, his sonorous voice ringing clearly through the air so that those on the roof could hear every syllable. "We come only for supplies. You are not soldiers, and we intend no harm. Nor shall we leave you with nothing. Surrender what you have and we shall take only what we need."

"How do you know there aren't soldiers here?" This came from down below, a man's voice but not Achaniel.

Llyr was sure that the lead Ghostbrand smiled beneath his hood.

"Trust me, we know. Now what do you say to our offer?" In response, a gout of intense flame spouted from the lower floor window, tracing a defensive line around the edge of the building. Within seconds, a raging wall of fire was burning between the Ghostbrands and UCE. From her perch on the rooftop, Llyr could see a couple of the hooded marauders venture towards the conflagration, only to jump back as the unbearable heat began to burn their flesh. The Ghostbrand leader's eyes widened as he surveyed the now impassable barrier.

"We may not be soldiers, but we're not stupid!" The Ghostbrand scowled before raising his hand to signal to his companions. In a mass of crackling flames and rustling cloaks, the invaders whipped primitive rifles from the folds of velvety material, crouched in the soft ground and opened fire, streams of bullets peppering the brickwork. Seren grabbed Llyr's arm and pulled her to the floor as a hail of brutality crested over the edge of the building. One of the other evacuees was not so quick, the hurricane of steaming lead pounding into him. He turned to face the cowering girls momentarily, a vacant uncomprehending look on his rapidly paling face. A line of crimson roses bloomed across his chest where the bullets had hit. As Llyr looked on in horror, the doomed man gurgled hopelessly before collapsing backwards. Seren gasped as the man's legs caught the lip of raised bricks and he toppled over. With a brief flap of his jacket, the man plummeted out of sight.

The young Airbrand found herself grimly fascinated by what she had just witnessed. These weren't the jets of colour, bright and fantastic that she had seen powering from the force muskets of the AotE - the Ghostbrand rifles fired needles of solid metal, driving into warm flesh to seek out the life and snuff it mercilessly. Up to this point, she had only ever thought the war was a case of the AotE blasting the Ghostbrands across the city – she had never considered what horrific wounds the Ghostbrands could inflict in return.

Smoke poured into the sky as the defensive immolation charred the earth, and the air was awash with the cracking of rifles and the fainter chinking sound as the bullets ricocheted from glass and stone. The symphony of destruction was punctuated occasionally by the screaming and hollow thudding of a flesh hit. After a year-long couple of minutes, the rifle fire died down – time to reload, time to capitalise. The evacuees on the roof heard Achaniel's voice roaring into the atmosphere and suddenly the sky was a sheet of rainbow psychedelics as the Encrafted retaliated.

Llyr didn't hesitate to jump up and peer over the edge. Down below, she saw the Ghostbrands bolting for cover, cloaks flaring. The flames thrust higher, and the ground was shaking the tiny figures like toy soldiers. As she watched, one of the invaders grasped his throat desperately as a torrent of murky water gushed through his clenched teeth. A few seconds later, the figure was nothing more than sodden heap of spluttering liquid. Seren popped up by her side and began whipping up a frenzy of miniature tornados, sending them spinning across the quad, pinballing into walls and Ghostbrands alike. Llyr scanned the area, her eyes roving across the twisted and broken limbs as she searched for the Ghostbrand leader. If she was going to put any effort at all into a fight, then she wanted to be sure she made a difference.

As the rifle fire burst once more into loud existence, the Airbrand spotted the leader standing by one of the oaks. His face was straining with concentration as he

fiddled with something she couldn't see, and either side of
him there was a guard, each laying an arc of fire across the
quad. Llyr spent a moment contemplating what to do.
What was the most painful thing she could inflict on this
creature? She could blow him into something painful? Or
perhaps blow something painful into him? As she
pondered, the soil in the quad stopped churning as the
Earthbrand who was causing it died with a scream. Then
she had it. She wanted to see the leader's face before she
killed him. Clearing her mind, the young woman focused
on the air particles directly around her. In the distance of
her mind's eye, she could see the yellowish pinpricks
flowing in currents, twisting and swooping as the other
Airbrands manipulated them. She summoned the closest
particles towards her, intent on her macabre purpose. Llyr
intended to hoist the Ghostbrand leader into the air so she
could see the look on his face as she dropped him from the
sky and sent him crashing into the cruelly unyielding earth
below.

Llyr squinted, once more picking him out and
preparing to channel her intentions into physical action.
Before she could pluck him from the ground however, the
Ghostbrand leader and his guards broke into a sprint and
hared away from the oak tree they were hovering around.
Seconds later, the vast trunk shattered as a deafening
explosion tore through it. Splinters of bark flecked the
quad and everything momentarily drew to a halt as all eyes
turned towards the sacrilegious destruction of one of the
UCE oaks. As the rifles silenced and elemental flares died
down, an air of solemn wonder was palpable on the
campus. The only sound was the groaning of the wounded
tree, underpinned by the soft fluttering scraps of oak that
were now floating back to the ground. The mighty column
seemed to hang suspended for a few seconds, wavering

slightly as if deciding which way to topple, but soon enough the oak tilted towards the John Terrence block.

The evacuees on the roof heard the rush of air being forced aside moments before the shadows shifted over the rooftop like skeletal fingers. Llyr and Seren slammed themselves into the concrete as the entire building shook with the force of the impact, while the sounds of smashing glass, snapping branches and scraping furniture resounded around the quad, hitting the opposite buildings and echoing back into the chaos. A monstrous plume of dust billowed from the stairwell as the innards of the building were displaced, and the girls crouched amidst the snowfall of destruction, waiting for the fragments to settle and for their ears to recover. Deafened by both the explosion and the collision, Llyr could make out faint yells, but she couldn't decipher if they were shouts or screams. It sounded as if she was listening through a thick substance, like the air had somehow solidified around her. Scrambling to her feet, she stumbled over to the edge and forced herself to peer over. There was still a lot of plaster drifting through the air, but the young woman could see the Ghostbrands rushing forwards through the quad. As the Airbrand stared, the cloaked marauders began to climb onto the fallen tree, which now lay across the fire that Achaniel had cast. Like filthy rats the Ghostbrands swarmed along the perfect bridge that they had created and poured through the gaping rent in the side of the building.

Wide-eyed, Llyr turned back to where Seren was brushing herself off. The scientist was massaging her forehead, bewildered and ashen. Llyr began gesticulating wildly, shouting to the other woman but of course the words jumbled together into a single incoherent vowel. Frustrated, the Airbrand shook her head and emerged through the aural shock with a sudden rush of sound.

"We have to hide, now!" she screamed frantically. Unquestioning, Seren nodded and led the way into the stairwell. Dust was still swirling out of the entrance, hazing the visibility but the scientist thrust her palm outwards and the pale flakes curved aside. The two women plunged into the gloom, taking in the amount of damage caused by the toppled oak. In the lower corridor, branches were lancing across, spearing through every available gap to block the way. The floor was now even more littered with debris and the Airbrands had to hop and weave in order to avoid the larger chunks of stone and wood.

From the floor below, the music of conflict picked up once more as the encroaching Ghostbrands entered the building and sought out the occupants. Twice, the young women had to change direction, the muzzle flashes bright and threatening just around the next corner. As they fled through the shrouded halls, Llyr began to lose hope. Every corridor looked the same, in disrepair and offering no cover, until they came to an alcove set into the left hand wall. This particular hallway was lined with lockers on either side, and a set had fallen across the alcove so that the girls almost ran straight past the obscured storeroom door that lay behind the steel containers.

The harsh notes of battle drew closer as Llyr and the scientist scrambled across the lockers and burst through the door into the cramped room. Luckily, most of the contents had been scavenged or looted previously and there was just enough space for the two women to stand amongst what remained. The lights however, did not work.

The two women cowered in the pitch darkness for what felt like days, with the crescendoes of hate-fuelled death echoing around them. At one point, the thudding overhead was so furious that Llyr felt the light sprinkle of plaster falling onto her forehead as she stared pointlessly into the darkness. After a time, the Airbrands caught the whisper of voices rushing towards them along the corridor. Pounding footsteps thundered across dusty tiles, then there was the resounding crack of gunfire accompanied by the defeated thud of someone hitting the floor. A man groaned in pain – not dead.

"Should we help?" Seren whispered.

"If we open that door, they'll kill us." Llyr had no intention of putting herself at risk. "Hold on…" As the Airbrand strained with concentration, the now familiar specks of citrine flickered into existence. Like stars cast across a velvet sky, constellations of air particles ignited and swirled together until the two young women were looking at a join-the-dots version of the corridor beyond.

A human shaped form lay sprawled on the ground, propped up against one of the overturned lockers. It was clutching at its side, obviously wounded. A second figure was standing nearby, a pistol in its hand. The particle replica was not detailed enough for the Airbrands to ascertain the identity of the figures, nor even tell which was Ghostbrand and which Encrafted. The standing form strode forward confidently, placing his foot on the chest of his wounded prey.

"You shouldn't have started this." It was the Ghostbrand leader. "We only wanted supplies but once more, the Encrafted have driven us to bloodshed." The fallen figure tilted his head and spat onto the floor. "You are weak," the intruder continued. "A group of foolish civilians hoping for Transcendence." At this, Seren gasped and Llyr turned on her hungrily.

"That means something to you, doesn't it?" she murmured. In the pale glow of the twinkling molecules, the scientist nodded.

"Everyone here is linked to Spyrus somehow," Seren whispered. "The company will choose four people to aid them when the time is right." Llyr scowled in disappointment - the poor woman obviously had no idea what the Protocol actually was. "We don't know who it's going to be, but that's the reason we're all here." Llyr was glad for the encumbering darkness as she couldn't help but smile as she turned back to the display of glittering air. Seren didn't know that she had been chosen. That would make things easier.

Their attention back on the conflict in the corridor, the two young women spoke no more. The Ghostbrand was still gloating over his unidentified victim.

"Go on," the wounded man spat once more. It was Achaniel. "Finish me off if you're going to." The Ghostbrand paused for a second, and Llyr could picture him considering the Firebrand's challenge. Would he do it?

"As I said, we only came for supplies."

"That's why you're going to lose this war." With a final exertion, Achaniel raised his hand to send a spluttering bout of flame arcing towards the Ghostbrand. The tiny storeroom was awash with light as the replica Achaniel imitated the motion perfectly. Drained as he obviously was, the jet coughed and then drifted off to the side, glancing against the other man's cheek. In that one thoughtless second, the Ghostbrand raised his own hand and pulled the pistol trigger. Click – no bullets. He tilted his head in frustration before regaining his cool composure. He rubbed his cheek casually, as if he had only been warmed slightly by the attack.

"Maybe next time," he warned. "There's still plenty for us to come back for." The Ghostbrand turned on his heels and retreated from the scene, leaving Achaniel to pull himself upright and stagger away, grunting as he disappeared around the corner.

It was only then that the two young women noticed that the background din had vanished, and UCE was now eerily quiet. The marauders had either left or been subdued. There was a moment's lull before Seren finally spoke.

"I guess it's over."

"For you it is."

Incomprehension spread across the scientist's face. "What do you-"

Llyr knelt softly in the gloom, closing her fingers around one of the few metal poles that lay in the dust. "I can't let you Transcend," she murmured. "This is my only hope." Llyr closed her eyes as she swung the length of iron, wishing she could close her ears also.

Once the deed was done, the remaining Airbrand rubbed her dusty palms over her face and awkwardly removed Seren's coat, all the while trying to tilt her head to avoid looking at the result of her cursed desperation.

Two nights passed. The first day was dedicated to recovering those lost in the battle and trying to do what they could with regards to a funeral. The few Ghostbrand casualties were buried together in the quad, the Earthbrands joining together to complete the task. By the evening of the third day, Llyr and the others were gathered in one of the foyer areas as usual. She had taken to covering her hair with an old baseball cap she had found in one of the classrooms. Nobody had mentioned Seren's absence, nor the fact that Llyr was now wearing her coat. The others must have assumed that she had fallen to the Ghostbrands, and Llyr found herself wondering if the scientist had made any friends while she was at UCE.

A ripple of excitement coursed through the group, forcing her from her reverie. People were standing and

craning their necks to see what was going on at the front.
Llyr's eyes widened as she saw the cause of the commotion.
Two AotE soldiers had emerged from the stairwell, led by
one of the others. Before she could even come up with a
plan, the male Captain strode forward and hoisted her
bodily from the crowd.

"Are you here to save us?"

<u>Emrys' Fight</u>
<u>October 29</u>

Chapter 19 – A Taste Of Resistance

It had been a fortnight since Etain left, and the farmhouse seemed to have doubled in size since his departure. It was amazing how a single person could leave such a momentous gap, and Emrys wondered if the void would be similarly as large if it was his sister that had gone. Probably not.

The Earthbrand was perched in his favourite spot on the wall at the bottom of the garden, his back to his home and his eyes to the vast freedom of the countryside that rolled away before him. The light caused the crops to erupt into a burst of golden fire as the sun hit its zenith and began the slow descent towards night.

There was no work to be done, and Emrys soon grew annoyed with his parents' constant skirting around the subject of the war. He was well aware that it was an inconvenient time to be a Ghostbrand, but he was reminded of it every time his mother had to stop herself from talking about the you-know-what or the you-know-whos. It wasn't that he agreed with the war – of course he couldn't – but he had to accept it was happening, even it was away on the other side of the city. Neither army had any use for the forest or the farmland his family owned.

Sliding from the wall, the young Earthbrand decided he would slip away for a few hours and have a look around the city. Obviously he wasn't going to inform his parents of his whereabouts, as he could just imagine his mother's disapproving looks while she flapped around spouting reasons why it was dangerous. As far as he was concerned, the majority of the city was fine as long as he didn't venture too far north towards the plains that had become the main field of conflict.

He sidled around the shadowed side of the farmhouse, ducking underneath the sill of the kitchen window where he could hear his mother chirruping contently as she did the washing up. He would have plenty of time before he was missed.

As he strode across the meadows, trailing his hands through the stalks of campion and ox-eyes, Emrys was struck by the change in the cityscape he had grown up in awe of. It seemed darker somehow, the windows less glinting, the spires less shining. Even the sentinels of Spyrus and the Temple of Branding no longer seemed to be standing proud. It was as if they were reluctant to stick out tall and commanding, and now wanted to cower in the silhouettes, nestled together with the lower buildings.

As the young man drew closer to the outskirts of the city, the tension became palpable and he began to regret his decision. There was not a sound and the air became cloying, as the absence of the bustling crowds was stark. It was like passing through a barrier that surrounded the area, and once he was well within the twisting streets, the feeling abated as the signs of life became apparent. It was in the hurried voices behind closed shutters, the echoing footsteps as people ran from building to building. The closer to the centre he got, the more like normal the city became, with shops open, albeit somewhat warily. The only blemishes on the high street were the boarded up businesses that used to belong to Ghostbrands. They had either been hounded out or had withdrawn of their own accord.

Emrys' winding route took him through the shopping district and around the base of the Temple of Branding. As he passed, he gave a casual wave to Faronarai, the Archpriest of the Craft Diocese, who was sweeping the entrance to the grounds. The Archpriest was an elderly man, well respected throughout the city and indeed country. He seemed to bear no ill feelings towards the Ghostbrands, perhaps because he had witnessed the parental disappointment that came with discovering a child who lacked the craft on numerous occasions. It was his job to oversee the branding process, and countless times he had had to deliver the news that most parents would dread.

Emrys was too young to remember his branding, but he shuddered with the memory of the day he was unbranded. It was shortly after his tenth birthday, and even the excuse of him being a late developer was running thin - after all, Etain had been exhibiting for almost two years. One weekend, Emrys had sprinted to the Temple to see Faronarai. He was in tears because he still hadn't managed to summon any of the powers of Earth, and the older man had confirmed his predicament – he was a Ghostbrand.

The journey home that afternoon all those years ago was fraught with torment. Emrys considered keeping his problem a secret, he even toyed with running away from the shame he thought he would cause his family, but he never quite made that rash leap. By the time he reached the farmhouse, his parents were in bed – in the countryside they were used to the children staying out past sundown, lost in the realms of the imagination, fighting off some evil and saving the world with nothing but a stick for a sword.

He edged into his parents' bedroom and shook them awake, the tears in his eyes causing far more panic than was due.

"I've got something to tell you," he whispered so the adults couldn't hear his ten year old voice cracking with anguish. Typically his mother had panicked, expecting death and destruction, when Emrys started to cry, forcing the words out between sobs. "I'm… a… Ghostbrand." His mother instantly swept him on to the bed and hugged him so tightly that he couldn't breathe.

"Is that what you've been so upset about? That doesn't matter to us," she said consolingly. "We aren't going to leave you outside like a dog!"

Since that time, he had grown to live with the fact that he would never be able to make the earth move, so to speak, and never be able to watch a seed flourish and blossom in the palm of his hand. He and Etain would never experience the Twin Connection – the ability to communicate with one another through thought – something that only identical twins were supposed to be able to do, but he had also got used to that too. Granted, he wasn't as comfortable as Ardent was but so what? He was still a living, breathing human being.

As the young man traversed the winding lanes, he could hear a number of voices shouting and whooping. Hurrying cautiously forwards, Emrys rounded the next corner and saw a crowd of people disappearing up the street. Some of the figures were holding placards, and every few paces one of them would toss a handful of flyers into the air, a periodical paper fountain of fluttering scraps. The Ghostbrand knelt, deftly scooping up one of the rectangles of glossy paper.

The flyer was plain white, save for a symbol in black, dead centre. At first it looked like it was one of the four Elemental Brands, but it was recognisable as neither Fire, Water, Earth nor Air. The logo was a circle with a single vertical line through it, and as Emrys studied the image, he realised that the image meant "Ghostbrand". The circle represented the traditional brand and the line mirrored the scars that those who lacked the craft gave themselves, and that Emrys himself wore.

He jogged along until he caught up with the rearmost members of the procession, slipping into their ranks unnoticed. Normally, the conscientious young man would never have thought of joining a bunch of strangers, but his curiosity was piqued. Now he was amongst them, the meaning of their shrieking became obvious – they were protesting about the war and Emrys was surprised to see a pleasant mix of both Ghostbrands and Encrafted.

The cheering rabble wove its way through the city until eventually it reached the City Hall. There was a wide space before the smooth granite steps that led up to the domed building in which the Element Council met once a month. Either side of the steps was a large stone lion, staring impassively down as life passed them by. Here, the protesters unfurled a large billowing banner with "No To War" sprayed crudely across it in red paint. The rivulets of colour that ran from the letters made the phrase look as if it was weeping blood, spilling its own life in order to stop the fighting. With a tumultuous roar, the crowd began to chant the same phrase.

"No to war! No to war!" Exhilarated, Emrys found himself joining in, letting an uncharacteristic yell burst from his lips.

It didn't take long for the City Hall security guards to come pouring out of the building like an avalanche of black body armour and force muskets. The mounting faction shrieked louder and the Encrafted members raised their palms defensively when they saw the guards finger the triggers on their guns. With a smile, one of the armoured men pointed upwards to where an elemental dampener had been mounted above the arched doorway. The councillors had obviously been expecting trouble sooner or later – after all, they couldn't afford another loss like The Everrulers. With a smirk, the guard folded his arms and watched.

It looked to Emrys like the protesters were being mocked – the guards knew they couldn't do anything, they just had to stand watch until the inconvenient noise-makers went home again. Nothing would ever change unless the anti-war campaigners were truly heard. Before his brain could register his actions, the young Ghostbrand was already ducking into the crowd, his rough countryman's fingers grasping a stone that lay on the floor. With the dampeners humming their peacekeeping across the area, it was the Ghostbrands who now had the upper hand - and Emrys was going to show the guards exactly what he could do with the powers of Earth.

With a fierce battle cry, he swung his arm over his head and sent the chunk of rock flying towards the steps. With a dull thud, it struck the heavily padded shoulder of the lead guard and skittered away across the worn flagstones. For a second or two, there was a lull in the passionate demonstration as each party eyed the other in disbelief as Emrys tried to look as innocent as possible. As if on some inaudible signal, the guards decided they weren't going to stand for such behaviour and charged down the steps. Half a second later, the protesters sprang forwards to meet them in a tangled clash of angry muscle.

The two groups traded blows for a couple of minutes, twisting limbs and bloodying noses when one of the guards broke away from the carnage and rushed back up the steps. Nobody noticed him slip around a pillar and press his grazed palm against a panel secluded there, but everybody heard the alarming halt of the elemental dampener. As soon as the comforting hum had ceased, the guards shouldered their force muskets and took aim at the rapidly fleeing rebels, who were once more shrieking and whooping like a troop of feral children.

Amidst the thundering blows of pounding footfalls, Emrys ran hare-like through the twisting lanes of the Old Town. His heart was filled with the mischievous joy that he had not felt since his school days, and the fact that he could be apprehended any moment made the experience all the more exciting. The idea that the guards might actually seriously injure the retreating revellers had not even crossed his mind.

The further into the historical part of the city the Earthbrand sprinted, the fewer of his previous companions he saw. One by one, they had ducked into doorways or secluded themselves in the shaded alleyways. Such was the thrill of the chase that Emrys had quite lost himself in the meandering dash – his bearings were well and truly spun.

He slowed to a jog as he rounded the next corner, then staggered abruptly to a halt. He had run himself into a dead end, all three sides in front of him blocked by quaint three storey buildings that probably housed cafes and boutiques on the ground floor, with spacious apartments above. Of course they were closed now, but Emrys could still glimpse the essence of the high society life that would have inhabited the trendy courtyard. As he rested his hands on his knees, finally allowing himself a pause for breath, he heard the telltale signs of footsteps echoing from the buildings behind him. They were fast, and he reasoned that he at least was still being chased.

In the calm of stillness, all the thoughts that had been flushed out by adrenaline came crashing back to reality, each new paranoia a resounding rockfall in his consciousness. What if he got arrested? What if they simply shot him when they saw he was a Ghostbrand? All he'd done was throw a stone, but there was the war – he wouldn't put it past people to lie and exaggerate the charges if it meant getting rid of one of the enemy.

The footsteps grew louder and Emrys began to panic, wishing he'd never felt that surge of youthful rebellion. As silhouettes began to rise and sweep across the far wall, the young Ghostbrand closed his eyes and waited for the cruel grip of iron fisted guards. What would his parents say when they found out? Would they be informed, or simply discover their son's fate on the news? What if Emrys' recklessness somehow got Etain into trouble? He was jolted from his despair by a strong pair of hands grasping him around the waist and hauling him backwards. The shock of being touched made the Ghostbrand open his eyes, but it wasn't the guards who had caught him - their shadows were still plastered onto the walls as they ran towards the square. Emrys caught a glimpse of gloved hands as he was pulled through an archway, then everything went dark as a secret stone was fixed back into place. When the guards arrived seconds later, there was nothing but an empty courtyard, with brightly striped awnings fluttering gently in the afternoon breeze.

Chapter 20 – Evacuation

The blackness was solid as Emrys' eyes struggled to adjust to their sudden plucking from sunlight. Rough hands shoved him along what felt like a stone tunnel, continually prodding and jabbing in different places so that he could not tell exactly how many people were jostling him along.

The Ghostbrand had heard rumours that there were secret networks of passageways that connected hidden cellars and secluded catacombs, but he had always dismissed them as a childhood legend. One of the greatest games from his youth involved roving around endless streets trying to find the entrances to these notorious burrows which could contain any amount of treasures.

With a sudden jolt, he was thrown roughly into a large open space, a cellar or vault of some sort. Losing his footing in the darkness, Emrys stumbled forwards, catching his forearms and knees on the uneven surface. His limbs stung, four crimson pressure points, and he grunted in the gloom.

With a faint click, the chamber was bathed in light. Electric, not Craft – so that meant Ghostbrands. A number of figures stood against the walls, which were natural stone. The passage must have led into a cavern of some sort. Emrys couldn't think of anywhere in the city that could hide something like this, and he hadn't noticed a descent as he was being pushed along the dark tunnel.

The harsh lamps suspended from the cavern roof on rusted chains were so bright that the men lurking at the edges of the chamber were nothing more than silhouettes, but the young Ghostbrand could tell that they were all looking at him, their unseen eyes boring into his flesh and rooting out his soul. As he squirmed internally under the visual onslaught, a new figure descended silently from a staircase carved into the rock. He stepped onto the ground and glanced questioningly at the other men. Unlike the henchmen, the newcomer held himself with an air of command. He was dressed in the combat uniform of the Ghostbrand fighters, a large cloak draped over his shoulders. The man also had a rifle slung across his back.

"Well?" he asked.

"This is the one who threw the stone." At this, Emrys shifted uncomfortably, turning his head away from the piercing gaze of the Ghostbrand leader, who was now watching with a hint of curiosity.

"Is he now?" He stepped forward until his face was inches away from Emrys' cheek. The country man could feel the fighter's breath on the side of his face, tingles flickering across his smooth skin. "And why did you do that? You caused quite a fight. We have a bad enough reputation as it is."

Emrys considered the question carefully, coming to the conclusion that honesty was indeed the best policy. These men didn't look the types to suffer liars gladly.

"I…" he paused to take a deep breath. "I got carried away. I think the war is wrong." As simple as that. He hoped that they would be able to discern between honesty and deliberate bluntness. There was an unbearable pause, then to his surprise, the men started to laugh.

"You're right about that," chuckled the leader as he offered his hand. Emrys took it and was lifted to his feet. "I'm Morgan. I used to be called Airbrand but, well…" He shrugged the cloak back to reveal the brand with the telltale scar across it. In reply, Emrys showed his own scar and the two men nodded in recognition of their shared plight.

"What was all that about?" Emrys asked, rubbing his forearms tentatively, peering across to check the damage.

"You can't be too careful. We had to be sure you were really being chased by the guards."

"Thanks for that, by the way. I don't know what I would have done if they'd caught me."

Morgan smiled wryly. "Thrown some more stones, maybe?" The two of them laughed. With a wave of his hand, Morgan dismissed his companions and then led Emrys up the steps. They walked a complicated path of tunnels and caverns, each with a number of doors bolted hastily into the rock. Eventually, the two men emerged into a comfortable looking chamber with a low ceiling. Complete with a naked light bulb hanging down over a couple of threadbare armchairs, the area looked like a typical student hangout rather than the headquarters of the Ghostbrand fighters. Morgan noticed the other man's expression of bemusement.

"We don't have much," he said apologetically. "We've scavenged as much as we could, and any money we had we've put towards other… projects." He sank into one of the chairs and motioned for Emrys to do the same. As Morgan began to explain the history of the Ghostbrand resistance, Emrys took the opportunity to study him. He had dark hair that curved down either side of his face in thick spikes, and occasionally he would shake his head quickly to swing the strands out of his vision. His hazel eyes seemed to glow with passion, matching every lilting word that came from his mouth as he explained how his group of men and women had banded together in the underbelly of the city. Gradually they had pulled nearly every Ghostbrand to them in a giant web spanning most of the country, and were coordinating these volunteers into what was essentially a battlefront on the outskirts of the city, where they camped out ready to lay siege to the city if the time came. It was clear from his words that the rebel leader had no doubt that it was the Encrafted that were responsible for the trouble.

"Of course," he went on. "Not everybody chooses to fight. We have a number of scientists, engineers, medics. You name it, there's a Ghostbrand version working for us."

"It would have taken years to sort all this," Emrys said, waving a hand around the room. "Much longer than the war has been going."

"You're right," Morgan said with a shrug. "The Resistance has been around for much longer, although resistance was not always our purpose. We used to be much more political, rallying for equal rights and the like. It is only comparatively recently that our ideals have turned more militant."

Whilst Morgan had been fervently talking, Emrys had been looking around the sparse chamber at all the charts and notices, but one in particular caught his eye. It was a list of five names – names that everybody in the world knew almost as well as those of the Elements or the Everrulers.

Tier Waterbrand
Aeris Earthbrand
Kyan Firebrand
Jade Earthbrand
Cobel Airbrand

They were the names of those executed for killing the Everrulers, and it stood to reason that the Ghostbrand rebels would wish to remember them. As he looked at a bracelet that hung with the list – a silver half heart with an L engraved onto it - a question began rumbling inside Emrys' mind. When the incessant rattling reached a deafening peak, the young Ghostbrand interrupted the rebel leader.

"Is it true?" he blurted. Morgan paused mid sentence, scrutinising the younger man. "Did Ghostbrands kill the Everrulers? I have to know. I feel like it's a part of me somehow. Part of who I am."

Morgan's face fell. "That's how they want you to feel," he sighed. "They want every Ghostbrand in the world to feel guilty about it so we are easier to subdue. If we all feel sorry for ourselves, we won't fight back as hard. I'll tell you one thing though. I don't know if it's true or not, but if they discovered it was Encrafted that killed the Everrulers, you think they'd declare war on themselves?" Emrys thought for a second. Of course they wouldn't. "When people are treated as bad as we are," Morgan went on bitterly. "It doesn't take long for something to crawl out of the dirt and condemn us." Emrys nodded and glanced around the sparse chamber.

On the wall next to the door there was a map of the city and its surroundings. Several locations had been circled in red, but there were no labels indicating what this could mean. Morgan seemed to have fallen into a lull of private musings and the silence was growing increasingly uncomfortable. The country man shifted awkwardly in the armchair, the ragged threads scratching through his linen combats.

"I should probably be going…" he drifted off, hoping Morgan would interject with his agreement. Instead, the rebel leaned forwards, eyes glinting powerfully.

"It's not safe out there at the moment."

"We've been down here for ages, I'm sure the guards will have gone by now." Before Emrys could move, the older man's hand shot out, catching his arm in an iron grip.

"I'd rather you stayed." As the country man twisted awkwardly in Morgan's unyielding vice, he imagined the rebel's eyes bursting with ferocious energy, unwilling to acquiesce to any but his own will. In a second, the vision was gone, and the older man had released his captive with an exaggerated flick of the wrist, his eyes now simmering back to their tranquil hazel. "As you wish," he smiled wanly. "Come back any time."

The country man sprang from the moth-eaten seat and hastened away down the corridor, with only a single backwards glance at Morgan, who had already turned back to the map on the wall as if nothing had happened.

After ten minutes of encountering dead ends and doubling back on himself, Emrys finally emerged into the sunlight once more, although the sky had taken on the rosy glint of the day in wane. How long had he been underground? He glanced back at the secret entrance, already indistinguishable from the rest of the walls with the Temple of Branding rising up on its mound behind. A lot of the Ghostbrand network must be underneath or even inside the hill that supported the temple. Fitting really, he mused, to see the shrine of the Encrafted blissfully unaware atop the shrine of the Uncrafted.

The streets were silent once more, but just to be cautious he skirted around the City Hall in case he was recognised. As concrete became grass and orange became indigo, the ground shook violently, pitching Emrys to the floor. The convulsions were followed seconds later by a succession of deafening booms mixed with the lamenting wail of sirens and alarms.

Scrambling to his feet, the Ghostbrand turned back to the city, which now had several plumes of smoke roiling into the air. Teasing tongues of flame were licking the edges of a few buildings and there was a definite sense of absence in the skyline, although Emrys could not place exactly what had gone. As he stared, Morgan's words came into his mind. The rebel leader had said it wasn't safe outside. Had he known this was going to happen? Had he planned it? Emrys suddenly felt sick, as if he was contaminated by his contact with the other man. His arm flared into an agonising itch where Morgan had grabbed him, and clutching his wrist, the young man spun on his heels and ran the rest of the way home.

When he pushed open the heavy door and stepped into the farmhouse kitchen, Emrys was instantly swept into his mother's arms. Her face was tear streaked and puffy, and for the first few minutes, she said nothing although her son fully understood the relief she must have been feeling. Mr Earthbrand was standing in the corner, his hand pressed firmly against the humming stone that stood there. The mind beacon was no doubt awash with messages about what had just happened. After a moment, he pulled his palm away and came to join his family, a severe expression clouding his face.

"First of all, Etain is fine." At this, Mrs Earthbrand released a long held in breath. "He wasn't near any of the trouble. He wants to see you in an hour Emrys, says it's important. Usual place, whatever that means." Despite the seriousness of the situation, Emrys smiled when he thought of the meeting place.

"What happened?" asked Mrs Earthbrand.

"Ghostbrands," the man stated, making no effort to evade the word. "The news is saying that they bombed a number of crucial buildings all at the same time."

"What sort of crucial buildings?" Emrys murmured, unable to shake the idea that he had been with the man responsible just moments before the horrifying event.

"Factories mainly," continued his father. "Places where they make AotE weapons and armour. The war effort has been severely crippled."

"All those people..." began Mrs Earthbrand, shaking her head in disbelief.

"It was evening, so I'm sure most of the buildings were closed. But there's bound to be some casualties." There was a pause in which nobody spoke, each locked in their own thoughts. Emrys shifted on his feet, eying the clock in the corner. Already, twenty minutes seemed to have slipped effortlessly by.

"Well, I better..."

"Yes of course," began his mother, sniffing away a tear. "Tell your brother..." Emrys nodded - the request was as good as rhetorical. "And you be careful out there." With another nod, Emrys pushed open the wooden door, the night air rushing to greet him.

The young Ghostbrand's mind was blank as he hurried across the fields towards the edge of their land. He had no idea what Etain wanted him for, but he was surprised at how much he wanted to see his brother again. Being faced with the idea of meeting him once more only emphasized how much he missed his twin.

The ground became uneven as Emrys crossed over into the next field, this one freshly ploughed. Breathing heavily, he slowed to a jog and scanned the horizon, picking out the familiar shape in the treeline. There was a minute pinprick of light hidden amongst the blackness that was the forest that bordered the Earthbrands' farmland. That must mean he's there already! Emrys thought with a grin. His pace quickened into a sprint and he leaped the fence into the woods, weaving inbetween the branches and trunks as he raced towards his brother.

The ramshackle shape grew larger as he approached, and he was now able to pick out specific details in the lichen covered sticks and twisted wire. He and Etain had assembled the den when they were eight – he had collected the wood and Etain had moved it into position with his power. As it was, the eight year old vision of perfection was far from structurally accurate, the den leaning precariously against the trunk of a pine tree. The roof listed to one side, giving the whole thing the impression of straining to get away from the trees and ground that held it in place.

The den had been the twins' fortress throughout their childhood, providing shelter from whatever monsters or aliens they had been "fighting" at the time, and later when they had outgrown such games, the boys had used it as a parent-free refuge for smoking, drinking and meeting girls. To be honest, Emrys was surprised that the den had survived this long, although he suspected that Etain had protected it somehow from the inevitable scars of time. The thought of seeing his brother again once more rose up inside him, strong and indestructible, a rock of emotion that caused the Ghostbrand to hover outside the door to their sanctuary. What should he say when he stepped inside? They didn't exactly part on a high note, and of course it had been Emrys' fault. Why couldn't he have just been happy for his brother instead of internalising everything and acting selfishly? Should they hug? Was that too gay? Maybe a handshake to start with? Should he speak first or wait for Etain to greet him?

Emrys shook himself, dislodging the stupid thoughts he was having. It had only been two weeks, it wasn't going to be awkward, and besides, he and Etain had fought lots of times before. That was what brothers did, not worry about whether they should hug each other.

The Ghostbrand took a deep breath and pulled the flimsy set of planks that represented the door. He had to stoop slightly as he stepped inside, as the door was at the lower end of the structure. As he raised his head expectantly, his face fell – a swan dive of betrayal. Etain wasn't there. There was a note resting on the upturned crate that had served as the brothers' table, all seeming infinitely small and insignificant since they had grown up. Emrys stepped forward and reached for the note, unfolded the official government headed paper with trembling fingers. An envelope slipped from the folds as his brother's familiar scrawl began.

Emrys. There wasn't time for me to stick around – I only managed to get an hour off work…

The young Ghostbrand read this with a smug and self-important voice in his head, even though he knew that Etain would never have intended it to sound that way.

It's not safe in the city anymore. Tohelnar and the Council have organised evacuations – the fight is coming here! In a few days, I'll be sent to one of the evacuation centres, I don't know which one yet.

More importantly, in the envelope are papers for Mum, Dad and Eir – they leave the day after tomorrow for somewhere in the hills I think. But that's not it! I asked the people I work for to get a special permit for you Emrys - you're gonna be evacuated too! I know it doesn't sound much, but there aren't many Ghostbrands that get the honour. You're not on the same bus as the 'rents, but you are going to the same place, so at least you'll all be together. You go the day after they do.

To be one of the only Ghostbrands to be removed from the danger zone, what luck, Emrys thought grimly. He doubted he would be accepted with open arms while people like him were probably killing the loved ones of those he was forced to shelter with. As if reading his mind, his brother's final paragraph offered a glimmer of hope.

I'm not saying it's going to be easy, but I've stuck a little something in the envelope for your own protection. Don't touch it until you know the time is right. I trust you Emrys, and remember what I said.
See you again, in this world or the next.
Etain

Emrys didn't even unwrap the velvet package tucked into the envelope. Instead he glared, fists clenched and his brother's words pounding in his head like a thousand angry boulders. How dare he sweep in and out leaving nothing but orders like he was the better brother? As the rage rumbled upwards, Emrys felt a clashing of jealousy and sorrow, two flints scraping against each other in the confines of his head.

With a fierce yell, he thrust his palm out, just like he'd seen Etain and all the others do so many times. Nothing. Not even the slightest whisper of movement or power. Emrys glared at his traitorous hand before kicking out at the crate, ignoring the spears of pain that shot up his leg as the wooden box sailed into the wall. He became a whirling quake of flailing arms, tearing and lashing at everything he encountered, the concerto of destruction layered with cries of anguish.

Before he knew it, the young Ghostbrand was on his knees, sobbing into bloody knuckles until he felt a reassuring arm on his shoulder. He didn't even bother to ask how Eir knew he was there, he simply leaned into her, knowing that once this was all over, the moment would remain between them. She would understand.

The next day and a half passed like fleeting seconds, and Emrys quickly found himself standing at the bus station with his family, bathed in the orange glow of the late afternoon sun. There were strict rules issued, stating how much luggage each evacuee could bring with them, and it struck the young Ghostbrand that his entire family life and childhood could be packed away into a couple of bulging suitcases.

As he had predicted, his mother was already sobbing into her handkerchief, despite the constant reassurances that he would be following her the next day. Mr Earthbrand had his arm around his wife, an amiable expression on his face. For him, this was just a short break to the mountains. The normal people would leave, the army would quash the resistance, and everyone would be back in time for tea.

The rusting coach gave a blast on the horn, slicing through the various sounds of hushed murmurs and mournful farewells. There were even a few AotE soldiers there, making sure their loved ones were safely removed from the danger area. As the driver blew the horn once more, people began to shuffle onto the bus, with those left behind peering anxiously through the windows, searching out their relatives and friends behind grimy glass.

The engine rumbled into life and the vehicle lurched forward, gathering speed as it turned out of the station. Emrys felt something tugging inside him, some connection being stretched until it was a taut bowstring drawing his family away from him. As the coach vanished around the corner, Emrys could almost see the link snap, sending stinging tendrils snapping back into his own heart, leaving vicious internal scars of separation.

Chapter 21 – Torn Epiphany

Emrys' mind was a landslide of random thoughts as he wandered through the city from the bus station. His family was safe, and he had a free ticket to join them tomorrow, so what was he having second thoughts about? Was it the fact that if he evacuated, he would be giving in? Handing over victory and submission on the proverbial silver platter? The young man wasn't even paying attention to where he was walking, and before he realised, he had emerged into the square. He had started thinking of it as the centre of all the action in the city: after all, this had been where he had thrown that fateful stone, and more importantly it had been the last place those executed Ghostbrands had seen.

Emrys skittered across the open space, sticking to the shadows. Although there was nothing going on, he still had vivid images of the AotE soldiers pouring down the steps and advancing on the crowds. Now it was him on his own, he was even more reluctant to encounter them.

"Please don't!" A cry rang out and the young man instinctively pressed his back against the wall, his face sinking beyond the veil of darkness. Seconds later, a figure stumbled roughly into the square. He flopped forward, spilling into a pool of light and sprawling on the ground. Emrys looked on as three of the AotE soldiers he feared so much strode casually into the wide space as if it were some sort of arena.

"Get up," one of the soldiers spat viciously at the cowering figure. The others watched as their victim hauled himself to his feet. They roughly shoved him until he was backed against one of the solid pedestals upon which lounged one of the stone lions. All three soldiers raised their force muskets threateningly, accompanied by another bout of sobs. "Turn around." Visibly shaking, the poor man turned to face the stone, placing his hands against the smooth surface as if bracing himself. "Any last requests, Ghostbrand?"

"Please, don't kill me."

The leading soldier laughed. "I'm not going to kill you."

"Then what do you want me for?" There was a pause, the soldier smirking sadistically. It was clear to Emrys that they were just prolonging it, abusing the control they had over their victim.

"Get his trousers…" The two lackeys stepped forward menacingly as the third soldier reached down for his flies. As he was held against the wall, their prisoner turned his tear-streaked eyes to the side, seemingly looking straight at Emrys hiding in the darkness. Emrys' heart skipped a beat. The man was no older than he was, though a lot thinner – a boy of the city rather than of the country. His eyes seemed to be screaming out for help, although he made no more sound through his gritted teeth.

Unable to watch or help, Emrys slipped away, pressing his hands over his ears so that he wouldn't have to hear the inevitable sounds of pain that were going to come. No doubt the bruised and violated body of the young man would be discovered later. They would check his brand and hush it up, calling it another legitimate casualty of the war. As soon as he was far enough away, Emrys leaned against the wall and threw up, the bile stinging his throat as he fought to stop his own body from convulsing.

Guilt tore at his soul like talons, ripping away his humanity. He should have done something to help, should have run into the square and made his presence known. And then what? he told himself. He was a Ghostbrand, what could he have possibly done to stop it? The other young man already looked worn and defeated, so at best it would have been three against one and a half. If he was lucky, they would have turned their despoilment on him. If he was unlucky, they would have paused briefly to kill him outright before continuing with their pillage. Emrys was powerless to help one man, let alone stand against the onslaught of oppression that all Ghostbrands now faced. Or perhaps not. There was, after all, a sprawling network of underground tunnels that housed the Ghostbrand Resistance. And by showing him round, Morgan had as good as invited Emrys to join, hadn't he? At least he would be doing something to help his cause that way. But what about the evacuation papers he had tucked into his pocket? Would he really give up the chance to be safely with his family? The face of the young man in the square flashed in Emrys' mind, cementing his decision. Of course he would.

He shook the aftershocks of his retching out of his system and began to stride purposefully through the empty lanes until he reached the secret door into the resistance bunkers. Once inside the cool tunnels, Emrys slowed his pace. Walking through the streets, he had been full of confidence and the energy that follows big decisions, but now he became cautious. He didn't want to catch anyone by surprise before they recognised him. Even then, only a few of the resistance – Morgan and a handful of his companions – knew who he was. Emrys doubted that the Ghostbrands would take kindly to a trespasser in their midst.

The corridor he was in twisted left and right, but still he saw no sign of anywhere he recognised. He was hoping to stumble across the shabby room with the moth-eaten sofas, or perhaps the domed cavern where he had first been dragged, but he saw neither. The only features in the roughly hewn tunnel were randomly spaced blank doors of rusted iron. Some of the doors only just covered the gaping holes they were set into, but every time Emrys peered through the gaps, he was greeted with a void of both colour and sound.

After what felt like hours, Emrys finally heard voices from further up the corridor. As he approached, a faint glowing light became more and more pronounced until it set itself into the rectangular halo of a door left ajar. The familiar gravel-toned voice of Morgan Ghostbrand penetrated the silence, and Emrys strode confidently towards the door.

Morgan was standing in the doorway with another man, midway through a heated conversation.

"It's not like I've learned anything useful," the stranger complained. "They have me working behind the reception desk, it's hardly the inner circle."

"We're lucky Spyrus even hired a Ghostbrand," barked Morgan in response. "Give it a couple more days, Rayne. If nothing has presented itself by then, we'll pull you out."

It was at this point that Emrys announced his presence with a light cough. The two rebels immediately halted their exchange, both staring at the newcomer. Rayne looked annoyed at being interrupted, but Morgan wore the smug smile of someone that had just won a new recruit for his cause. With a nod, Rayne shuffled past Emrys and disappeared into the dimly lit tunnels.

"Rayne is on a mission, of sorts…" Morgan said, smiling warmly but shrewdly through the strands of hair that covered his face. He ushered Emrys into what looked to be some sort of lab, although the complicated chair in the centre of the chamber made it look increasingly like a dentist's surgery. From where Emrys was hovering by the doorway, he could clearly see the back of somebody's head, a tuft of short brown hair emerging from the backrest of the clinical seat. A network of tubes and cables were draped over the arms of the chair, and a single limp hand could be seen occasionally twitching on the armrest.

"I knew you'd come back," Morgan began. "You've got a taste for resistance now." Emrys ignored him as he moved towards the chair. He nodded towards it, a look of concern playing across his features.

"Is he injured?"

"Him? No. He's just Caliban – we look after him." If Morgan was uneasy about Emrys seeing the chair-bound figure, then he gave no hints. Emrys moved around and gasped. It wasn't a man – it was a boy of about fourteen. Tubes pierced his arms and chest, and although his eyes were closed, he wore a mask of excruciating pain. Emrys scanned the boy, paying particular attention to his shoulders – Caliban had no brand.

"We acquired him as a baby, before he was branded." Morgan spoke as if he was reading Emrys' mind and anticipating his questions.

"You mean you stole him," Emrys commented astutely. "Why is he here?" At this, Morgan's chest seemed to swell with pride.

"How do you think we've been shielding ourselves in battle? How we've been protecting this place? The Encrafted don't realise that it's one of their own that's fighting against them."

"You make it sound like he has a choice," Emrys snapped angrily. His expression softened as he stared at the boy's furrowed brow. He was frowning, the corner of his mouth curling slightly every time his arm twitched. "Does he... I mean, can he feel?" In response, Morgan flicked Caliban's bare shoulder. The boy didn't move, although Emrys thought he saw his expression deepen slightly.

"He can't feel anything. The chemicals we give him keep his mind isolated from any physical stimulus. He knows only to shield our troops. That's it." At this moment, Caliban shuddered, the numerous tubes rippling outwards like spider's legs. "The movements are involuntary nerve reactions," the Ghostbrand leader continued. "His brain doesn't interpret them."

"I don't know what's worse," Emrys muttered softly. "The fact that you've taken this boy and kept him sedated his entire life, or the fact that you can talk about it like it's an everyday occurrence for you. Just another day at the office."

"I don't see what you're getting so worked up about, he's just one of *them*." At that moment, any respect that Morgan had garnered, any vestiges of the courageous rebel leader crumbled to dust. The years of lies and half truths that Emrys had built up about the resistance being noble and honourable cracked and tumbled until he could see himself standing alone on top of the rubble. Deliverance.

"He's not one of them, one of the *others* that we should be afraid of. You are." Emrys saw the casual demeanour of the man before him flicker as he began to realise the potential recruit he had just lost. "Do you know why I came here tonight?" Emrys continued. "I saw something so… inhuman that I thought I was absolutely clear on which side is right and which is wrong, but here I'm seeing something just as bad. Rebels, AotE – it doesn't matter. It's not two sides, it's just people. Misguided, stupid and cruel people doing what they think should be done in the name of whichever banner they stand under. Sod you both!"

"You can't do that, Emrys. This is a war. Black and white, you have to choose a side!"

"I choose grey." At this, Emrys shouldered past the older man and hurried back through the tunnels, ignoring Morgan's muffled cries.

Once outside, the young Ghostbrand ran home, being sure to avoid the square. He didn't want to run into the soldiers or anything they might have left behind. He was in a state of clarity, his mind was made up and the last thing he needed was to be shocked out of his new-found resolve.

As he stalked through the heather atop the last rise, he looked mournfully down towards his home. Usually beaming with light and bristling with activity, the building now lay dormant, cold and lifeless. When would its lamps be lit and its rooms filled once more? Overlooking the farmhouse was a tall birch tree which had been barren since he could remember. On special occasions, the family would sometimes hang the branches with lights, ribbons or other adornments, but the one permanent fixture was an old-fashioned hurricane lantern hanging from one of the lower branches.

Emrys ran a finger restlessly across the peeling silver bark of the trunk as he fumbled in his pocket for the book of matches he always carried. Unlike a Firebrand who could summon a flame with a click of the fingers, Emrys had to provide his own.

Once the lantern was lit, Emrys sat against the tree, hugging his knees against the cold of the night. Before long, the young man felt his eyelids drooping and he forced himself to recite some of his old school lessons to keep his brain active.

"At the beginning, there was nothing. Nothing until the five Elements decided to create the world," he muttered quietly to himself. Earth came first, then it was Air. It was not long after these fundamental lessons in creation that Emrys and his brother had been taken to the Temple of Branding – everything had changed after that. Whilst for a time he had been angry at the Gods who had not seen fit to bestow their gifts upon him, he had still not forgotten their creation story.

Whilst he was running through his memories, he heard the soft footsteps he was hoping for. Scrambling to his feet and shaking his head to wake himself up, Emrys turned around to see Ardent making his way out of the gloom. The hurricane lamp was something the three of them had worked out when they were younger – Etain saying that it was only fair considering the other two couldn't use the mind beacon. Whenever the lantern was lit, they would convene at the tree to discuss whichever current matter was most pressing, from the time that Etain's girlfriend had dumped him to the time that Ardent had contemplated dropping out of college. Now, the two men looked at each other for a few seconds, taking in the severity of the world they now lived in. Not only was it the first time that only two of the friends had been able to reach the lantern, but both men knew in their hearts that tonight's meeting was going to be a lot more important than girlfriends or school. For both of them, it could mean life or death.

Chapter 22 – Shadow Ties

"I can't do it!" Ardent shouted a final time as he paced back and forth, kicking up plumes of dust with his boots. Emrys had just explained his idea, but he hadn't expected his friend to react so negatively.

"Please," Emrys begged. "Etain told me to fight – well now I think I've found something to fight for."

"Then why can't I help you?"

"It might be dangerous."

At this Ardent scowled. "What about when we camped out in the woods and it turned out to be the AotE training ground? I wasn't bothered about danger then, and I'm not now."

"This isn't the same," Emrys replied indignantly. "Back then, the soldiers weren't trying to kill us."

"They aren't now," Ardent reasoned. "We haven't done anything wrong."

"I don't think that matters anymore," Emrys muttered wistfully.

Ardent narrowed his eyes in response. "Why do you say that? Em, what's happened?" Emrys paused, the echoes of the yelping guy in the square pounding through his mind. The flash of those desperate eyes in the lamplight would haunt him forever and he didn't want his best friend to share the sickening image.

"Nothing," he lied. "We're at war, Ardent - nobody's safe."

"That's a lame excuse."

"Then do it for me. I want somebody to make sure my family are all right, plus Eir deserves a treat." Ardent blushed slightly but Emrys saw him consider the point, saw the acquiescence creep across his face - however reluctantly - until eventually he nodded.

"Alright – I'll do it because you're my best mate, not because I like the idea." Emrys jumped forward, catching Ardent in an awkward hug, aware that he was pricking himself with all the safety pins and spikes his friend was wearing.

"You know generally, you're not huggable." Ardent smiled. "You'll be needing these then." Emrys pressed the evacuation papers into Ardent's hand.

"Won't they know I'm not you?"

"Etain left me this too," Emrys said as he handed over the small velvet wrapped package. "All he said was that it's for protection, maybe it'll help?" Ardent didn't seem too impressed. "Ok, look at it this way. They're expecting a Ghostbrand, and they'll get one. I don't think they'll look too closely."

"Well you've totally reassured me on that one mate," Ardent sighed sarcastically. "Apart from the fact that our brands are completely different colours, surely they're *more* likely to notice me if they're as against all Ghostbrands as you say… But I'm a big boy now. I'll be fine I guess."

"You could always smear some dirt on it or something," Emrys offered with an apologetic shrug. There was a moment's silence as Ardent put the parting gifts into one of his many pockets.

"Just tell me one thing. Is it anything to do with the Resistance?"

"Why would you say that?"

"I saw you the other day," Ardent shrugged. "It was the day all those buildings blew up. I was coming out of the Ink Studio over on Eastside and you… you appeared out of nowhere. Everybody knows there's caves and stuff under the city, it wouldn't surprise me if the rebels were down there somewhere." Emrys could feel Ardent's eyes on his face, searching for a giveaway.

"I was in one of the clothes shops, that's all. You must have missed me coming out." Emrys felt bad lying to his best friend, but didn't want to worry him. If he said that he'd met the leader of the Resistance, he would never hear the end of it, and worse still, Ardent would probably refuse to go and check on his family. He only hoped that Ardent wouldn't have remembered that all the shops would have been closed at the time he had emerged from the tunnel into Eastside. There was more silence as his friend worked things over.

"Alright, I trust you… just don't do anything stupid ok?"

"You too."

"I'm sneaking into an evacuation centre pretending to be somebody else, what's stupid about that?" The two of them laughed, breaking the mood as it came to saying goodbye. Neither one of them wanted to say it, and it felt for Emrys that once they walked away from each other their journeys would be difficult and lonely. In the end, it was Ardent who made the final gesture. "Well, if you angle it like this," he began, tilting his body to the side and bending slightly, "you'll find I *am* huggable." With a smile, Emrys hugged his friend one last time and then stepped back as Ardent turned to leave.

"Ardent?" The young man turned back quizzically. "Be careful."

"Lame!"

"I'll see you on the other side?"

"That's even worse!"

"Ok, ok." Emrys was desperately trying to say something that didn't sound clichéd, but it just came out like he was stalling for time. In the end he settled for simple gratitude. "Thanks."

"Don't mention it. Now I really am going. I don't want to make you late for blowing up the Council or whatever it is you're planning." With a final jangle of chains and a casual wave, Ardent faded into the shadows, leaving Emrys to his thoughts. He'd just given away his chance of evacuation so he was stuck here now and he still wasn't entirely sure what he was going to do. The only thing he knew was that he would start with Caliban and go from there. After all, it was the sight of the boy that had driven him to abandon faith in either side of the damned war.

He took a final look at the birch tree as he blew out the lantern and headed down the hill towards the farmhouse. As he was fishing his keys out of his pocket, there was a sudden rush of air. Emrys whirled round in the blackness but there was nothing to see. The whole atmosphere seemed to smell of ozone, and the young man's fingers tingled as he rubbed his hand through his hair. What was happening? Was it some sort of new weapon? Perhaps a bomb that had the power to charge the air somehow? A crackling sound built in pitch until the whole field was alive with it, and Emrys fell to his knees with his hands clamped over his ears. He wondered if Ardent was experiencing the same thing, and if he was home yet. His concerns were shattered as the sky itself seemed to turn brilliantly white for a fraction of a second. Thunder boomed high above like something blasting through the sound barrier and then darkness. Emrys' ears were ringing, and he could still hear the crackling sound. He looked up in horror as he saw that a patch of grass in the field ahead was smouldering, a ring of flames surrounding a shadowy object.

Abandoning his fear, Emrys ran towards the fire, his mind full of falling stars or crashed jets. He froze, taking in what was in the centre of the flames that were quickly becoming embers. It was a person – a man a little younger than he was, and wearing jeans and a hoodie His dark hair was stuck into immaculate spikes and when he heard Emrys gasp, he stood up, holding his hands out in front of himself defensively.

"Who are you?" Emrys shouted. "Where the hell did you come from?"

The other guy thought for a second. "I was in the forest. The others were there, then there was fire and now I'm here."

"What's your name?"

"My name? My name is Chase Rivers."

Etain's Extraction
November 16

Chapter 23 – The Other Path

"Are you here to save us?" piped up one of the women in the crowd of refugees. In the aftermath of the Ghostbrand attack, the two AotE Captains who now stood amidst the rubble of the UCE corridor were a welcome sight. Etain was surprised that nobody had charged forward already, but the force that the male Captain had shown whilst hauling one of the girls out of the crowd seemed to be enough to keep the tentative crowd at bay. The Captains looked at each other awkwardly before replying.

"No," the female Captain stated. "We're looking for Etain Earthbrand. Spyrus has specifically requested that we extract these two immediately." What? Etain must have misheard. Did she just say his name? It must be some sort of mistake. Etain didn't even know any AotE soldiers. "They are coming to collect the rest of you later."

"Right. We all know how this ends," said the Firebrand policeman, Achaniel. "Spyrus aren't coming for us; they've chosen their golden quad." Another mistake surely? Etain had nothing to do with Spyrus, and certainly wouldn't be part of any group they might have. Maybe it was some sort of joke, or worse. But then again, the Captain had used the word 'extract' – that meant he was going to be taken away from here, maybe reunited with Emrys and his family. Etain began to push his way through the evacuees towards the front of the group, hoping that the soldiers would see him before they decided to leave. He worked his way beside Achaniel, hoping to say goodbye before he left. For many, Achaniel had been the guiding light during their time at UCE. He had personally welcomed a number of them and had been instrumental in the defence of the campus from the Ghostbrands.

Suddenly the policeman grabbed him, his rocky arm curving perfectly around Etain's neck. The young man's eyes widened and he yelped, gasping for air as his captor's arm tightened. He tried to reason with Achaniel, but he couldn't force any words through the crushing grip. Etain panicked as he saw the soldiers raise their weapons. What if they thought he had somehow started it and shot him?

"Screw Spyrus," the policeman spat. "And screw you." With a flick of his wrist, the light bulbs in the ceiling exploded, the gas heating up and bursting into a wall of flame between the soldiers and the refugees. For a moment, Etain could see nothing but raging orange and yellow swirling and lashing from floor to ceiling. There was a scream from the other side of the fire – he doubted it was the female Captain.

Suddenly the fire bulged outwards and Etain felt the heat graze his cheeks as he struggled against Achaniel's grip. There was the crack of a force musket, and the Firebrand's arm went slack. Etain pushed the hand away from his throat and Achaniel fell backwards, crystalline fragments of ice jutting from his chest, quickly melting into a cool crimson.

The female Captain leaped through a gap in the flames, dragging the girl Seren Airbrand behind her. Whilst Etain hadn't really got to know anyone at UCE, he recognized the lab coat she was wearing. The soldier proceeded to grab Etain's shirt roughly, before spinning him round and heaving him towards the other captain. As his world twisted through fire and smoke, the young man tripped, crashing hard onto the concrete and grazing his elbows through his dusty and smudged work shirt. He was vaguely aware of movement around him and numerous voices.

"Run!" someone shouted directly above him – the male Captain. There was another rush of blasting heat and the young man was hauled off the ground, then out of nowhere, the two men were running, ducking the fallen beams and turning the corner of the corridor. They were confronted with a dead end, a large plate glass window directly before them, but nothing else.

"Where're the stairs?" the Captain shouted above the roar of the flames. Etain pointed aimlessly back the way they'd come – through the wall of fire. He was certain that the Firebrand Captain would be able to extinguish the barrier with the flick of his hand, but surely he wouldn't shoot his way through the crowds on the other side? The Captain cast his eyes around the corridor they were trapped in, realising that the only way out was through the window that looked out onto the street below. He stepped forward flexing his palm, and for a second Etain thought he was going to use his power to melt the glass, but instead – lightning fast – the soldier flicked his padded elbow, breaking the glass and sending a shower of diamonds into the sky.

"You're an Earthbrand, right?" he barked. "Can you get us down?" Etain ran to the ragged hole and peered down at the tarmac, his mind racing out of focus.

"I… um…" At that moment, the relentless growling of the fire faded. Either the gas had run out or another Firebrand had emerged to take control. The soldier's eyes flashed as he weighed the options. He seemed to look the young Earthbrand up and down, as if sizing him up.

"Jump on my back!"

"What?" Of course the soldier looked a lot bigger than the young man, but he wondered how much of that was armour.

"You think they'll just let you walk out of here if they catch you?"

"But you said Spyrus was coming back for them?" The Captain glared and Etain realised that, in truth, nobody else was coming. "Ok, ok!" he blurted, hurrying forward and awkwardly hopping onto the Firebrand's back, wrapping his legs around the older man's waist. He wasn't quite sure where to put his arms as the Captain's shoulders were so uneven - one of them bulged with armour and was strapped up with a map and a comms stone whereas the other was bare and smooth. In the end, he hooked one arm into the shoulder pad's webbing and let the other hang free.

"Ready?" the Captain asked, placing one leg over the window ledge.

"No." Etain heard the soldier chuckle to himself as the two of them swung onto the outside of the building. The first thing the young man noticed was the drop in temperature from fire-warmed corridor to moon-kissed open air.

There was a drainpipe by the side of the window, which the Captain moved towards, grunting with every step and occasionally rearranging Etain on his back. He gave the pipe an experimental tug, and when it didn't move, he stepped from the window ledge and clung to the drainpipe. Bracing his legs against the wall, he began to climb upwards hand over hand.

"Shouldn't we be going down?" Etain asked.

"Not yet," the soldier managed. He was obviously feeling the strain but didn't want Etain to see it. "Now keep quiet until I say." He kept ascending the pipe until they were well above the top of the window frame. The window

of the next floor was less than a foot above Etain's head.
Here, the Captain locked his arms and waited in silence,
breathing shallowly through narrowed lips. Etain tried to
copy as best he could but his legs were getting tired, and he
had to repeatedly hitch them up to stop himself from
falling off the soldier's back.

Sure enough, after less than a minute, a head thrust
inquisitively through the shattered window below. Etain
couldn't recognise which of the evacuees it was but he
tensed up, trying to suck in his stomach and tighten his grip
around the soldier's waist. The person peered down at the
glass shards littering the concrete and cast an idle glance
either side. *Please don't look up, don't look up…* Etain found
himself willing the person beneath them so strongly that his
own voice was reverberating inside his head.

After a tense minute, the scout drew back inside the
building and the two men clinging to the bricks breathed a
collective sigh of relief.

"Ok, now we can go down," whispered the soldier.
He loosened his grip on the drainpipe and slowly began to
abseil down it. They kept on in this fashion until about
fifteen feet from the ground, where the pipe abruptly ended
in a rusted stump. There was no sign of the bottom section
on the path below. Etain waited to hear the Captain's plan
with bated breath. "Are you holding on?"

Before the younger man could answer, the soldier
pushed them both away from the wall and they plummeted
towards the concrete, two deadweight rocks falling to earth.
There was a split second of roaring air before the inevitable
crash and Etain's world spun wildly. The Captain crumpled
beneath him and he rolled off the older man's back, grazing
his temple as he skidded across the stone. He lay on his
stomach in stunned silence as he waited for the world to
right itself. The young man's head was throbbing and he

wondered if he was concussed. Looking to his left, he saw the soldier had propped himself against the wall. He was holding his ankle, gently prodding it and grimacing every time he did so. Etain groggily raised himself onto his hands and knees.

"Why the hell did you do that?" he asked, bewildered. "I could have used my powers to help, or at least jumped myself so you didn't take both our weight."

"It was a 'don't think, just do it' moment." The Captain shrugged before returning to his ankle.

"Is it broken?"

"Looks like it. But don't worry," the soldier said as he caught Etain's look of horror. "There's a medikit back at the jeep. Help me up."

Now it was Etain who took the strain as he supported the soldier, the two of them shuffling slowly around the side of the building. They stuck as close to the wall as they could so that they would not be seen by anybody casually looking out of the windows. As the young Earthbrand shifted the weight of the other man's arm across his neck, he noticed a droplet of blood fall to the ground as a single crimson raindrop. The Captain did not seem to notice - he was too intent on keeping the weight from his ankle as he hobbled along. Etain snatched a swift look behind them and clearly saw the scarlet Morse code dot-dashing across the tarmac from where they had landed. Broken ankles didn't usually bleed did they? He found himself flicking through the first aid training he'd received when he'd started work, but was sure that the soldier would have a great deal more knowledge on the subject, even if he'd inflicted most of the content rather than treated it.

The road rounded the last corner and they saw the jeep waiting outside the twisted gates of UCE. It struck Etain that the everyday mode of transport had now become their beacon of reassurance as they hobbled towards the vehicle, eager to find the medikit and escape. Once there, the soldier slumped into the passenger seat and threw his force musket into the back. He turned around and reached back for the medikit, but at the look on the poor man's face, Etain rushed forward and fetched it for him. The soldier nodded his appreciation as he shucked off his helmet, then leaned back and closed his eyes. Etain opened the camo-green box and rifled through the contents. There were bandages, tablets and even some hypodermic needles, all bearing the Spyrus insignia.

"What do you need?" Etain asked.

The soldier sat forward wearily. "Start with morphine…"

"What's your name?" The young man was hoping to distract the soldier as he administered the morphine shot just underneath the man's red Firebrand. Also, it would make talking to him easier if he had something to call him.

"Talyn." Etain wiped the spot with a cotton pad before carrying on, his voice wavering like the bearer of bad news.

"Right Talyn," he began. "You're bleeding, and I don't think it's your ankle. There must be something else. Can you feel anything?" Talyn opened his eyes and saw the scarlet splatters for the first time. His mouth opened in surprise as if he didn't quite believe Etain at first.

"You just gave me morphine – I can't really feel anything anymore. You'll have to look." He lifted his arms and cast his eyes across his body, but the younger man saw it instantly. Underneath Talyn's right arm, where the shoulder pad met the side of his armour there was a wide streak of red, picking a zig zag course down the buckles and straps and pooling in the dirt beneath the man's feet. Etain could actually see the waves of Talyn's heartbeat,

pumping the blood around and out of his body. Drip drip
drip pause… drip drip drip pause…

"I'm going to take your armour off, ok?" Talyn
nodded as Etain began to unclip the various fastenings,
each buckle ticking off the seconds until they could see
what was causing the bleeding. Etain tried not to think
about what he might see, he just concentrated on breathing
regularly and trying not to panic in front of somebody
older and more experienced.

First, the pad lifted off and revealed the paler
shoulder. Everybody's branded shoulder was a little darker
than the other because it was constantly exposed, and it
had been a primary playground game of teasing people
whose shoulders looked the same, calling them "Cover-
Ups" and other ridiculous names.

Next, he worked his way down the side, popping the
catches as he went. With the last clip, the main body
armour cracked open like the shell of some cyber-
crustacean. It was hinged on the left, with the front chest
plate sculpted into an angular polygon vision of muscle,
and the back lined with air and fluid tubes fused into a
central spine over a layer of sweat mesh. The young
Earthbrand could only guess at what it was all for –
protection or cooling, he couldn't be sure. Etain set the
complex equipment aside and turned back to Talyn.
Underneath the armour, he was wearing a simple black
short sleeve top stretched over his chest. The entire right
side was glistening in a rose blossom that was already
seeping across the front. There was a ragged tear in the
fabric about the size of Etain's thumb, and he studied the
area carefully but still couldn't see what had caused the
wound.

Slowly, he peeled up the shirt, feeling Talyn's
stomach tense as the cold air hit his skin. There was a

ripple of six pack abs then the soldier relaxed. That was
when Etain spotted it. If Talyn hadn't moved, the
Earthbrand wouldn't have seen the twinkling star set
amongst the blood red backdrop. He leaned in.

"What is it?" murmured Talyn. Etain didn't answer
immediately. There was a shard of glass embedded under
the soldier's skin. Only the tip was still visible. The young
man thought back to Talyn smashing the window for their
escape. The glass had sprinkled the ground below, which
they had then landed on. The sliver must have found a gap
in the fastenings and worked its way inside, deeper and
deeper as the men had moved. For a second, Etain was
overwhelmed by how lucky he was, considering he was
only wearing his work shirt which was now scuffed and
grubby. "Well?" Even after the morphine, Talyn still
managed to convey the authority he had as an AotE
Captain.

"It's glass. Deep." It was all Etain could bring
himself to say. He was no medic and had no way to gauge
how serious the wound was.

"Right. You're going to have to pull it out." Talyn
said this so bluntly that Etain wasn't sure if he was being
serious or not.

"Are you sure that's a good idea?" Even with his
rudimentary medical knowledge, Etain was sure he'd heard
something about not pulling foreign bodies out. "What if it
makes it bleed more?"

"And what if it burrows deeper inside? It might not
have hit anything vital yet, but it will do if you don't take it
out. I can handle bleeding, but probably not a punctured
liver. Sorry for laying this on you." The Captain looked up
softly until Etain gave a reluctant nod. "But you've got to
keep me talking, ok? I don't think the morphine will be
enough."

"Enough for what?" Etain exclaimed with wide eyes. "You've had more training than me, what could happen?"

"I might scream like a girl." As Talyn chuckled, Etain released the breath he had been holding. It occurred to him that as a soldier, Talyn might well have been injured before – maybe even worse than this, but if Talyn was making bad jokes to reassure him, Etain would go with that. "Whenever you're ready Etain." Talyn leaned back and clenched his teeth in anticipation.

"So, um…" The Earthbrand faltered as he clutched for random straws of small talk. "What made you join the army?" He assessed the wound, unsure of whether he should just yank the glass or try to pop it out somehow. The shard might be jagged and he could end up doing even more damage.

"The money. Simple as that. I want my boy to have the best he can. Rees is ten. I'd show you a picture but I'm kind of busy." Whilst he was talking, the shred of glass had burrowed even deeper between Talyn's ribs. There were only a couple of millimetres left outside. If Etain didn't catch it now, he'd lose it and he didn't want to attempt amateur surgery propped up against a jeep in the middle of the night. He made up his mind. He was going to pull the glass out.

"Tell me more about him."

"Rees is my world," Talyn began. Etain could hear the man's voice swell with pride when he thought about his son. "He's going to be tall like his dad, but he has his mum's eyes. Liana is an Earthbrand like you – bright green eyes too. Rees is the first Firebrand I've seen with such emerald eyes. He'll be a looker all right, bu- ARRGH!" Etain tore the crystal shard out swiftly, then clamped his hand over the wound while he reached for a bandage. As he tied a crude knot in the strap he'd created, he looked at Talyn sheepishly.

"Sorry about that…"

"No, you did it very professionally," Talyn said, breathing heavily against the system shock. "Have you considered a career in-" The soldier's face froze, his mouth open and eyes wide with surprise. He slid out of the passenger seat until he was standing against the side of the vehicle. At first Etain thought something had gone drastically wrong with his emergency treatment. Images of punctured lungs and severed arteries flashed through his mind before he heard the clicking of a rifle. He followed Talyn's gaze and met the curious stare of a dozen Ghostbrand fighters. A number of barrels were trained on him and Talyn, and Etain cursed himself for not hearing their approach whilst he was busy with his foray into medicine.

The trickling sands of time seemed to slow down further as the young Earthbrand turned from the snarling rebels. In what felt like excruciatingly slow motion, he registered Talyn's force musket lying out of reach on the jeep's back seat. He cast his regretful eyes over the discarded body armour then saw his own expression of shocked concern mirrored on the other man's face. Talyn nodded resolutely.

Time jumped into super speed as everybody leapt into action. Etain spun around and down into a crouch, jamming his fist into the concrete. The tarmac rippled like water and a seismic wave pulsed outwards from the two men, sending the jeep crashing over onto its side, the windows shattering as it crunched against the pavement.

At the same moment, three of the Ghostbrands fired their weapons, bullets flying in a frenzied arc as the men were thrown backwards in the earth tremors. Talyn gasped, a spray of scarlet spreading across his unprotected chest. The Ghostbrands were flung mercilessly, cracking skulls and twisting limbs as they landed on the once more solid ground.

The following silence was alien after the split second of roaring anger, and Etain turned to the soldier now slumped back on the tarmac. The slight rise and fall of the man's chest indicated he was still alive - barely. Etain cast a wary glance at the devastation he had caused. At the perimeter of a thirty-foot radius lay the Ghostbrands in various states of injury, not to mention the jeep, which was now completely unusable. The young Earthbrand could tell that the men, however, would still be able to get up and shoot him as soon as they regained consciousness.

He hastily hooked his arms under Talyn's and dragged the soldier onto one of the side streets, out of sight of the fallen rebels. He gently rested him against the side of one of the student halls, long abandoned and boarded up. In the chill quiet, Etain fancied he could almost hear the long lost echoes of raucous student parties and drinking games that had graced UCE Garnsworthy Hall. He was interrupted as Talyn coughed, spilling a fresh wave of crimson down his already soiled top. The Earthbrand leaned over him, surveying the line of bullet holes, punched in from the soldier's left hip to shoulder. Talyn's head was lolling as if he was trying not to fall asleep, and Etain didn't have to be a medic to know that if the Captain fell asleep this time, it would be over.

"Talyn," he began, shaking the older man gently. "You're hit pretty bad. Just tell me what to do." Talyn coughed once more, blood bubbling at the corner of his lips. He turned, eyes slipping in and out of focus.

"I think this is a bit above your capable skills," he managed.

"No!" Etain could hear the desperation in his own voice. "Now tell me what to do."

"Go back to the jeep and fetch my armour and my force musket." He slumped his head forward as Etain ran back, mind intently focused on retrieving the items and not on their purpose. None of the stricken Ghostbrands had moved, although Etain heard a few moans as he was scrabbling through the overturned vehicle to rescue the force musket. Arms full, he hurried to where he'd left Talyn.

"Ok, now what?"

"Put them on." It was only as Etain was buckling up the armour that he realised Talyn hadn't asked for the medikit. He stood, a poor imitation of a soldier with body armour fastened over a shirt and tie, and a helmet sitting loosely over ruffled hair. He looked as if he would have done anything to avoid touching the force musket that hung at his side, like the two of them were physically repelling each other. Etain wore a grim frown – he had realised that Talyn wasn't planning on coming with him.

"Spyrus Tower," Talyn murmured. "You know where it is?" Etain nodded. He'd never been before, but the giant mind beacon was visible gleaming in the moonlight for miles around. *Everybody* knew where Spyrus Tower was. Suddenly, Etain remembered the groans he had heard back at the jeep.

"What about you? The rebels..." In response, Talyn held up his hand and clicked his fingers weakly. Despite the obvious effort it took him to do so, a fearsome ball of flame ignited at his fingertips, which he then cupped into his palm.

"I can handle it," he said grimly. "Now go! Stick with Captain Waterbrand, she'll sort out the Ghosties." With his last ounce of strength, the soldier pushed Etain out into the street. The younger man stood hopelessly lost for a second before turning awkwardly in the bulky armour and jogging towards the beacon of Spyrus Tower. He was a couple of blocks away when the rifles cracked once more, accompanied by a final roaring burst of flame.

Chapter 24 – Transcendence

Etain's teeth were beginning to chatter as he made his way across the city. The tower was steadily growing taller and more ominous as the young man approached, although after numerous identical blocks of boarded up windows, flickering streetlamps and cracked tarmac, it was almost as if he hadn't moved and the looming building was creeping up on him, ready to swallow him into the unknown void of the Transcendence Protocol.

The young man passed beneath the cover of the concrete arches that pierced the ground from the base of the tower like some immense crouching insect, and he immediately became aware of movement. A figure shuffled into view, walking with a limp and trailing dust like he was physically billowing clouds of smoke with each clumsy step. As the stranger registered Etain's presence, he paused, scanning him up and down with fearful eyes.

Before either one could speak, a flash of recognition lit up the limping man's eyes, his mouth widening with disgust. He shook his head, releasing a shower of debris from his pale crew cut.

"You!" he accused. "You're a soldier?? A traitor?" Etain looked down and silently cursed the AotE armour he was wearing.

"No, I'm not… hang on, I don't even know who you are?"

"You don't remember me from down in the tunnels? You went to see Morgan. You're the new favourite? I wondered why nobody came to get me out." At this, the young man's body trembled as he fought to control himself. "When they suspected me, I was chained to that desk for over a week. You could have done something!" Etain shook his head indignantly. He had already decided that the poor man was not right in the head. Maybe he had witnessed something terrible inside Spyrus?

"I don't know any Morgan, and I haven't been in any tunnels lately," he muttered as he shouldered his way past. He could make out the glass doors a few feet along the wall and was anxious to catch up with Seren and the other Captain.

"But he looked just like you!" Etain froze. After a second, he spun round and grabbed the man by the shoulders, ignoring his frantic yelping.

"Exactly like me?" The man nodded. "When was it?"

"Um," he stuttered. "No more than a week ago. What's so important?"

"You saw my brother…" Etain drifted off into his own thoughts as the other man stared, bewildered. "He should have been evacuated by now." The Earthbrand looked questioningly at the stranger, hoping he would have some answers.

"You'd better hope he wasn't," the stranger muttered under his breath.

"What do you mean by that?"

"Didn't you hear? The whole reason the AotE are on the move is because the evacuation centres got hit." Got hit? Etain thought frantically. That could mean anything!

"Which centres?" he demanded. The other man paused briefly before awkwardly continuing.

"Well… all of them. Within the last couple of days. That's probably why you've been called for this transcendence thing – to make sure Spyrus has somebody left after the war."

"I don't work for Spyrus."

"Well whatever, it's not like they told me anything. Did I mention I was chained to a desk?" He held up a cuffed wrist with the remnants of a shattered chain hanging from it. Etain could clearly see the area on the man's wrist where the skin had been worn down, red and blistered from hours of desperate tugging at the bonds. Etain swallowed.

"Were there any survivors?" he asked, half of him not wanting to hear the answer. The stranger shook his head solemnly, such a gentle movement to rock the very foundations of Etain's life as he realised his entire family was gone. But not Emrys. For some reason his twin had not gone to the evacuation centre. The young man took a deep breath, aware that he was not crying for his loss. "The Ghostbrands did it?" He wasn't sure if he was asking or stating it. The stranger nodded apprehensively.

"That's what they're saying."

"And this Morgan you mentioned? I'm guessing he's the leader? Is he capable of doing something like that?" The other man thought for a second before nodding once more.

"Yes."

Etain prepared himself to ask the final question, hoping in his heart that this man had been mistaken. "And my brother was meeting with him?" Another nod of dreadful confirmation, and that was when the tears began to fall. Crushed, Etain leant back against the concrete whilst the stranger hovered tentatively in the gloom of one of the support struts. As tears silently rolled down the Earthbrand's cheeks and trickled down his neck beneath his armour, he realised he truly had lost everyone. His parents and sister were dead, and now it looked like his brother had played a dreadful part in their murder – no matter how indirectly. It felt like hours before the stranger stepped forward and offered a comforting hand on his shoulder.

"Are you still going to Transcend?"

Etain looked at him through red rimmed eyes. "What choice do I have? There's nothing left here. Whatever the protocol is, it has to be better than this."

"Then you want the top floor," the stranger turned to leave. "I'm sorry you had to find out like that."

"I'd rather know. Thank you…"

"Rayne."

"Thank you, Rayne. Good luck." With a nod, Rayne vanished into the shadows, the dust clouds making it look as if he had disappeared with a puff of smoke. Etain watched the empty space for a second before prising his back reluctantly from the icy concrete. Half of him felt he should remain in the frozen discomfort of his grievance, but he had resolved now that whatever the Transcendence Protocol was, he wasn't going to let it happen without him.

The first thing the young man noticed was how luxurious the building was inside. When all he had seen for the last couple of months was boarded up windows, out of business shops and graffiti vying for both sides of the conflict, the gleaming crystal and polished brass of the Spyrus lobby was like walking into a five star hotel. The only sign that there had even been a war was a patch of dust and debris littered around the reception desk. As Etain edged closer, he saw half a chain bolted into the counter top, and immediately recalled the half-chain that Rayne had around his wrist. He didn't want to think what had been going on here – after deciding that the Transcendence Protocol was a positive move, the last thing he needed was to have doubt cast over the merits of the Spyrus company.

Deliberately facing the other way, he rounded the desk and made for the corridor beyond. The short stretch ended in two sets of mahogany sliding doors, and as the young Earthbrand approached, one of them hissed open with a chime, uncomfortably cheerful in the grim silence of the lobby. Etain jumped back as his own reflection stared out at him from the shining interior of the lift. For a moment he had forgotten he was wearing Talyn's helmet and armour. He took a moment to admire himself properly, conscious that he looked as ridiculous as he had suspected, like a child trying on his father's uniform.

He stepped into the lift, warily scanning the panel of over a hundred buttons. Only the very top one was illuminated, the others a dull and lifeless grey pearl. With a deep breath, he prodded the button and waited apprehensively as the doors slid shut. Almost immediately, the sleek wooden doors were sliding apart once more, and Etain stepped out into a vast area that reminded him of a studio apartment or penthouse suite in a grand hotel.

The girl from UCE, Seren, was standing by a vast floor to ceiling window that took up an entire wall, and the female captain was kneeling by what looked like a model of the battlefield. Both women turned to face him as he emerged, wobbling under the weight of the armour.

"Where's Captain Firebrand?" the soldier asked, although from the look in her eyes when she saw Etain alone in AotE uniform, she already knew the answer. Etain gave an apologetic shrug.

"He didn't make it," the Earthbrand began to explain, but the soldier had already turned back to the table, engrossed in the miniature figures that seemed to be moving, writhing around the surface like a swarm of ants. Seren continued to look at him, a flicker of disgust crossing her face. He couldn't tell whether it was directed at him, Ghostbrands, or the whole situation.

"Well I guess this is it then," she began. "Do we just wait here or what? How do we transcend?"

"What is the Transcendence Protocol?" Etain asked. The young woman had spoken with a confidence that implied she knew what she was talking about. He wished he had gotten the chance to speak to her back at UCE, but they had never really mixed.

"She doesn't know anything," cut in the soldier acidly. As Etain stared at her indignantly, she slung her force musket and marched towards the lift. He had barely opened his mouth before the doors had shielded the soldier from view.

"Well some man you are," snorted Seren. "You didn't even try to stop her."

"Are you kidding me? She's a soldier!"

"Well you're dressed like one. Didn't you ever play dressing up when you were little?"

"Not really," Etain began. "I've kind of worked on the farm since-"

"Tch," Seren interrupted. "A country boy. Great."

"Hey! It's not like-" The lift chimed once more, the bell ringing the end of the verbal boxing match. The Waterbrand captain stepped out once more, a look of subdued anger sweeping over her features. Behind her came a man easily in his fifties, wearing an immaculate suit. He wore a simpering smile and seemed to be purposefully ignoring the obvious bad mood of the soldier.

"Aha! Etain Earthbrand," he beamed. "I'm Firaire. So good to meet you. And..." Firaire faltered as his eyes scanned Seren. "Well this isn't what I expected at all."

The young woman braced herself, locking her knees and standing firmly in front of the Spyrus man. It looked to Etain as if she was physically daring him to challenge her.

"Did you really think you could fool Spyrus?" Firaire continued. "You look exactly like your father – and no amount of dirt is going to hide that. I only hope you didn't hurt her..."

"What?" the soldier cut in, unashamed confusion replacing the broiling anger she was wearing. "What are you talking about?"

Firaire smirked as he considered his answer. "This isn't Seren Airbrand. Her real name is Llyr – daughter of Erion. He was a councillor, but sadly passed away on Election Day." As if to emphasise his point, Firaire flicked his wrist, the dusty cap that the girl was wearing tumbling off her head. Red hair cascaded down onto her shoulders. "Now I must ask where the real Seren is, and what you hope to achieve by masquerading as her."

"UCE was attacked before the soldiers arrived," Llyr said with a nod towards the captain. "Seren didn't survive. I had heard that the Transcendence Protocol was some sort of salvation – that it would protect me from the war."

"Who did you hear that from?"

"My father. They were pretty much his last words."

"Ah," the old man nodded knowingly. "So Tohelnar was right, your father did know too much, although he was wrong about the Protocol. Salvation indeed," he chuckled. "Now I suggest that you leave before my amusement fades."

"No way," Llyr stated indignantly. "You have to take me!"

"And why is that?"

"My father told me some other stuff too – about a meeting he was at nineteen years ago." It was then that Etain noticed a perceptible shift in the conversation, and he could tell that the AotE soldier had seen it too. Firaire seemed to stand a little bit shorter, as if the confidence had been knocked out of him. They both watched as Llyr leaned forward and whispered something into the older man's ear, his face contorting with anger as he listened. Llyr stepped back once more, a satisfied smile on her face. "You're taking me, deal with it."

For Firaire, that was the final straw. The older man clenched his fists, and the atmosphere began to hum as if charged with static electricity. Etain could feel the hairs along his arms stand on end and tingles run up and down the back of his neck. He swapped a nervous glance with the soldier and could see his own expression of curiosity mixed with apprehension reflected on her face. As sparks flickered from between Firaire's fingers and jumped into the air haphazardly, he looked as if he was considering his options. Etain could tell that there was a lot of information that he was unaware of, but that was weighing deeply on Firaire's consciousness. Eventually, the older man seemed to reach a decision and he unclenched his fists, returning the atmosphere to a tolerable calm.

"Fine," he muttered. "It is of no consequence to me – I just hope you don't run into trouble. Seren and Etain were chosen for their skills, and we have no guarantee that you can match her."

"What skills do I have?" Etain asked, eager to prevent the two of them from having another showdown. "I'm just a lackey really, not even been there six months." At this, Firaire smiled warmly.

"You have a number of skills you are yet to show, my boy. The Acolytes of Transcendence are always chosen on the same merit - a diplomat, a scientist and their armed guards." As soon as the older man turned away, Etain felt his chest swelling with pride. He had been chosen specifically for this. There were tons of others that had been doing a much better job than he had, but they had chosen him. If only his family could see him now. No, he chided. Don't think about them. Stay strong for them, for Emrys. At the thought of his brother, his stomach churned. Could Emrys really have had anything to do with the resistance? If only there was some way of finding his twin so he could discover the truth. "It's time we got on with this," Firaire muttered. "Follow me and I'll explain."

The Spyrus employee gestured for them to step once more inside the gleaming lift, this time pressing the button for the lowest basement level. As the lift descended, he gave them a brief summary of the situation.

"It's quite simple really," he began. "One of our operatives has travelled a great distance in order to collect four items of great importance, and we have lost contact with him. The Transcendence Protocol is a quick method for you to reach him, then bring him back. Llyr, as the scientist, it will be your job to ensure a return is possible. Captain Waterbrand is charged with your protection and Etain, it will be your challenge to... reason with our man and convince him to come with you. You'll be briefed in more detail on the other side."

The young Earthbrand thought that Firaire had raised a vast amount of questions – far more than he had answered, but before Etain could ask for any clarification, the lift chimed its impossibly cheerful tones and the doors slid open onto a small, square waiting room. There was a low bench on one wall and a potted tree in the corner. Firaire walked straight through the room and threw open the double doors at the end.

Etain stared in awe as he was confronted with a vast chamber of purest white. He couldn't even tell what was floor, ceiling or wall, so that it felt as if he had somehow fallen out of the world. He stamped his feet just to convince himself the ground still existed, drawing confused looks from his companions.

"Just checking," he smiled sheepishly. Firaire stepped forwards, indicating a structure that loomed in the centre of the room. As Etain followed his gaze, his heart seemed to slow down, an intense and paralysing chill creeping through his body. He had seen the five jet-black spires before, surrounding a group of cowering Ghostbrands awaiting their execution. This time however, all that stood within the obelisks was a rough circle of discolouration, a smudge or burn in the smooth and glossy flooring. "Whoa," he breathed, suddenly wondering why he had become the voice of the group. "I'm not stepping inside that." Why weren't the others raising any objections? Firaire looked at him quizzically.

"They're dampeners," he stated simply. "They stop magic getting through."

"Haven't you ever seen Chargeball, country boy?" sniped Llyr. "They're for protection, right?" The Spyrus man nodded.

"I know what they are," Etain retorted. "And I'm pretty good at Chargeball thankyou very much, but does this look like a Chargeball court to you?"

"What about that burn mark?" the soldier asked, frowning.

"It's true, Transcendence does require a significant amount of energy, but the dampeners are there to make sure it remains contained."

"So what do we actually do?" the soldier pressed. It seemed to Etain like she was anxious to cover all the details and he had to admit, he wasn't fond of being thrown into the unknown either.

230

"All you need to do is stand in the circle. There will be a brief jolt, and you'll be somewhere else," Firaire said triumphantly.

"Just like that?"

"Just like that." Llyr strutted forward, defiantly planting her feet in between the glinting pillars. With a sigh, the soldier also stepped forward, leaving Etain standing open mouthed as Firaire scrutinized him.

"You're going for it?" Etain questioned, sure that the soldier would be able to read the disbelief plain on his face. She was supposed to have all sorts of army training that would have stopped her from doing something so rash, so why was she marching in blind?

"I may not like her," the captain said with a sideways glance at the other woman. "But if she went charging in and died, then there would definitely be some sort of feeling about it." Etain thought he detected a sly grin beneath her helmet, and considered his options, hovering on the edge of the ring of towers. Going with the girls would be an adventure, a chance to extend what he'd started when he'd got his job in the city. Since he had been in high school, Etain had known he didn't want to stay on the farm, and getting the job had been amazing enough, but here was another opportunity to broaden his horizons, to be more than just the country boy that people like Llyr looked down their noses at.

Whilst he was deep in thought, the soldier held out her hand invitingly which cemented the deal. Suddenly, he felt useful, rekindling the feelings that had swelled within him when Firaire said he had been specifically chosen. If this was his calling then he wouldn't throw it away. He stepped forwards and put his hand into the captain's gloved palm. All three of them were now inside the circle.

"I guess we're going on a trip then," Etain muttered.

"Glad you decided to join us."

"What's your name?" the Earthbrand asked quietly. "I can't keep calling you 'the soldier.'"

"It's Myst," she said with a smile. Etain smiled back at her, only just glimpsing Firaire out of the corner of his eye. He was briefly aware of a shimmering violet glow building in the older man's palm, then the universe was a blinding lilac and everything was gone.

Chase's Becoming
October 31

Chapter 25 – System Shock

As one, the four threw their papers into the fire. As the
little scraps of white floated down into the flames like
moths attracted to the fatal candle, a figure burst into the
circle from behind one of the ruined walls… The four
cloaked men turned to face the newcomer, his jaw jutting
with determination. It was Chase. A similar expression of
confusion, anger, fear and surprise appeared on five faces
as a cry echoed through the clearing above the crackling of
the fire.

"You!" The four initiates turned to face each other,
while Chase stared at them all, faltering. They had all
shouted at the same time. A multitude of questions floated
through Chase's head, but he could not make words come
out of his mouth. Suddenly everyone was focused on the
bonfire in the centre of the clearing. The first of the scraps
of paper fell into the heart of the flames and the fire
exploded outwards. There was a blinding flash as the
column of flame shot skywards. The four initiates fell
backwards in their compass directions, a quartet of
directional chaos. Chase was rooted to the ground as the
flames blasted outwards.

He was engulfed, screaming as the fire surrounded
his body. It felt oddly cool however, and Chase wondered
if his senses weren't being tricked, like plunging into
freezing water that burns just as much as boiling. The
furious orange got brighter and brighter until it passed

through intense white and into pale lilac. Chase's eyes
stung, and then in an instant there was blackness.

A chilling breeze blew into the young man's face and
he blinked, trying to get the sight back into his eyes after
the blinding glare of the fire. There were a number of
twinkling lights glinting far in the distance. Stars? Had he
been thrown onto his back before blacking out? No. Chase
looked around carefully, taking in the lack of the trees that
had previously surrounded him and cloaked the mysterious
events in darkness. The pinpricks of light were the
windows of a distant city, wide and sprawling over the
rolling hills. He was crouched in the centre of a field, a
smouldering halo encircling him, the grass frazzled and
blackened. He patted himself down, expecting to feel the
sting of raw skin, but instead his clothes - and more
importantly his body - were intact.

Off to his left was a large farmhouse looming out of
the night-blue grass, and growing steadily nearer was the
persistent padding of someone charging across the field
towards him. Chase stood up, palms raised in defence.

"Who are you?" shouted a man a little older than
Chase. He had the muscles of someone used to manual
labour, with short brown hair that curled a little at the ends.
The man's eyes were a vibrant green, and they were now
surveying him with a mixture of interest and apprehension.
"Where the hell did you come from?"

"I was in the forest. The others were there, then
there was fire and now I'm here."

"What's your name?"

"My name? My name is Chase Rivers."

The man stepped backwards, his voice softening.
"I'm Emrys." Chase relaxed a little, as if the swapping of
names had broken down some sort of barrier – they were
now both just guys, even if one had just avoided being

burned to death. "Rivers?" Emrys continued. "So you're a Waterbrand?" Chase shook his head, having no idea what a Waterbrand was. "Well what then? Airbrand? Firebrand?"

"I'm not sure what you mean," Chase stammered, wondering if this was some sort of code. Was he expected to give a correct answer? Maybe he should have just picked one and lied? Emrys rolled his eyes as if he was dealing with an invalid.

"Roll your sleeve up," he said with a nod to Chase's right arm. Without questioning, the younger man did so, revealing his shoulder, smooth and thin. The only blemish there was a small white spot where he had had his TB jab at secondary school. Emrys recoiled, a look of shock and confusion flickering across his face. "Are you like Caliban? Do you know him?"

"Caliban, like from Shakespeare?"

"Shakespeare? Is that where you're from?"

"No, Shakespeare's not a place. He's a dead writer – like really famous?"

"Your words are confusing," Emrys muttered with a shake of his head. "Look, it's late. Let's go inside and we can talk in peace – I reckon I have some cider left." Chase nodded, reassured that wherever he was, they still saw the general problem solving abilities of casual drinking.

Moments later, Chase was sitting at the kitchen table, can in hand while Emrys was wantonly chucking bacon, mushrooms and eggs into a frying pan. The young man had insisted that they both had something to eat before they continued their conversation, and Chase was secretly glad that he had been given a small amount of time in which he could collect his thoughts. By the time Emrys had placed a plate piled high with fried goodness, Chase had managed to collate a reasonable story, which he proceeded to tell as the other man listened intently.

Chase covered everything from when he received the text message (which, for some reason he had to explain) telling him to go to the forest, up until the point when the fire erupted. Emrys remained silent until he had finished, and in those awkward moments, Chase felt like he was being scrutinized – after all, his tale did stretch the boundaries of belief. To his surprise, Emrys did not discredit anything he had been told, instead commenting on the description that Chase had given of what was occurring in the woods when he had arrived.

"It doesn't sound like any ritual I've heard of," he said absent-mindedly. "Although I guess I'm no expert." The word ritual stuck in Chase's thoughts, as he remembered what he had guessed before he stepped into the fateful clearing. He was sure that Matt, Josh, Rich and Scott had been talking about some sort of craft – and now Emrys mentioning rituals confirmed something in Chase's mind. This was witchcraft. Again, he thought of a secret code and wondered if he had stumbled into some sort of cult. Perhaps the other students from UCE were members, and so was Emrys. Perhaps he had blacked out in the clearing and been brought here and this was some sort of initiation test.

A vague idea of what had befallen him seemed to slot into place within Chase's brain. Matt was the ony one who had really known Chase, even if it was just a ruse for Matt to get his homework done. Matt must have for some reason convinced the others to let him join in their secret club or whatever, and had sent him the anonymous text calling him to the designated spot. They were probably watching him even now, to assess his reactions. As such, he decided he would go along with Emrys to show that he wasn't afraid. With any luck, this would set him in good stead and the others would end this prank.

"Faronarai would know," Emrys continued to himself. "But no, too late now. We'll have to wait till morning." He jolted, refocusing on Chase. "We should get some sleep. There's someone I know that can probably help you out, but we'll see him tomorrow. You can have my brother's room, he's… well, he isn't here." Chase thought he detected a note of bitterness in Emrys' voice but decided not to comment as he was led up the stairs.

He was put in the room at the end of the landing, and the door still bore a nameplate in childish scrawl, "Etain", as did the other two doors, "Emrys" and "Eir". Emrys informed him that his parents had given the children a floor of their own, with the older generation preferring the loft conversion.

Once he had heard Emrys tread softly out of the bathroom and close his door, Chase began to look around the room in more detail. There was a wardrobe, a double bed and a bookshelf that contained a collection of tattered volumes that looked like they had not been touched in years. There were books about science, maths and poetry. No Shakespeare though, Chase thought with a sly grin. He leafed through the pile, and saw "Taliesin High School" stamped on the inside cover of many of the books. It reminded him of his own stack of textbooks that he hadn't returned after his A Levels.

Next, he moved across to the wardrobe, wandering if there might be something inside that would fit him. He didn't particularly fancy sleeping in his clothes. He was out of luck. The only garment inside was a peculiar cross between a sleeveless top and body armour. The shirt itself had an elbow brace sewn onto one side, and a number of buckles that held together the padded front and back. A large baby blue T was embroidered on the chest.

On the bottom of the wardrobe next to a crumpled pair of shorts was a small golden figure. Chase bent down to retrieve it and realised that it was actually a sports trophy. The shining figure was clutching a ball, and seemed to be wearing a similar outfit as was hanging from the clothes rail. The inscription on the base read "Etain Earthbrand – Taliesin High Chargeball Captain". Chase had no idea what Chargeball was, but judging from the kit they wore, it looked like it could be fun. Maybe he would ask Emrys to show him tomorrow. He lay back on the bed, and without realising how shattered he was, fell instantly to sleep.

Chase awoke to the soft tapping of Emrys knocking on the door. There was no clock in the room, and the light from the window was a dull and cloudy grey.

"Did you sleep ok?" the older man asked quietly. He bustled in holding a plate piled high with pancakes and fruit, setting it down on the bedside table. "Don't get the wrong idea about the breakfast," he chuckled. "The strawberries were turning." Chase hungrily grabbed the cutlery with a nod. "What's on your necklace?" Emrys asked, pointing to the silver chain that hung around Chase's neck. After swallowing his mouthful, Chase reached under his hoodie and pulled out his crucifix, the simple cross glinting in the sunlight.

"It's just a cross, I'm not really religious or anything, but I guess I like the idea of something better after we die." Chase spoke candidly, surprised at how easy he found it to talk to Emrys.

"We have something like that," Emrys said. "A lot of people like to believe that when we're gone, we go up the palace in the stars to celebrate with the Gods."

"But?"

"But I'll believe it when I see it. There doesn't seem like much to celebrate right now."

Emrys left Chase alone whilst he finished the breakfast and got out of bed. Afterwards, Chase lumbered down the stairs to where the other guy was waiting.

"What time is it?" Chase muttered, running a hand through his hair. There was nothing that even resembled hair gel in the bathroom, and he was desperately trying to make his spikes look half respectable.

"It's just after four," Emrys said. "You kind of crashed out." Chase couldn't believe that he'd slept for almost a day, and nodded sheepishly. "Don't worry about it," Emrys continued with a shrug. "Although there's not much point going into the city today." Chase thought for a second, weighing the disappointment he felt against the prospect of having someone actually treat him like a friend, even though no homework was involved.

"Why are you helping me?" Chase asked. "I wouldn't just let some stranger crash at my house."

"My family are away. It seemed stupid to have the whole farmhouse to myself. And besides, I'm only going to take you to Faronarai, it's not like you're moving in or anything. But since we aren't going today…"

"Maybe we could just, you know, hang out? Hey, you could show me what Chargeball is?" Chase looked across at his companion hopefully – perhaps Chargeball was something like the volleyball he used to play. Emrys frowned, and Chase wondered if he had said something he shouldn't have. He felt the need to explain himself. "I'm sorry, I saw the uniform in the wardrobe…"

"Ah. Well Chargeball will have to wait, I'm afraid. I'm uh… not very good at it," Emrys said ruefully. "I could take you to this hut me and Etain built though?"

"Yeah," Chase said, relieved that he hadn't killed the conversation. "I'd like that."

Emrys jogged up the stairs and Chase heard the banging of various cupboard doors before the older man returned pulling a sweater over his head. He casually threw a spare jumper to Chase, who gratefully pulled his hoodie off and replaced it with the heavy woollen top. The jumper was homemade, but well done. As he was sliding the jumper over his spikes, he tried to imagine what a sweater made by his own mother would look like, and came to the conclusion that he probably wouldn't have donned it so readily.

When he was ready with the jumper hanging loosely over his slender frame, he noticed with amusement that Emrys had turned away while Chase had taken his top off. He coughed to signal that it was safe for Emrys to turn around once more and gave a nod of thanks for the change in clothing.

Emrys had packed a bag with the remaining cans of cider and they both drank one as they meandered through the woodland. It was totally different to Chase's last foray into the countryside and he felt completely relaxed rather than on edge. Emrys regaled him with tales about how he and his brother had climbed this tree, or explored that hollow, and Chase was content just to listen, soaking up the details of what a proper childhood should have been like.

Eventually they reached the ramshackle den that the two brothers had built. Despite its sloping roof and warped wooden supports, Chase could tell that a lot of time, effort and love had been poured into it. They stepped inside and sat on the pieces of chipboard that formed the floor, cracking open another can each.

Emrys continued to talk about his family and his childhood and in turn, Chase gave a detailed rundown of life at UCE and working on The Rag with his colleague Ed.

To finish off the last of the drinks, Emrys introduced him to a card game, Conch, where forfeits were assigned to particular cards, and by the time Chase flopped onto his bed once more, his cheeks were glowing and his mind was filled with the delights of actual friendship. His dreams that night were a mix of desires, both to return home and to stay here where he was treated as an equal.

The next morning, Chase had just finished dressing when Emrys knocked on the door.

"If you're ready, we should head out," he began. "That man I mentioned, Faronarai, he's in the city. It's a bit of a walk."

"So this dude, what is he?"

"What is he? Like what brand?"

"No, I mean like is he a doctor, scientist, therapist, what?"

"Oh right. He's the Archpriest of the Craft Diocese at the Temple of Branding. He oversees the brandings and runs all the ceremonies and stuff." There was that phrase again – brands and branding.

"Tell me about this branding thing," Chase asked as they stepped into the sunlight. Once more, Emrys seemed to flinch again as he had the other night. At first it seemed to Chase like he wasn't going to say anything, but in light of the distance they had to travel, Emrys began to speak as they walked into the meadows that separated the farmland from the suburbs of the city.

"Every kid gets branded right? After you're born, your parents take you to the Temple of Branding, and you're given a brand – either Earth, Water, Fire or Air, the four Elements."

"So which are you?" In answer, Emrys turned slightly so that Chase could see his bared shoulder. There was what looked like a tattoo – a greenish circle with a crooked line through it. However, on top of that design there was a straight white scar cutting the tattoo in half.

"Mine's technically an Earthbrand, meaning I should be able to manipulate the powers of Earth."

"But?"

"But I'm a Ghostbrand," Emrys said slowly, as if forcing the words out. "A nothing." They walked on for another couple of minutes before Emrys continued his explanation. "Sometimes, a kid doesn't have any power at all. The trouble is, they are branded long before their power manifests, so you end up with people like me. People who were branded when they were little, but their power just never came. So we slash the brands as a symbol of this."

Chase was trying his hardest not to say anything that would offend Emrys, but his companion's story certainly begged belief. Believing in witchcraft was one thing, but this guy seriously believed that every single child got tattooed at some temple? Funny how none of Chase's classmates at UCE had these tattoos, his mum didn't have one, nor had he ever seen one before. Chase had been caught in an accident in the woods, he knew that much was true. Somehow in a daze he had stumbled out and bumped into Emrys, which again he could accept with minimal doubt, but the rest of it?

Chase began fleetingly to think of how he could get away from the country boy if things got out of hand. He looked at him casually, pretending to be looking into the background. His first assessment of Emrys still stood: the man was built but lean and graceful. There was no way Chase could take him if it came to a fight. The only advantage Chase could possibly have was speed. He was light and wiry - good at sprinting. Simple then – if Emrys suddenly came at him with a tattoo needle then he would just run for it – as soon as he got to the city, he could find his way home. Chase began to laugh to himself, realising just how stupid his last train of thought had been. Emrys had been perfectly hospitable to him, even treating him like a friend – why would he suddenly turn on him?

"What's so funny?" the Ghostbrand asked.

"Nothing, I was just thinking ab-" Chase froze as the view unfolded before him. The sharp burn of tears stung the corners of his eyes and he sank to his knees. This was not his city.

Emrys knelt next to him and Chase was already crying freely, all ties severed from the life he knew. He was in an unfamiliar place, and for all he knew, all the stuff Emrys had told him was true.

"What's up?" Emrys asked, brow furrowed with uncertainty.

"This isn't my home…"

"Yeah, I know. It's fairly obvious you aren't from round here."

"Except... bits of it are the same. I don't understand," Chase sniffed. Emrys put a hand on his shoulder.

"What do you mean?"

"Well, like the land is the same, with the hills and the river and stuff, and some of the buildings are the same. I know that tower," he said as he pointed to the largest building in the city, the silver S on the roof glinting in the sunshine. "Also, those are the oaks of UCE, but everything else is different. That castle thing is not from my city."

"That's the Temple of Branding, it's where we're headed. Look, I'm not gonna deny that some of this doesn't make sense, but if we just go and see Faronarai, I'm sure he'll give you some answers."

With a resigned nod, Chase clambered to his feet and followed Emrys into the city.

Chapter 26 – Rehistory

The two young men peered disappointedly at the notice that was pinned to the gates of the Temple.

Closed until Midday

Chase felt his heart sink as once again, the possibility of an explanation was so close, yet unobtainable. Emrys seemed to notice the young man's face fall.

"Don't worry," he said, casting a glance at the sun. "We've got two hours, tops. We'll just wonder about for a while." Whilst Chase really didn't fancy drifting aimlessly through the city, he eventually began to forget his disappointment as he noticed all of the subtle differences that surrounded him. At regular intervals in the street stood large pillars that hummed slightly. Every so often, people would walk up and touch them, stand there for a few moments and then walk off again. From Emrys' description, Chase surmised that they were a bit like phoneboxes.

Another treat was the Museum of Natural History. Of course, there were the usual pots and statues, but Chase couldn't believe his eyes when they got to the skeletons. Standing in front of him was what seemed to be a horse skeleton, but with one major difference.

"You're kidding," Chase breathed. "A unicorn?" Emrys looked up, nonplussed.

"Yeah, they died out like ages ago. People dig them up and stuff. Same with dragons and griffins. I reckon I found a horn once at the top field, but Etain said it was a broken bit of leg."

"Like dinosaurs?" Chase asked. Emrys looked blank.

"I don't know what that is." Rather than try to explain, Chase simply smiled and they continued through the museum until it was time to head back to the temple.

If the Temple of Branding was impressive from the outside, sitting upon its mound like a trophy on a pedestal, it was even more magnificent on the inside. Once through the doors of burnished mahogany, the main hall opened up into a cavernous congregation chamber lined with pews. It reminded Chase of the cathedral that stood resolutely in his own city. All along the walls were alcoves containing statues of various robed figures looking out into the hall with lifeless eyes. Chase tried to imagine what it would look like crammed with people all listening intently to whatever the speaker at the lectern was saying.

The two of them crossed the flagstone floor quickly, footsteps echoing somewhere high above them in the arched ceiling. At the back of the hall was another archway leading into a second chamber. This one was no less grand than the first, although a little smaller. From the entrance, there was a deep purple carpet leading a path through the hall towards the other end. The carpeted aisle wove between four statues of what looked like Roman or Greek gladiators. The four figures were a little taller than average, bedecked in armour, helmets and spears. Each was holding out his right hand, and balanced in their palms were large crystals, polished to a shine. One green, one red, one yellow and one blue. Around each figure's neck was a pendant, made up of a small circle with a different shaped line across it, and as Chase stared at them he felt a stab of familiarity. He couldn't place where he had seen necklaces like those before, but they didn't seem strange to him. He looked questioningly at Emrys.

"These are the Elements," Emrys explained. "When you're taken to be branded, you walk along the Branding

Line. You pass the Elements and they choose you when their crystal glows. Whichever Element chooses you, that's what you're branded with."

"What happens if someone gets to the end without being chosen?"

"That's never happened before. You always get chosen."

"You think it will work for me?" Before Emrys could reply, Chase took a halting step onto the plush violet, the green crystal bearing statue looming in front of him.

"Wait!" Emrys hissed. "You can't do that! Only those to be branded may step on The Line!"

"Well I haven't been branded, so what's the problem?" Chase started walking, treading softly on the carpet. He approached and passed the green crystal bearer, whose stern eyes looked down on him disdainfully, then the statue clutching the red stone. Still nothing happened as he walked past the yellow gladiator, and finally the warrior holding the smooth and polished blue gem. Chase's shoulders sagged as he reached the end of the Branding Line. This was yet another group that for some reason he couldn't be a part of. He turned back to Emrys who shrugged apologetically.

Chase scuffed his feet angrily on the floor as he stepped off the carpet. He felt like pushing the statues over or spitting on the carpet – anything to show that he wasn't bothered about not being chosen by this stupid place and its customs. In the end, he settled for yanking a curtain that covered an alcove at the back of the hall. The material tore from the brass curtain rings and fluttered to the stone floor as Emrys jumped forward, his mouth open in shock. A part of Chase was glad that he had broken something that meant something after all. He turned to look at Emrys, hoping to make some snide remark, but nothing came as he realised that Emrys wasn't staring wide eyed at the ripped curtain, he was staring at what lay behind it.

Shoved hastily into the cramped alcove was a fifth statue. Whereas the others stood proudly, chests puffed out beneath gleaming breastplates, this one crouched almost cowering in the shadows. He was turned to the side, looking out over his shoulder, eyes narrowed beneath his helmet. He looked like a beaten man, resigned and defeated. His outstretched arm ended at the wrist, the hand presumably grasping a coloured crystal snapped off and lost. An old statue perhaps? No. The look on Emrys' face told him that this was something more.

"So who's this dude?"

"You should show some respect," Emrys snapped. "The Elements are not dudes. They created the world."

"Well he looks kind of shoddy compared to the others."

"I believe this is Dielunasar, the Element of Spirit. He is equally as powerful as the other four – maybe even more so." Chase looked once more at the forlorn figure.

"He doesn't have a pendant on," Chase said, nodding towards the bare neck of the statue before him.

"I can't explain that," Emrys said thoughtfully. "I assume he should have one – perhaps it was a mistake made by the sculptor. We tend to believe that the pendants are a symbol of the power of the Gods."

"Kind of like their proof of Godliness?"

"I guess you could say that."

"If he's an equal, why isn't he out there on the Branding Line?"

Emrys sighed as if only just remembering that Chase knew nothing about the beliefs of his people. "There's no such thing as a Spiritbrand. It cannot be. Look at it this way – if I was a proper Earthbrand, I would be able to manipulate the ground, summon rocks, and even earthquakes if I thought hard enough. Now what do you suppose the Element of Spirit governs?"

Chase thought for a second, casting his mind back to distant RE lessons. "Like, personality and soul and stuff?"

"Exactly. If Spiritbrands existed, they would be able to control people's thoughts, their actions, their spirits." Chase stared into the eyes of the Spirit Element and was struck by the similarities between the God and himself. Dielunasar was filed away, outcast from the others just like Chase had been throughout his life. He had never been one of the popular kids when he was growing up, and this had only cemented itself as he had progressed through his A Levels and into University. It was somewhat reassuring to know that the same thing could happen to someone as powerful as the armour clad figure before him.

Chase tried turning away but found himself held by the stony gaze of the statue. It was if the figure of the Element had connected with him somehow, and didn't want him to leave. He began to step subconsciously forwards until their eyes were level, both grey – light and dark boring into each other.

"I didn't even know that a statue of Dielunasar was made," Emrys muttered in the background. "After all, why would they need one?"

"A very good question, Emrys Earthbrand." Both young men whirled around to face the newcomer, an elderly man with laugh lines dancing across his face. He smiled warmly at Chase, as if he could somehow sense what the young man had just been feeling.

"See anything you like, young man?" Chase shook his head. "And back to your question Emrys, the statue was made before it was decided against Spiritbranding. That is all. It would have been hugely disrespectful to destroy an image of an Element so we kept the statue here." The old man paused, and although he was still smiling, Chase suspected he was waiting for an explanation as to why they had snuck into the Branding Hall.

"We came to look for you, your worship," Emrys began. "Chase here... has no brand. Also he – well, he just appeared." Emrys looked like he was floundering so Chase jumped in with the rest of the story. After he had finished, to his surprise, Faronarai smiled.

"Chase is from the other world," he stated, as obviously as if he was naming bits of furniture.

"Wha-?" Emrys stammered awkwardly.

"Tell me the creation story, Earthbrand."

Chase turned to watch Emrys as he recalled the tale.

"Ok. First Ehraifir moulded the world. Then Ainarai made the atmosphere and Wonaitohelrai made it rain and rain until the seas were made. Farinaraiel made all the creatures and then Dielunasar gave them spirit."

"All true," nodded Faronarai. "Then what?" Whilst Emrys thought about the next part of the story, Chase thought about how different it was from the ones he had been taught at school. One God being able to create everything seemed so farfetched when placed next to this mantra. At least here, the roles were divided and everything could be assigned into one of the five broad Elemental categories.

"Once humanity emerged," Emrys continued, "it looked like we were having trouble keeping our powers in check, so the Elements created The Everrulers to maintain a balance. And that's where we've been ever since. Up until they were assassinated, that is." Emrys took a deep breath and looked at Faronarai anxiously. His expression reminded Chase a little of his dog Pepper. When he was a puppy, he would drop some rag or a ball at your feet and then look at you as if to say "Have I done right?" Faronarai smiled mischievously as he shook his head.

"That's the part everybody gets wrong," he said. "But don't worry my friend, it's not your fault – that's the way they teach it."

"What really happened then?" Emrys asked, and Chase had to admit, his curiosity was piqued too. The Elements creating representatives to keep the peace seemed fantastical enough – what else could possibly top that?

"Are you sure you want to know? It will change the way you see this world." Emrys nodded defiantly. "Very well then, perhaps we could sit in the vestry?"

The two young men followed the Archpriest into the plainly decorated antechamber, where they seated themselves on hard backed chairs.

"The truth is," Faronarai began mournfully, "the Everrulers were not a gift. They were a punishment. When humanity finally developed, the Elements disagreed on whether we should be able to use the Craft. Dielunasar believed that his gift should be accessible to all – every man to be an equal. However, the other four were proud. Even though the Elements were planning on returning to their palace at Elohelmarelnartoh, they did not wish for us to share their powers. As it was four against one, Dielunasar was overruled and humanity was unable to use the Craft."

"Hang on," Chase interrupted. Even though he was new here, he could still spot the contradiction in the old man's version of events. "That doesn't make sense because Emrys said everyone here can use powers."

"I'm getting to that, young man. The initial world formed by the Elements is the world *you* call home. Not the world Emrys and I do. Somewhat understandably, Dielunasar was angered by the decision of the others. In secret, he forged another world of his own, a world in which humanity could use the powers of the Elements."

"But wouldn't it have taken aeons for humanity to develop on this second world?" Emrys asked. "How could Dielunasar even know that humans would develop? We might have come out as something completely different on his world."

"You're forgetting what Dielunasar is," Faronarai countered with a wag of his finger. "The Element of Spirit has dominion over souls. He vowed that every soul that passed in the first world would be reborn in the second, and vice versa. As such, there is only ever a fixed amount of life on the two worlds, they just swap between the two after each expiration. As soon as the first humans began to reach the end of their lives, they were reborn in the second world. This world. So in truth, we are merely one lifetime behind the world that Chase came from." Chase could tell that Emrys was stunned, and he couldn't blame him. He himself was feeling a strange sensation. The news was ground breaking, yes, but Chase was somehow unsurprised by it. He had, after all, spent his entire life being shunned by those who felt themselves better than him. It made sense that there was a whole other world where people could use magic, and that somehow he had found himself there – a fresh start, so to speak.

"So where do the Everrulers come into this?" Emrys managed breathlessly.

"Well naturally, the other Elements found out about it. Not even Dielunasar could hide an entire world. Once again, the Elements were split. Farinaraiel wanted to destroy the world and all the souls that the Spirit Element had stolen, but in the end it was Ehraifir that formulated the solution. The second world was allowed to continue, on the condition that the Everrulers were created to keep it in check. Think of them as prison guards if you will. And *that's* where we've been ever since."

"What happened to Diel...the Spirit Element? Did they just give him a slapped wrist and be on their way?" asked Chase fervently. He found himself sympathising more and more with the Spirit God. The Archpriest sighed and shook his head wistfully.

"Not at all. Dielunasar suffered the worst punishment imaginable. The others stripped him of his Element status and bound him to one of the souls he had stolen. It was their reasoning that if he loved his world so much, he could live there forever. That was when the Elements left. Earth, Water, Air and Fire abandoned their Spirit."

"So what happened to him?" pursued Chase. "After he was stranded, I mean." Faronarai looked warily at Emrys lapping up every word intently and shook his head.

"That will have to be for another time, I'm afraid," he said. "Now Emrys, I thank you for looking after Chase thus far, but I really do think it would be better if he stayed here with me. I can help him, and it might not be prudent to let an unbranded person wander about in these... difficult times." Chase realized that Faronarai was trying to get rid of Emrys on purpose – he obviously didn't want him to learn any more about the Spirit God. Perhaps it was dangerous in some way? For a second, it looked as if Emrys was going to object, but Faronarai obviously held a position of power and respect, as the country man said nothing. With a nod, Emrys stepped towards the door.

"I'll maybe see you around then," he said to Chase softly. "Take care." He strolled out of the Branding Hall with his shoulders hunched. Chase heard the wooden doors creak shut behind him, and felt a pang of sorrow for Emrys. He was all alone in that large and echoing farmhouse. He had had company for one night, and even that was taken away from him.

"Now then young man," the Archpriest said sternly. "Let's get you sorted."

Chapter 27 – Deification

Immediately after Emrys had left, Faronarai began to bustle about the vestry collecting the various trinkets and belongings that were on the shelves and the desk. He was throwing them roughly into a satchel whilst muttering to himself as Chase stood awkwardly in the corner.

"Can I help you at all?" he asked tentatively. The older man jumped as if he had for a moment forgotten that Chase was in the room.

"Not at all! You must not lift a finger - you are... well, that will do I think. Come on, we must go across the city to Spyrus."

"Spyrus?" Chase exclaimed. "How can a medicine company help me get home?"

"Our Spyrus is very different to your Spyrus"

Within moments, they were hurrying through the alleys and side streets of the old town that clustered around the base of the temple mound. Chase was struck by how different everything looked when bathed in the afternoon sun rather than the light of early morning. Everything seemed to be bleached out, the colours faded and the cracks visible. He could truly see that this was a city that had fallen on hard times – everywhere he looked there were signs of conflict; broken glass, boarded windows and barricaded doors. Random squads of armoured and armed soldiers were marching through the streets, but none of them paid the two of them any heed.

No matter what they passed, the Archpriest kept smiling at Chase as if he was going to shatter at any moment, gently leading him by the arm as they approached the Spyrus Tower. They stepped through the sliding doors and marched straight across the cavernous lobby. The receptionist didn't say a word as Faronarai skirted round the desk and made for a pair of lifts, all with Chase in tow. Once inside, the older man pushed the button for one of the floors near the top, and Chase felt his stomach lurch as the lift shot upwards.

The doors opened onto a large conference room with a long table that was a smooth polished black. There were thirteen padded chairs surrounding the table, which was immaculately laid out with note pads and glasses of water. At one end of the table was an obelisk of a dark stone. It was towards this that Faronarai purposefully strode. He rolled up his sleeve and placed his palm directly onto the obelisk, which was giving off a slight humming sound. After a few seconds, he stepped back from the obelisk and sank into one of the chairs. He gestured for Chase to sit next to him, and then they waited.

Less than five minutes later, the lifts chimed again and a flock of suited men descended the small flight of steps into the conference room. They were all of a similar age, with silvery or salt and pepper hair, and all equally dressed to perfection. They flowed around the table like a tide of grey, filling up the seats next to Chase and the Archpriest. The last man to emerge from the lift carried a large leather briefcase, which he set gently at the head of the table before surveying the other men. Chase found himself shrinking into the soft chair. He was surrounded by important men, men with power and as usual they would probably ignore him and leave him out of whatever this was. The man at the head of the table cleared his throat.

"Welcome, Chase," he said warmly. Chase sat forward, rubbing his ears to make sure he'd heard correctly. Maybe one of the others was called Chase too? But no. His cheeks reddened as all eyes turned his way. "I am Oynarel, and we are the heads of Spyrus. There should be thirteen of us, but two are elsewhere. Anyway, I imagine you have a lot of questions and confusion, but before you ask, perhaps a little explanation might clear some things up. I trust my colleague has explained where you came from?"

"I know about our two worlds and how they're linked," Chase nodded. "But I don't know how I got from my world to yours."

"We'll get to that," Oynarel said. "Now, as you know, our Lord was punished severely for creating this world. He had to live among us for eternity. You would think that mankind would show him some gratitude, but alas, the majority chose to follow the Everrulers, and Dielunasar was exiled. Luckily, he managed to gather a group of the faithful, a group that came to call themselves The Spiri, followers of Spirit.

The soul that the Elements bound Dielunasar to was weak and soon died, unable to contain the divine form. Our Lord found himself jumping from host to host in an attempt to maintain any semblance of life. What the Spirit Element really desired was to live in the first world - after all, it had been created by all five Elements together, and was by nature alone superior to this world." At this point, Chase's chest swelled with pride. He came from the superior world! "However, every time one of Dielunasar's hosts passed on, he was always left behind. What he needed was a host that had been born in the first world, but of course, he could never get there in order to inhabit one. He tried once, but the effort nearly cost him his life."

"Can Elements die?" Chase asked, incredulous.

"They can't be killed, except by each other, and they don't age, but they can... over exert themselves. If an Element were to completely exhaust their energies then they would fade away into nothing. Now where were we? Ah yes! Dielunasar eventually grew tired of his existence, flitting through lifetimes. He chose not to inhabit a new host and instead sealed himself away until such a time arose when he could achieve his goal of getting to the other world.

His followers, The Spiri, continued on through the generations, eventually forming the Spyrus Corporation. We have dedicated our time to finding a way for Dielunasar to get to the other world, and I'm pleased to say that some years ago now, we discovered a way to safely transcend between the worlds without the death of the host."

"Is that how I got here?"

"In a fashion, yes. Although how your friends in your world managed to do it to you, I have no idea."

"They aren't my friends!" Chase cut in acidly. Oynarel paused slightly, narrowing his eyes at the younger man's venom.

"Be that as it may," he continued. "We discovered that by combining the four physical Elements, we could produce a force strong enough to send souls through to the other world. At first it was difficult: we had to collect four consenting subjects, one of each brand, but we eventually found a way around that too." At this point, all of the Spyrus men stood up. As one, they rolled up their right sleeves until the shoulders were exposed. Chase could clearly see eleven brands just like the one Emrys had shown him except these were violet, and instead of a crooked line running through, they had what looked to be a cross or a figure of some sort.

"Spiritbrands," Chase said. "But the only way you could get them is to be chosen by the statue of Dielunasar, and that's broken."

"Such a sure knowledge of our ways," mused Oynarel with a smile. "You are right, the statue of Dielunasar would be the only way to get a Spiritbrand, but these are not Spiritbrands, they are so much more. Imagine a brand that gives you the power of all four Elements!" The fervour in Oynarel's voice rose to fever pitch as if he was delivering a sermon.

"Good for you," Chase muttered sarcastically. "I'm surprised you didn't go the whole shabang and combine all five."

"I don't deny that would be a far superior goal; however, a brand was never cast to accompany the statue. There can never be a Spiritbrand."

"Fine. But I still don't see what this has got to do with me. You said you found a way to cross between the worlds. If Dielunasar is already in my world, then you've done it, end of, right?" Oynarel shook his head.

"You're forgetting something. Dielunasar sealed himself away. He designed his prison so that he could only be released by someone from the first world. That's where you come in."

"All right," Chase sighed. "So I set your God free, then you'll send me back to my world?" He had decided that he would do whatever these people wanted. Despite lamenting about how pathetic his life at home was, he was missing it desperately, if only because it was *normal*. Chase would even have said he was starting to miss his mother if anybody had asked. "Promise?" Chase asked again. Oynarel raised his eyebrows.

"You have my word," he said with a sly grin. He then reached forward and unfastened the clips on the briefcase he had brought in. There was a slight popping sound as he lifted the lid. Chase stood up so he could peer over and see into the case, but whatever was in there was shrouded in a silk wrap. Oynarel lifted the object gently and theatrically held it aloft as he removed the covering.

He was holding a lump that seemed to be half rock and half crystal. With a gasp, Chase recognised it as the hand that was missing from the statue of Dielunasar, but whereas the gems held by the other four statues were polished and gleaming, the purple crystal of Spirit was rough hewn and jagged. As Chase watched, the gemstone began to shine, faintly at first, but growing brighter and brighter.

"All you have to do is touch the stone," Oynarel said casually. Chase held out his hand, hovering inches away from the glowing crystal. The stone seemed to call to him, a flurry of whispers echoing at the back of his mind, drawing him forward. It reminded him of when he'd been in the forest and had been pulled inexorably towards the clearing. That was what had led him here, across worlds and now this was his chance to get back. He couldn't care less what Spyrus were going to do with the returned God, as long as Oynarel kept his word.

With a deep breath, Chase took the final step and seized the violet stone. There was a flash and Chase was thrown back, sprawling across the ebony table. He felt a strong charge pulsing through him and coming to rest behind his eyes, even though he was no longer touching the rock. He lost all awareness of the other men in the room and lost control of his limbs, though he could see them twitching out of the corner of his eye. It was odd, but Chase's final thought wasn't anything honourable, or witty - the only thing the young man could think was *don't be sick, please don't be sick!* Chase blacked out on his back, surrounded by the heads of the Spyrus Corporation.

<u>Deus' Return</u>
<u>November 2</u>

Chapter 28 – The Second Detriment

Dielunasar's eyes flickered open. Bright lights flooded his skull and he blinked, trying to regain focus. He was looking at a ceiling, fluorescence pouring down on him, enveloping him. He flexed his fingers, testing them, experimenting with his new form. It had been so long since he had occupied a body, and he was revelling in all its wonders. He sat up, twisting and flexing, stretching his arms and wiggling his toes.

Someone cleared their throat, and Dielunasar whipped his head around to face them. A crowd of suited men immediately dropped to their knees and prostrated themselves before him, their noses almost touching the floor. *Sycophants*, he thought maliciously. Wherever he went, there were always those too enamoured with his power to leave him alone. He opened and closed his mouth a couple of times, preparing to speak with vocal chords that he hadn't used in centuries.

"You may rise," he rasped. The men clambered to their feet, which for some of them was more difficult than others.

"My Lord, we have done it!" one of them said, stammering slightly. "We have successfully returned you into being." At that moment, Dielunasar recalled the task he had given his followers before sealing himself in the statue.

"You? You are my Spiri?" The men nodded warily as Dielunasar counted them. "You lie. Thirteen Spiri there always are, and here you are only eleven."

"Sarinexa is out hunting, my Lord," the leading man said. "And Farinavirel is in the other world. That's right, we found a way to send people through. Farinavirel offered to be sent through many years ago, in order to create a Spyrus there as well."

Dielunasar was above the matters of mortals, but he was slightly impressed that these men had actually managed to do what he asked.

"What is Spyrus?" he asked.

"Well," Oynarel said, "in your absence, we have grown in power and influence under the guise of The Spyrus Corporation. Tohelnar is a part of The Element Council now, and tha-"

"I smell conflict," Dielunasar cut in, throwing his head back and inhaling deeply.

"I was getting to that my Lord. Thanks to some pioneering work, we developed Airtox – to the outside it was branded as an air purifier, but it was laced with a simple Anger enhancer – a derivative of the Hybrid Onslaught. We released this at the same time as some disturbing evidence regarding the deaths of The Everrulers."

"About time too," the Spirit Element spat. "Puppets of my punishers. Am I right in assuming that you were responsible?"

"Yes, my Lord," Oynarel said smugly, again puffing out his chest. "Their deaths provided us with a catalyst. Ghostbrands were blamed, and with the help of the Airtox in the atmosphere the country fell into war. By the time the Airtox dissipated, it was too late to turn back."

"Of course, we will be supplementing the AotE battalion with Airtox during their major battle campaigns, and soon, the world will be rid of the Ghostbrand curse," chipped in one of the other men. Dielunasar turned to observe Firaire smirking at him and his insides churned. If Gods threw up, then this was how it would feel. The Element found himself wondering how his loyal followers had allowed themselves to become driven by greed and power. There had been a time when they lived only for him, and now during his isolation his men had found other motivations.

"What next, my Lord?" asked Oynarel furtively, breaking Dielunasar's thoughts of disgust. The Spirit paused for a second whilst he formulated an answer.

"As you know, I intend to travel to the other world. It has always been my goal. I will collect my gifts and use them to create the new Order."

"You mean to go ahead with your initial plan, my Lord?" one of the Spiri said, awe and apprehension clear in his voice. "You will overthrow them?"

"In time. However, I would spend some time here first. This is my creation and I've been gone so long, it would please me to see how it has changed. We-" He was interrupted as a thunderous booming cracked the sky and the tower shook, causing a fine haze of plaster to drift from the ceiling like snowfall. The Spyrus men immediately dropped to the floor, cowering unceremoniously under the furniture while Dielunasar turned to face the panoramic windows that overlooked the city.

The tower stood at one end of a long boulevard and curious people who had remained in the city were now creeping out of hiding, all to stare in the same direction. Beyond the Temple of Branding, a large plume of smoke was billowing from the highest of the distant mountains, the Eye of Fire. Tendrils of thick black ash snaked into the sky as the main cloud bloomed and spread until the sky became a dark grey.

As the terrified populace watched, a bright orange tongue seemed to flare from the peak of The Eye. If it was clear enough to be seen from the city, then Dielunasar could only guess how monstrous the flames were up close. Seconds after the flash, another deep resounding rumble shook the city, this time accompanied by blaring alarms and the tinkling of broken glass. The onlookers below fled shrieking – some back inside to fetch belongings or simply to hide, others sprinting down the street in the opposite direction.

The volcano glowed brighter still as the buildings shook more and more violently. Dielunasar did nothing more than raise an eyebrow as orange cracks appeared spidering across the tarmac. The fissures widened and began to spew gloops of molten rock, splashing and frothing as they incinerated whatever they landed on amidst a choir of hissing, cracking and screaming. With a further rumble, the apartment block opposite was swallowed up as a fissure erupted beneath it. Like a sinking ship, the building vanished into the swirling neon waves, melting and twisting as it was sucked into the bowels of the earth. And then there was stillness. The lava ceased to bubble and receded back into the cracks it had poured from, and the road resettled into a set of jagged and uneven steps. The Eye of Fire had only a single wavering column of smoke rising into the shimmering air as the ash cloud from the eruption drifted and dispersed back into the previous blue.

Dielunasar found himself chuckling as he turned back to his minions, ashen faced and trembling as they were.

"The Gods are coming," he said with a grin. "And they are vexed." He waited for the understanding to play across the faces of the hapless men before him.

"You mean," stuttered Oynarel, "that was…?" Dielunasar nodded with satisfaction.

"It changes nothing. If anything, it will make my job easier. As I was saying, we shall reconvene in just under two weeks, on the fourteenth. For now, I wish to explore my world alone." Dielunasar swept out of the room, immediately sensing the notes of relief permeating the stench of fear emanating from his followers – the only thing the Spirit Element could not determine was whether they were more afraid of the volcano or of him.

Chapter 29 – Judgement

Dielunasar spent the next few days roaming the extent of the world, expecting to revel in the progress his children had made during his long slumber. Instead, he was disgusted.

He had strolled through AotE barracks and seen thousands upon thousands unsure of why they were even fighting. He donned armour and spoke to many of them, learning how their initial drive and rage had faded almost as soon as they had signed their souls away to the hungry war machine.

On the other side of the frontline, Dielunasar saw Ghostbrands, persecution beaten into their hard and worn faces – commiting the same acts of violence for different reasons.

Further afield, the Spirit Element saw countries that were so poor that their citizens were dying from diseases that the Spyrus company could heal with a single remedy, yet nothing had been done. Overflowing with the despair he gained from being amongst such impoverished masses, the Spirit found himself using his infinite power to heal vast crowds with a single touch, and despite this miracle, not one of them saw him for what he truly was. Had he been gone so long that his world had forgotten its creator?

He travelled back lamenting the fall of his world. True, everyone had treated the Everrulers like heroes, and he was glad that they had been eliminated, but what had his Spiri done in the twenty years since? As the God of Spirit, Dielunasar was flooded with emotion – a tide of sadness for his waning creation and a flow of anger aimed at those who had sat by and grown rich on its demise.

Finally, he wandered towards the familiar lights of the city, although its once ordered and regular outline was now crooked and jarring. As he approached, he saw one light twinkling off to the side – a beacon of innocence and hope in a world of corruption and greed – Emrys' farmhouse.

When he entered, the Ghostbrand was fussing around the kitchen, which looked like the rest of the city. Furniture was overturned and the floor was a mosaic of smashed crockery. Emrys was on his knees collecting remnants and stuffing them roughly into a bag.

"Did the volcano do this?" Dielunasar asked.

"No, Spyrus did." Emrys finished collecting the debris before looking up. His stony expression softened as he recognised his visitor. "Oh, hey Chase." Dielunasar blinked at the familiarity but ignored it. "I wasn't sure I'd see you again… I washed that hoodie," Emrys said with a smile.

"So how do you know Spyrus did this?" asked Dielunasar, trying to sound like the teenager he appeared to be. At this, Emrys dropped the bag of ruined kitchenware, clambered to his feet and moved towards what looked like a store cupboard. He casually flicked the door open and turned to Dielunasar with a guilty grin. An unconscious young man with a bloodied temple had been folded into the small space.

"This guy told me. Before I panned him." At this, Emrys nodded towards one of the heavy cast iron pans that was hanging from a bar across the range. Dielunasar felt a great swelling of pride as he took in the power of this seemingly powerless Ghostbrand. The Spirit Element couldn't help laughing gleefully for a second before reassuming the persona of Chase Rivers.

"Won't he kill you when he wakes up?"

"Well yeah, I guess he'd like to have a go. I only got lucky the first time. I don't reckon he was expecting me to fight back so… creatively. But I'm not planning on being here when he comes round." Dielunasar looked more closely at the unconscious man. He was younger than Emrys but older than Chase. He wasn't dressed in the uniform of the AotE, but instead was wearing a simple black top with black trousers. There was even a bloodstained balaclava that Emrys must have removed. All of it made him look like the amateur assassin he was trying to be. "I just need to grab some more stuff from upstairs," Emrys began. "Then we really should get out of here." Dielunasar nodded as the Ghostbrand jogged across the room and up the chunky steps.

As soon as Emrys' footsteps were overhead, Dielunasar knelt next to the unconscious intruder, placed his hand on the young man's bloodied forehead and closed his eyes. Like an imprint on the back of his eyelids, the Spirit God could see the man's brain lit up with thoughts, memories and personality. Within seconds, Dielunasar had located the pathways that had closed down when the man had been knocked unconscious and reignited them.

Both men's eyes opened instantaneously, but whereas Dielunasar's were narrowed shrewdly, the prisoner's were wide and flicking swiftly back and forth.

"When my father hears about this, you'll be sorry," he hissed venomously as he tried to prop himself shakily up onto his elbows.

"Quiet!" whispered the Spirit Element with such authority that the intruder flinched. "I will give you one chance to talk to me of your own free will, then you will talk by force. Why did Spyrus send you?"

"Go to hell," the young man spat, features burning with resentment. In another time, Dielunasar would have been impressed by the boy's courage, but today he needed information quickly.

"You had your chance," he muttered as he reached inside the other man's mind once more, rerouting energy and altering synapses. Of course, he could have done this from the beginning, but he wanted to test the boy's resolve. The young man's eyes immediately went blank, his expression slack faced and vacant. "Why did Spyrus send you?"

"The Ghostbrand may have learned too much," the prisoner replied in lifeless monotone. "He spent time with the Archpriest and the host. He had to be eliminated before he could pass on any possible information." Dielunasar nodded. 'The host' obviously meant the body he inhabited, and it was true that the Archpriest's story about the other world made Emrys the only person outside of Spyrus who knew the truth. However, Dielunasar was feeling less and less inclined to act with Spyrus' best interests in mind.

"Why did they choose you? Sarinexa is usually used for things like this." Of the many different roles his Spiri traditionally occupied, the one designated as Sarinexa usually took care of the wetwork.

"Sarinexa did not return after the Eye erupted. I begged my father to let me prove myself."

"And you are?"

"Kier, son of Tohelnar." At this moment, Emrys' footsteps once more resounded on the steps.

"Well Kier, son of Tohelnar, it's not your day is it?" Dielunasar smirked as he punched the boy solidly in the temple and laid him back down in the cupboard. True, he could have simply reached inside Kier's mind and shut him off, but Dielunasar thought the boy probably deserved a smack. The Spirit jumped to his feet just as Emrys appeared. The Ghostbrand's eyes flickered from Dielunasar to Kier and back suspiciously.

"Any trouble?"

"Nope," Dielunasar shrugged. "He's still out of it."

"Good. Well I really have to leave. No doubt Spyrus will send more men when this jackass doesn't come back. Sorry I couldn't be of more help – I hope coming to see me doesn't get you mixed up in all this," Emrys said ruefully. "Did you have any luck with Faronarai by the way?" This was as he headed through the door. Dielunasar followed him out into the farmland.

"I'm seeing him again tonight actually. We're going to be making a lot of progress."

"Ah, good. I hope he can help you get home." *Oh, he's going to help me...* Dielunasar thought to himself maliciously. "Well, I'll see you." Emrys hovered, decisions and uncertainty weighing heavily on his mind – and that was when the Spirit Element saw it. The Ghostbrand's aura flared so brightly that Dielunasar didn't even have to close his eyes. As Emrys made some final choice to abandon his home, Dielunasar saw great tendrils of determination and resolution beaming out from the young man. The Spirit realised that Emrys was going to do something big. He also realised at that moment what he could do to aid the closest thing he'd had to a friend since he had come here.

"Emrys, wait," he said softly. The Ghostbrand turned to him on tiptoes, anxiously to be away before his resolve faded. He raised his eyebrows in question. "You have a strong sense of purpose about you."

"Uh huh?"

"I want to give you something to help you on your way." Before Emrys could reply, Dielunasar leaned in and kissed him, drinking in the waves of surprise that burst from the Ghostbrand like lightning. After a second or two, he felt Emrys straighten, straining to pull his lips away.

Dielunasar stood back and watched him awkwardly brush himself off, free of the radiating passion of the Spirit God.

"Um…" Emrys floundered, breathing out hurriedly. "I'm not a samer or anything so… that was like for luck, right?"

"Something like that," Dielunasar replied with a smile. "Go well, Emrys Earthbrand. We shall not meet again." Without another word, he turned and hurried into the fields. As much as he wanted to stay and see the young man succeed and grow strong, he did not even look back, all too aware of the effect his presence had on mortals. That was the one trick the other Elements had missed, never spending too much time amongst their creations. If they had, they would have seen the sometimes disasterous consequences of being subjected to the immense energy that emanated from the Gods. During his banishment, Dielunasar had had both men and women throw themselves at him in fits of uninhibited lust, had seen people fight for his attention and kill themselves when they didn't get it, and had even been set upon by victims consumed with murderous rage. He had caused ecstasy and death in equal measure and had the others known about this contamination, perhaps they would have thought twice about exiling him amongst such easy prey. Dielunasar had effortlessly enthralled the original Spiri and set in motion the plan that would eventually lead to his ascension to the first world.

As Dielunasar headed back towards Spyrus tower, he wondered if his Spiri's transformation into power hungry prejudice was a result of his presence or his absence. *Not that it really matters*, he thought. One way or another, Spyrus wouldn't be his problem much longer.

Shortly afterwards, Dielunasar was standing once more at the head of the grand conference table, ten of his men facing him expectantly.

"Where are Firaire and Sarinexa?" he asked.

"Firaire is attending to a last minute bit of business, my Lord." This came from Tohelnar. "And Sarinexa has not returned. I fear he was lost in the eruption." Dielunasar surveyed the ageing faces before him, reading their expressions with interest. A thick fog of uncertainty permeated the room, and it was obvious that the Spiri were not sure what to expect. It had been so long since they had been in the presence of the God that they had forgotten how he was. He would have to remind them.

"I am done here," he began. "Tell me how to cross over." Immediately the atmosphere lifted, relief pouring out of the suited men.

"It's quite simple really," Oynarel said, the confidence and cockiness returning to his voice. It was all too obvious that he was imagining himself sitting pretty on power and riches again once Dielunasar had left. "You are all too aware of the disasterous repercussions of trying to force a way through on sheer will power." Dielunasar remembered returning from his one foray into the first world, drained and fading, nearly all energy spent. He had had to burn through many souls to regain his strength, and that was when he began his long sleep, while his servants worked the problem. "We knew that only a Godly amount of energy could do the job," the old man continued. "Yet we each only possessed a slice of the power of one Element."

"You are lecturing me on a history that I predate," snapped the Spirit Element. "What of the method?"

"Of course my Lord," the Spyrus head simpered before turning to Faronarai, who resumed the tale.

"Using my access to the Element Statues at the temple, I managed to merge the energies of all four Elements into one brand. This gives you enough power to transcend."

"You have the brand here?"

Faronarai nodded eagerly.

"I will fetch it, my Lord," Tohelnar said with satisfaction as he made for the lift. Once the doors had slid closed, Dielunasar turned back to his men, a triumphant smile beaming from his face.

"Good. Now I have no further use for you, my Spiri." He waited for the realisation to sink in. Would his men stand up for themselves and fight for their survival, or would they resign themselves to the judgement of their God?

"My Lord?" Little by little, the air once more became rank with fear.

"I may be leaving this world, but it is still my creation. I love this world, and you have ruined it in my absence. Your war has divided mankind, and for what? I bore no ill will to the Uncrafted and now you have them all but exterminated, running scared and hiding in holes in the ground like vermin. That is not what you swore to me. You collectively bound yourselves to serve my ideals even whilst I slept."

"But that was generations ago," stammered one of the men from the back of the room. "So much has changed since you left."

"Indeed!" roared Dielunasar. "Devotion does not change, regardless of the circumstances. Yet here you are, poisoning the air and Gods know what else to further your own gain. Tell me how many innocent people have died in your rise to the top of your corrupt tower?"

"No more than the souls you usurped in your time here."

"I am a God - such is my right! It is not for mortals to play with the lives of entire worlds."

"I am sorry, my Lord," Oynarel said, taking a step forward. *At least one of them still knows his place*, thought Dielunasar angrily. "But if you will not leave this world quietly, then you will not leave it at all." The old man raised his right hand, which began to glow with an intense violet light, rose tinting the room like an ageing photograph. "Do you think your teenage form can contend with the power of all four Elements against you?" At this, the other nine men raised burning palms and stood resolutely against their creator. Dielunasar laughed openly, watching the men grit their teeth as his mirth fuelled their anger.

"You forget who you address, minion. You may have the power of the Elements, but an Element you are not. Not to mention that from the moment I walked in here, I have been planted in your very consciousness. I am Spirit – anything with a soul is my plaything."

"Do not listen to him," shouted Oynarel in steeled tones. "It is with words that he seeks to undermine us. If he was truly in our minds, we would have felt it."

Dielunasar smiled. "Oh, you'll feel it." The remaining nine Spyrus heads stood with mouths wide open as their number one turned to face them and serenely raised a hand to his face. His expression never changed as he dug his fingernails into the center of his forehead and peeled a vast strip of skin clean off. Blood poured onto the pristinely ironed suit as the man reached up for another chunk of his own flesh, still not uttering a sound nor moving an inch. Pink gave way to red, which in turn revealed the smooth and glistening white of Oynarel's skull, before he clawed his own eye from its socket and cast it onto the floor with a wet plopping sound. One of the others retched onto the polished table as the Spyrus head finally collapsed, pitching forward onto the pile of lumps and slivers that had once been his own face.

Not one of the violet palms remained ignited and Dielunasar tilted his head backwards, inhaling deeply. If the atmosphere had been thick with fear before, now it was fetid with absolute terror. The Spirit Element made short work of the others, turning the conference room into an image from a blood soaked nightmare and by the time Tohelnar returned, only Faronarai was still alive, sitting at the table repeatedly pounding his head into it, blood oozing from his shattered nose and creating increasingly large splatters over the tabletop. Dielunasar snatched the long iron rod that Tohelnar was holding, revelling in the old man's expression of sickened shock. Tohelnar fumbled with the buttons on his jacket.

"I have the tattoo of the council," he stammered, trying to muster some composure as he was surrounded by his slaughtered colleagues. Dielunasar laughed cruelly.

"I am a God! The parlour tricks of The Everrulers cannot protect you."

"Please," Tohelnar whispered pathetically. "I have a son..." Dielunasar thrust the branding rod into Tohelnar's chest, hearing his jacket rip as it emerged out the back. Tohelnar fell to his knees, eyes clouding over. Dielunasar knelt down in front of him.

"I've seen Kier," he whispered softly. "He was killed by the Ghostbrand you sent him to assassinate." Usually Dielunasar considered himself to be above lying, but it was worth it to see Tohelnar's heart break just seconds before it stopped beating.

Dielunasar removed the branding rod and stood, turning to face the large windows again, remembering the last time he had stood there as the Eye of Fire spewed molten rock across the city. It struck him as odd that for people who detested most of the world below, Spyrus had a lot of panoramic windows to view it with. *One last look*, the Spirit thought as he rolled up a sleeve and held the branding rod to his pale skin. He didn't feel a thing, and only the wisps of smoke curling from his shoulder told him that the brand was doing its job. That was another trick of the divine brands: no heat required. Power seeped into his heart, and he could feel the new energy of the other Elements mix with his own. He was Fire. He was Earth. He was Air and Water. He was Spirit.

Seconds later, he was staring at his own palm, held six inches in front of his face. This was it. He was finally going to the world he had but glimpsed before his exile. He had only taken that one walk across the earth in which he had bestowed the gift of soul, and that was aeons ago. His mind was filled with exciting possibilities, branching off into different existences the first world could have taken. It was one lifetime ahead of his world, and a lot could change in one lifetime.

He concentrated on the energy flowing through his body, somehow boosted and tempered as it passed through the brand on his shoulder and down towards his hand. His outstretched palm began to glow until Dielunasar's entire vision was blinding purple. With a final push, he forced the energy out of his hand and back at his own body. There was a resounding flash and the Spyrus conference room was empty save for the crackling scent of ozone and the eleven former heads of Spyrus.

The Rise Of War
November 17

Chapter 30 – Kiss Of Life

Morgan Ghostbrand hurried through the twisting network of tunnels. He had spent years of his life crafting them into a workable base of operations for the Ghostbrand Resistance. The AotE's Enforcement strike was pummelling the Ghostbrands hard, not to mention the eruption of the Eye of Fire, and Morgan was forced to take some of the lesser-used passageways as the main throughways had been blocked or had collapsed completely.

He cast a nervous glance over his shoulder, making sure he hadn't been followed. Within the last hour, the soldiers had somehow broken through the resistance, and all that mattered now was Morgan getting to one specific room. An explosion rocked the tunnel, shaking chunks of rock loose from the ceiling. Shielding his head with his arms, he charged through the miniature rockfall and twisted once more, constantly aware that at any moment he might run into an AotE grunt with a force musket who would end it all. His own rifle had been lost when the soldiers had first swarmed in like a plague of armed locusts. They had opened fire on him but luckily the gun had saved his life, its stock shattering with the force-musket impact rather than his own ribcage.

The corridor turned again, ending in a T-junction. Screams echoed from the left-hand branch, but again, Morgan's life was saved – his destination lay along the right-hand branch. He began to think about fate and destiny, gritting his teeth as another ear-shattering explosion enveloped him in dust. Funny how the supernatural forces that had seemingly abandoned him and his kind now appeared to be providing him with a safe route, ensuring he got the job done.

He rounded the final bend and breathed a sigh of relief as he saw his destination in front of him, the door still standing, and from what he could ascertain, unopened. He eased it open now, peering gingerly inside and casting his eyes over all the nooks that a soldier could be hiding in, and many that one couldn't, just to be sure. Finally satisfied, he slipped inside and closed the door behind him, immediately hefting a side counter across the doorway. This room was to be his last stand, his final resting place. He knew the war was over for him as soon as the AotE had breached the tunnels under the Temple of Branding. That meant that the Ghostbrands up on the battlefield had been eliminated or had been reduced to too few to stop the soldiers from discovering their headquarters. He would have held up his hands and let the rock pellets, or ice shards or whichever element power was to be his destroyer pummel him were it not for his final important action as leader of the Ghostbrand Resistance.

Once satisfied that the door was suitably barricaded, Morgan allowed himself a minute to survey the room and collect his thoughts. The lab equipment was just as he'd left it, and the sleeping form connected to the chair in the centre of the room had not moved an inch, save for the occasional twitch he had developed. Morgan wondered if Caliban really did have no idea of what was going on around him, about the countless lives that he had saved and taken in the battles that raged above. Now the war was coming ever closer to the slumbering boy and Morgan had

had to make the difficult decision. Despite his containment, Caliban was far too powerful to fall into the hands of Spyrus and the AotE.

There was much debate as to the effect of the branding process. Most believed that the Element Statues detected the power you would have and then that power simply developed as you grew up, but there were a small few, declared heretics, who believed that every child had a certain degree of raw energy. Only after being branded did it begin to take the form of one of the four divisions of power. If this train of thought was true, then Caliban still had access to this raw energy without the restrictions that branding placed, despite being past the age of power-maturity.

As it was, Morgan had decided that if the game was up, then Caliban would have to be terminated. Who knew what further oppression the Encrafted could pursue if they had access to someone like Caliban? All too aware of the lives that would still be lost without Caliban's protection, the alternative was too frightening. As he was musing, the door rattled as if a large blast of air had shot up the tunnel, followed by a collection of gutteral cries and the thuds of bodies being thrown against rock. It wouldn't be long before curious soldiers took a look inside the lab, gunned Morgan down and took Caliban for themselves.

He stepped forward and gently smoothed the hair away from the boy's forehead. He really did bear him no ill will, and wished that he had a chance to explain that it was nothing personal. Caliban had just been a part of something a lot bigger, and Morgan liked to think that if the boy knew what his sacrifice had meant, he perhaps wouldn't have minded making it.

"I'm sorry," he whispered calmly as he clenched a bunch of the life support tubes in his fist. All it would take was one tug and Caliban's miserable existence would be extinguished, his systems shutting down one by one. He tensed his arm for the final pull when the door exploded inwards, his barricade tumbling into the room and skittering across the floor. He steeled himself, hoping still to maintain an image of authority in front of the Encrafted scum, but as the rock dust cleared, it wasn't an AotE soldier. It was Emrys.

Emrys flexed his palm as he took in the scene inside the lab. Morgan was standing by Caliban's chair, a bunch of tubes curled in his fist. Without thinking, Emrys thrust his hand forwards and the sandstone floor beneath Morgan's feet rippled like water, throwing him away from Caliban and smashing him into the wall.

"How is that even possible?" Morgan gasped, winded from the impact.

"I don't know," Emrys admitted. "But I'm using it while it lasts." He had been feeling tingles ever since Chase said goodbye to him, and he had soon realised what Chase's gift was, but how or why it had happened, he had no idea. It was like being born again, a second chance to feel everything he should have felt the first time round. He could feel the vibrations in the rocks as fights broke out above, he could sense thousands of minute creatures going about their lives in the soil, and he could hear the whispers of the plants that were rooted in it. It was like seeing everything with fresh eyes, and Emrys was still getting used to the things he could now do.

"Don't think the soldiers won't shoot you," Morgan growled. "You'll always be a Ghostbrand to them – you've slashed your brand, that's all they'll see." In response, Emrys again turned his thoughts to the Earth, seeking out every hairline that separated the individual chunks of rock. Whilst Morgan was still fervently damning the Encrafted, a stone the size of a fist dropped onto his forehead and he slumped forward. Emrys had more important things to do than debate with the Ghostbrand leader – better to leave him to the soldiers who would carry out their own justice. Instead, Emrys hurried to the machines surrounding Caliban, desperately looking for a switch or a button that would release the boy from his captivity.

As he scanned the main console, all he could see was a simple slide scale that was labelled 'Sedatives'. He slid the guage all the way to the bottom, cursing himself for not forcing Morgan to explain this all to him before he knocked him out. Instead, he had to wait patiently to see if it had any effect.

After a few moments, Caliban began to stir restlessly, his movements more pronounced than his previous twitchings. He flexed his fingers as his eyes fluttered open, pupils wildly casting about the lab. He began to cry out as his newly conscious brain started to process all of the tubes sticking out of him at wild angles like some sort of spider. The boy's movements became more frantic as he clawed at the machinery and Emrys jumped forwards.

"Shhh," Emrys cooed, giving the boy an awkward pat on the shoulder. "It's gonna be ok." Emrys hoped it was true, but with gunfire still rattling through the tunnels outside, he wasn't so sure. He looked again at the various pipes protruding from Caliban's skin, and wondered when it was safe to take them out? Surely now that he was awake, Caliban was functioning on his own and didn't need all of the artificial systems? Keeping this thought firmly in his mind, Emrys chose a tube at random and yanked it quickly out, a bead of blood forming on Caliban's side. The boy winced as Emrys pulled out another one, but remained alert and conscious. "I'm going to get you out of here."

Caliban opened and closed his mouth, trying out new shapes as Emrys worked his way around the chair, disconnecting as he went and ignoring the various beeps he was causing. The consoles obviously thought that Caliban's life support was failing.

"Where... here?" Caliban asked in rough, halting speech. Emrys stopped for a second, looking at the boy with awe.

"You can speak?"

"I... listened."

Emrys nodded as he pulled the last plug and wiped away the blood before gently pressing a gauze pad over the wound.

"Can you stand?" He held his hand out, and Caliban looked at it quizzically. When he didn't reach for it, Emrys leaned forward and grabbed Caliban's own hand, gently pulling him upwards out of the chair. The boy wobbled uncertainly and instinctively leaned on Emrys for support. Even through his thick jumper, Emrys could feel Caliban shivering as he stood in nothing but a pair of shorts, his bare feet tentatively padding the rock floor. Emrys gently swayed Caliban over so he was leaning against the wall, then pulled off his jumper. "Take this." Caliban didn't move, but again gave his look of curiosity as his mind worked over the new information. Emrys smiled and Caliban imitated him.

"Arms up," Emrys said, raising his own arms above his head and watching bemusedly as the boy copied him once more. He pulled the jumper over Caliban's head and patted it down, wondering how many more of his mother's knitted jumpers he was going to give away to strangers this week. "There you go. Warm."

"Warm."

"Right, we need to make a move." Emrys slipped over to the door and pressed his ear against it. There were no immediate sounds outside, nor could he detect any vibrating footsteps in the vicinity. He turned and beckoned to his new companion, who made his way shakily across the room, leaning heavily on every bit of lab equipment that he passed. It looked to Emrys like Caliban was walking across the deck of a ship during a raging storm, and he realised that they would never make it out alive with him being so slow. He hurried back to the centre of the room where Caliban had only just managed to arrive and turned his back on the boy. Instead of wasting time explaining, he reached back and hooked one arm under Caliban's knee, hitching him up onto his back. He used his free hand to wrap Caliban's arms around his neck before securing it behind the boy's other leg and then locking his hands together across his own stomach. Laced together like that, even if Caliban didn't hold on tightly, it should have been relatively hard for him to fall.

Emrys shuffled out into the corridor, readjusting Caliban until he found a comfortable stride. Once he got going, he hardly noticed the weight of the half-starved boy on his back and they made quick progress through the tunnels without encountering a single soul. Caliban remained silent but he was constantly looking around, keeping all of his senses open to help him to interpret the world he had been a part of for almost fifteen years but was now only experiencing for the first time.

When they reached the door leading to Morgan's den, Emrys ducked inside without thinking. He went straight for the noticeboard and took the list of Ghostbrands and the silver half heart bracelet, shoving them hastily into his pocket before returning to the corridor. He couldn't really say why they were important, but he felt that he owed it to the executed Ghostbrands, not to let their names fade from memory once the war was over.

They came onto the final stretch of tunnel that would lead them back into the city, then froze. A group of soldiers were clearly silhouetted against the tunnel entrance, although thankfully they were facing outwards, obviously charged with stopping people getting in rather than coming out. However, there would surely be questions. Emrys took a step back into the shadows of the tunnel to think of any excuse he could use to get past the soldiers. It was only when Caliban started playing with his hair that the idea came to him. He shifted his weight once more and strode confidently along the tunnel.

Upon hearing his footsteps, the soldiers turned around, force muskets trained on him and Caliban. Emrys took a deep breath.

"Gimme some space, I got a casualty here," he growled as low as he could, trying to make his voice sound like what he imagined a battle worn soldier would sound like. In the next moments, everyone seemed to explode into action in the same split second. The soldiers, obviously unimpressed with Emrys' lack of uniform or weapon, opened fire. Almost instantly, Caliban shouted something about 'shielding the troops' and the two of them were suddenly surrounded by a shimmering pearlescent light. The various elemental projectiles dissolved or bounced off the barrier and the soldiers exchanged looks of concern as they broke fire for a second. In that moment, Emrys roared fiercely as he jumped into the air and landed, slamming his feet into the rock as hard as he could. Cracks spidered out from his boots, racing crookedly towards the soldiers until they were surrounded, trapped in place as the rock beneath them shattered like glass. With an ear piercing snapping sound, the ground collapsed sending men and rock tumbling down into one of the hidden caverns below. In less than a minute, the exchange was over and Emrys leapt heavily over the hole and sprinted as fast as he could, not stopping until he reached the forest that overlooked the city.

Safely under the shelter of the trees, Emrys slid Caliban off his back and hugged him tightly.

"You saved us!" he said incredulously. He hadn't been expecting Caliban to be able to do anything like that. "How did you...?"

"I... shield... the troops." That was when Emrys remembered what Morgan had said the first time he had seen Caliban. 'He knows only to shield our troops.' Something about Caliban protecting their base and their men from harm.

"What else do you remember?"

"Words... lots of words. I... listened. Spyrus. Ghostbrand. Rayne. Resistance. Encrafted. Caliban. Emrys."

"Emrys, that's me!" Emrys beamed, pointing to himself. "And Caliban is your name."

"Caliban..." The boy held out his hands and looked at them. "I am... Caliban. Words. Only words. But now pictures give them meaning. Emrys," he said, pointing at the other man's chest.

"Yep. Now Caliban, I need you to listen to me. This place is secluded enough – nobody will find you as long as you stay here. I need you to stay here while I go and find somebody ok? There's something I need to know. You understand?"

"I stay... here."

"Good man." Emrys patted him on the shoulders before turning to leave.

"Wait… Emrys. What shall I… do?"

Emrys thought for a second, then smiled. "We still don't know what powers you have. Have a play - like I said, nobody will find you here."

"Play?"

"Yeah, you know…" Emrys held out his palm and letters appeared in the soil just like he had seen his brother do countless times. "Just think stuff and see if you can make it happen." *Well done Emrys*, he thought. *That was the worst explanation ever.* But it would have to do. "I'll be back soon. I promise."

As Emrys disappeared into the foliage, he was backlit by flashes of light as Caliban experimented. As it was, Emrys was still getting used to his own powers, and he realised that he might never get a chance to find out how it had happened. It might already be too late if Chase had been sent home, but he had to try. Emrys was going to Spyrus.

Chapter 31 – Retaliation

Firaire had acted swiftly after discovering the mutilated corpses of his colleagues. It didn't take a genius to work out what had happened, especially after he saw the branding rod lying on the floor of the conference room. The first thing he did was go to the master beacon at the very top of the tower – a huge lump of magnetite suspended directly beneath the spire on the roof. From there he sent out the message that the Transcendence Protocol was now activated – the official procedure for just this event, because yes, Spyrus had suspected something like this would happen, and Spyrus always had a plan.

And so he had visited the soldiers in the trenches and sent them after the 'golden couple', but at the same time he had begun to gather a regiment of his own, a legion of those soldiers who swore their allegiance to Spyrus, and not the Element Council. He had sent a summons through the beacon and it was this force that he was on his way to meet now, as he strode through the echoing halls of Spyrus, which was now deserted. Even the spy-receptionist was gone. Pity, thought Firaire. He would have liked to teach the Ghostbrand a lesson.

As he moved through the bowels of the tower, he wondered what his colleagues would think of his current course of action. Of course, the official plan was to send the select group through in order to talk Dielunasar down and bring him back if possible, but Firaire found he could not forgive the God for the murder of his colleagues, many of them his friends – Especially after all they had done while Dielunasar did nothing, locked away in his precious little stone, helpless and cowering. Firaire almost wished they had left him there, but it was too late for such thinking.

He reached the end of the corridor where a lift was waiting. He stepped inside and pressed the bottom button. Moments later, he had passed through the waiting room and was standing in the white room, this time filled with fully armoured soldiers who instantly snapped to attention when he entered. He surveyed his loyal men for a moment.

"Soldiers of Spyrus," he boomed. "You have been pulled from the battles outside for a greater purpose. A bigger prize. The next step in the Ghostbrand war. Here, they are a minority – a plague that is easily exterminated - but there is another place, another world full of nothing but Ghostbrands. Imagine the victory that awaits us there! You will descend upon this Ghostbrand world like locusts – destroying all that opposes you until that world is purged!" The soldiers cheered as one, and Firaire allowed himself a satisfied grin. If Dielunasar wanted the first world so desperately, it would serve him right to see it overrun and ruined by the very men he had abandoned here. It was a win-win situation - the only situations Firaire ever liked to embark on. At best, Spyrus would claim dominion over two worlds instead of one, and at worst, enough of the first world would be wrecked so that Dielunasar could not enjoy it. If he was even himself anymore… Firaire wondered if his colleagues had explained the risks to the Spirit God before he travelled across. It was all very well sending a singular being through the world barrier, but Dielunasar was not a singular being – he was a God inhabiting a mortal body. Who could say what would become mixed up and contaminated during the journey? What emerged on the other side might have been just Dielunasar, just Chase, a twisted combination of both, or even worse, neither. *Either way*, he smirked. Myst, Llyr and Etain would unwittingly keep Dielunasar occupied whilst the invasion took his world by force.

"Now is the time," he shouted once more. "Take this world for Spyrus!"

"For Spyrus!" Amongst all of the cheering, nobody heard the soft chiming of the lift back in the waiting room.

Emrys stepped out of the lift, drawn down by all the noise in an otherwise empty building. He emerged into a box room with nothing but a bench and a tree, but through the open doors across the room he could see into a vast chamber full of people. There was a colossal legion of soldiers facing a man who had his back to the open doorway where Emrys hovered. He was wearing a fine suit and had grey hair. As Emrys hung back, the suited man raised his hand and there was a flash of intense lilac. As one, the thousand strong army vanished. Emrys couldn't help but gasp.

"You killed them?"

The old man whirled round and smiled. "Well, well, you must be Emrys," he purred. "You look so much like your brother."

"You've seen Etain?"

"Oh, I've seen all your family... I'm completing the set with you." Emrys' heart leaped at the mention of his parents and sister.

"Are my parents ok? They were evacuated."

The man smiled, a sickening imitation of sympathy. "Didn't you hear? The evacuation centres were attacked by the Ghostbrands. No survivors. I'm dreadfully sorry." Emrys' insides lurched as if the other man's words had been a bullet fired into his gut. Everywhere he turned he was confronted with death, whether it was from the sight of the vapourised soldiers, or the images of his family that were now flickering in and out of his mind.

"So much death," he muttered, tears stinging the corners of his eyes.

"Oh, those soldiers aren't dead," the man said as if it was obvious. "You were with that Chase boy so you've heard about the other world? I must say, after that I'm a little surprised to see you here." Emrys thought back to the assassin that had attacked him back at the farmhouse. "Anyway, they've simply been... *transported.*"

"But that was an army."

"An invasion to be exact. But now for you, my little Ghostbrand. I'm afraid I can't let you out of here knowing what you know. Kier may have failed, but it ends here and now. You are after all, powerless to stop me."

Anger coursing through his veins, Emrys held out his hand and narrowed his eyes. The tree growing in the terracotta pot in the corner flew into his hand, twisting and wrapping around itself until it formed a sword-like shape, complete with serrated edge.

"Not as powerless as you think."

The old man raised his eyebrows. "Well this is a surprise. I obviously underestimated you. May I ask how this is possible?"

"All I know is that it started after I said goodbye to Chase. I need to ask him what he did to me." The man smiled softly as if realising something that Emrys was unaware of. All traces of surprise were gone when he next spoke as if he had already slipped back into businessman mode, ready to turn the latest development to his advantage.

"I sent him home. If you really want to find out, I could send you after him?" Before Emrys could even reply, the old man's hand began to glow just as it had done in front of the soldiers. The only difference was that with the soldiers, the light was purple, and this time it was orange. "Just stand nice and still, that's it," he reassured. Emrys felt the tiny room getting steadily hotter and the air began to shimmer with the heat. He was sure this hadn't happened before.

"You thought that sending someone else in your place would save you?" the old man said softly as flames ignited in his palm. Emrys suddenly realized who the older man was talking about.

"What did you do to Ardent?" Emrys asked, dread pouring into his heart.

"So that was his name, was it? You know, I really should have asked before I set him on fire."

Without thinking, Emrys leapt across the room, slicing downwards with the treesword he had created, just as the other man tensed his arm ready to release a stream of burniong energy into Emrys' face. The serrated edge connected with the man's shoulder, tearing into the flesh between his neck and collarbone. Blood hit the floor as the old man screamed, the flames extinguished in his moment of agony. Emrys hacked again and the arm came loose, dropping to the floor with a wet smack, then he swung the sword round into the wide-eyed man's neck. Only when the crimson life had stopped squirting from the older man's jugular did Emrys allow himself to drop the sword and think about what he had learned. His parents and sister were dead. His best friend was dead. And if this sick old bastard had met Etain too, then he was probably dead as well. Emrys retched and fell to his knees, slumping against the wall, surrounded by blood, tears finally pouring down his scarlet splattered cheeks.

Chapter 32 – Spyrus Falls

Caliban lay down on a rock in the clearing that Emrys had left him in. He had done what he had been told and had 'played', but he could not really understand the significance of what he could do. He had no purpose. When he had been protecting himself and Emrys from the soldier's bullets, he had had a definite outcome to achieve – survival. Here, he had no such motivation. He had found that he could move some of the plants that grew around him, he could make flashes appear in the sky, amongst other things, but again, what was his purpose? Instead he had turned his attention to learning the names of things, putting the words he had overheard during his slumber together with the images he could now see with his eyes. Almost fifteen years of listening had given him a substantial vocabulary, and now that he was awake he found that by focusing his mind as Emrys had told him to, he could generally place the correct names to things. Grass. Soil. Tree. Caliban.

He had no idea of how long he had been teaching himself when he heard footsteps trudging up the path. Soon enough, Emrys appeared, looking tired and defeated. In one hand he was carrying what looked like a tree that had been fashioned into something different. A weapon. A sword. Under the crook of his other arm was tucked a bundle, wrapped in what looked like a sheet. A dark liquid was slowly soaking through.

"Any luck?" Emrys asked as he flopped down onto the rock next to Caliban. In response, Caliban clicked his fingers and a flame appeared in the palm of his hand. "Ah, so you're a Firebrand."

"Firebrand? But I can do this too…" Next, the boy held his other hand above the flame and water poured from his fingertips, extinguishing the miniature fire. Emrys sat up and watched curiously. "There are some things I can do that mirror all four of the Elements, but there is a lot I can't do."

"Your speech has improved a lot, that's for sure."

"I have been learning the names of things."

"Good."

"Did you find out what you needed to know?"

"No," Emrys shook his head, and Caliban glimpsed in his expression an indication of what the young man had been through. There was sadness in his eyes. "But I know what I have to do next." At this, Emrys unravelled the congealing bundle and out flopped a human arm. Caliban opened his mouth in surprise.

"I did not think we could function whilst incomplete, is this wrong?"

"No, we generally can't," Emrys said, suppressing a slight smile. "The owner isn't… functioning any more. But you see the tattoo on the shoulder?" He held up the bloodied stump and pointed towards the small violet circle with a cross shape in the middle. "Everybody is supposed to have a brand," Emrys continued, showing Caliban the green version that he wore on his bare shoulder. "It controls their power - maybe that's why you can do a bit of each, because you don't have one - but this brand is different. I think it's the key to getting to where I need to go. I've been trying to make it work, but I guess I wrecked it when I cut it off." Caliban took up the arm and peered at it inquisitively, bending the elbow and flexing the fingers, causing Emrys to look away and suppress a wave of nausea. "I need it to glow purple," he said whilst staring into the undergrowth and waiting for Caliban to finish his examination with his childlike immunity to the morbid.

After a few moments, when Caliban said nothing, Emrys turned back and gasped in surprise. Caliban was holding the arm up and the palm was glowing with the same intense light that Emrys had seen the man use on the soldiers.

"That's it!"

"This appears to be one of the things I am able to do. It just... flows right. What should I do with it?"

Emrys stood up and took a deep breath. "Aim it at me."

"What will happen?"

"I don't know exactly. But it will look like I've just disappeared."

"This doesn't seem like a good idea."

"You're still new," Emrys smiled. "You'll learn someday that sometimes you just have to jump in. My brother told me to fight, and that's what I'm going to do. But before I go, I want to apologise."

"In the short time we have known each other, I can't think of anything you have to apologise for."

"I meant in general. People have done terrible things to you, to thousands of others in the name of this war, but there's been guilt on both sides. I want you to remember that because I think you could be what this place needs. You're not constrained by anything, you're a mix of everything. You can truly bring balance here."

"A purpose?"

Emrys nodded. "So, you fancy it? When I come back I'm expecting rainbows and ponies, mind." Caliban tilted his head. "Ok I'm sorry, that was a joke. But will you try?" This time Caliban smiled, a warm smile of his own unlike the one he had copied from Emrys earlier.

"Yes Emrys, I will try."

"Right, now lets fire this thing up." Caliban held the arm out again and once more poured his energy into it so that it began to bathe the clearing in lilac. He looked apprehensive as Emrys closed his eyes and clenched his fists, then there was an immense flash as the energy burst from the palm of the severed arm and hit Emrys squarely in the chest. Instead of being blasted backwards however, Emrys simply vanished into nothing. Caliban remembered that the Earthbrand had been expecting this.

The boy turned away and strolled up the nearest rise, which commanded a view of the entire city. It was a field of twinkling lights and smoke, guarded at one end by the Temple of Branding, and at the other by Spyrus. When he looked at the Temple, all he could think about was his imprisonment in the tunnel network beneath it. Without a second thought, he raised his hand to the sky and a bolt of lightning split the clouds, a silver javelin striking into the grand domed roof of the temple. Stone, fire and smoke shot into the night sky as the temple collapsed in on itself. The fighting in the tunnels must have weakened the ground because in less than a minute, the mound the temple stood on was sinking and tilting like a dropped cake. *There's been guilt on both sides.* Too true. If Caliban left things as they were then Spyrus would still rule the world with its iron fist.

Once more, lightning shot from the heavens, this time striking the base of Spyrus tower. The building was much stronger than the temple, and Caliban struck it again and again, each bolt sending fountains of crackling sparks into the inky blackness. A pitiful groaning echoed across the city as some vital support strut began to bend – the first step in the destruction of Spyrus. Sure enough, the groaning was joined by more incessant screeching until there was a chorus of twisting metal. The tower was now visibly leaning – only slightly at first but the angle was becoming more and more pronounced. Windows shattered as loose furniture erupted out of the now sloping offices and crashed in splinters onto the concrete below. With a final rush of air, the tower began to fall in slow motion, the inertia now sending things crashing out of the other side of the building only to sink back into gravity's embrace and smash back into the mirrored glass walls. The tower crashed into the streets, kicking up vast waves of dust and debris before finally settling and the city was silent at last.

Chapter 33 – The Warning

Even with his eyes closed, Emrys could see nothing but bright violet light and he stood steeling himself for impact. The rough wooden handle of his makeshift sword was biting into the palm of his hand as he clenched his fists. All he felt was a light pat on his chest and then the world went black. Cool air caressed his face, and he opened his eyes. He was still in the forest. It hadn't worked after all. He turned to look for Caliban to persuade him to try again when he saw two men standing right in front of him, their mouths wide open with surprise. The first thing he noticed was that they were both wearing cloaks. Ghostbrands? *But surely everyone is a Ghostbrand in this world?* As his eyes moved up their bodies, he also noticed that their tops had both sleeves on like the men from Spyrus – yet another reason not to trust these people.

It was when Emrys finally studied their faces that he realised he was truly in a different world. He had seen these faces on countless pictures, on coins, in books and on statues. He would have recognised these two men anywhere, the short blonde hair of one and the deep brown curls and lopsided grin of the other. The Everrulers were alive! He stepped forward and sank to the ground in a low bow.

"Altair of Air and Dylan of Water," he said hurriedly. If anybody could stop the Spyrus forces that had been sent through to this world then the Everrulers could. "You are in great danger! Where are Dexamenas of Earth and Phoenix of Fire?" His eyes darted between them, expecting to see the other two Everrulers standing just behind. In his world, they had rarely been apart.

"Why do you want to know?" Dylan asked, sounding extremely young. But weren't the Everrulers middle aged? There would be time for questions later, Emrys reasoned. He had to get his message across so that Spyrus could be stopped.

"Because, my Lord Dylan. A war is coming…"

COMING
SOON

SUFFERANCE

ACKNOWLEDGEMENTS

Miguel and Looby – UCE still belongs to you
Mark, Tessa, Looby, Rummy and Bunty – The proofreading skills are always appreciated – maybe you should start charging!
Pigeon – Maybe you'll read this one…
Clamp, Pete, Dad, J Bailey, Sheila Price, Bunty, Meriel and that Random Kindle Person – Reviews let me know that I'm doing something right!
The Current 78 – Consider yourself superior to others
Geoffrey, Clamp, Pigeon and LJ – Pictures are fun!
The guys of Garendon and Burleigh – For all the lunchtimes spent playing Cropper-Soccer
Tom – Cheers for the sage advice about the Car Park
The Download Crew – "Modulate to Accumulate"
Ali – For knowing what's what
Smith – The King of 'Don't think just do it" moments
Nichala – Conch will always be half yours

Firainarkorsar faroyrai elvirelraiyohfirinanargia

About The Author

Philip T McNeill is an Earthbrand who currently teaches English in a Gloucestershire secondary school. He can often be found writing or drawing whilst he should be paying attention in meetings. He is fond of a cheeky dash and right now, he is listening to The Spirit Of Man from The War Of The Worlds – classic!

Check out his web comic 'Clamp Oswell's College Years' at www.clamposwell.com

@philiptauthor
@clamposwell

Facebook – The Locte Chronicles
Facebook – Clamp Oswell's College Years

Bonus Features – Book Selfies and Spyrus Sneaks

6843998R00177

Printed in Great Britain
by Amazon.co.uk, Ltd.,
Marston Gate.